BUDI DARMA

Olenka

Translated with an Introduction and Notes
by TIFFANY TSAO

PENGUIN BOOKS

PENGUIN BOOKS
An imprint of Penguin Random House LLC
1745 Broadway, New York, NY 10019
penguinrandomhouse.com

Set in Sabon LT Pro

LIBRARY OF CONGRESS CATALOGING-IN-PUBLICATION DATA
Names: Budi Darma, 1937– author | Tsao, Tiffany translator
Title: Olenka / Budi Darma; translated with an introduction and notes by Tiffany Tsao.
Other titles: Olenka. English
Description: New York, NY : Penguin Books, 2026. | Includes bibliographical references.
Identifiers: LCCN 2025037520 (print) | LCCN 2025037521 (ebook) |
ISBN 9780143138532 trade paperback | ISBN 9780593512616 ebook
Subjects: LCGFT: Novels | Fiction
Classification: LCC PL5089.B82 O4413 2026 (print) | LCC PL5089.B82 (ebook)
LC record available at https://lccn.loc.gov/2025037520
LC ebook record available at https://lccn.loc.gov/2025037521

Originally published in Indonesian by Balai Pustaka in 1983
Published by Noura Publishing (PT. Mizan Publika) in 2018.
This English translation published with an introduction, notes, and suggestions for further reading by Tiffany Tsao in Penguin Books 2026

Printed in the United States of America
1st Printing

The authorized representative in the EU for product safety and compliance is Penguin Random House Ireland, Morrison Chambers, 32 Nassau Street, Dublin D02 YH68, Ireland, https://eu-contact.penguin.ie.

OLENKA

BUDI DARMA is one of Indonesia's most esteemed and influential writers. He was born in Rembang, Central Java, on April 25, 1937. Due to the nature of his father's work in the postal service, his family lived in several different towns and cities in Java when he was a child, including Bandung, Semarang, Kudus, and Salatiga. After completing his undergraduate degree in English literature at Gadjah Mada University in Yogyakarta, he became a lecturer at Airlangga University in Surabaya. In 1970, he was granted a one-year scholarship from the East-West Center at the University of Hawaii in Honolulu to study humanities. In 1974, he received a Fulbright scholarship to pursue his master's degree in creative writing in the English department at Indiana University Bloomington. Following this, he received support from the Ford Foundation to complete his doctoral studies at the same institution. He received his PhD in English literature in 1980. Budi Darma won numerous national awards for his writing, including first place in the Jakarta Arts Council Prize for Best Novel Manuscript (1980), the Jakarta Arts Council Prize for Best Novel (1983), the Indonesian Government Arts Award (1993), and the Presidential Medal of Honor (Satya Lencana Kebudayaan) for his literary contributions to the nation. International honors he received include the S.E.A. Write Award (1984) and the Mastera Literary Award (2011). Even after technically retiring, Budi Darma continued to teach at the State University of Surabaya and be active on Indonesia's literary scene until his death on August 21, 2021, at the age of eighty-four.

TIFFANY TSAO is a writer and literary translator. For her translation of Budi Darma's *People from Bloomington*, she was awarded the PEN Translation Prize and the NSW Premier's Translation Prize. She is the author of four novels, including *But Won't I Miss Me* and *The Majesties*. She holds a PhD in English from UC Berkeley and lives on Gamaragal land in Sydney, Australia.

Contents

Introduction

New readers are advised that this Introduction makes details of the plot explicit.

The story of how *Olenka* came to be written is the stuff of literary legend. Toward the end of 1979, Budi Darma—then in his early forties and on the verge of completing his PhD in English at Indiana University Bloomington—happened to step into the same elevator as a woman and three boys. Due to their similar features, he assumed the woman was their mother. When the three boys stepped out of the elevator, the woman stayed behind. She was, in fact, not their mother and informed Budi Darma of the boys' circumstances—their mother had left the family and the father worked full time, so the boys had to fend for themselves during the day. Upon leaving the elevator, Budi Darma rushed into his apartment and began to write. He couldn't stop. In less than three weeks, he had finished the draft manuscript for his first novel—*Olenka*.

This is the account of *Olenka*'s origins that Budi Darma himself provided in the novel's afterword, which was written around three years later, in 1982, to accompany *Olenka* upon its publication in 1983 as the sixth of its seven component parts: parts one through five being the fictional narrative (including a coda); part six being the essay on *Olenka*'s origins; and part seven being a lengthy endnotes section comprising a whopping fifty-four notes in total, detailing the narrative's numerous literary, cinematic, and cultural allusions, supplemented by the occasional relevant anecdote.

The formal insistence on the importance of the supplementary afterword and endnotes section alongside the novel's fictional component; the extensiveness of its annotations—these weren't *Olenka*'s only unusual formal features. There were also the supplementary images inserted at intervals throughout the narrative: images of photos and text clipped from real-life newspapers and magazines, accompanied by captions explaining their relevance to the story and designed to imbue it with verisimilitude.

Then there were the unconventional features of the narrative portion: its characters and setting, to start with (namely, white Americans in the American Midwest); and despite the foreign characters and setting, the infusion of its Indonesian-language text with Javanese words and phrases, which would have lent the narration a homier quality for many readers. (While the official language of the state, Indonesian was not yet the language many people would have spoken at home, and most readers would have been Javanese, Indonesia's ethnic majority.)

There was also the narrative's departure from straightforward chronologically based storytelling—in the words of Budi Darma's afterword, his "leaps" ("*loncat-loncatan*")—via the narrator's lengthy ruminations and dreams, and, at one point, the interruption of the narrator's narrative with Olenka's backstory, recounted in her own voice via an extended soul-baring letter. Plus all the ways the novel combined seemingly incongruous elements, being a reference-heavy love story turned parody of a love story, turned genuine quest for meaning and purpose and eventual spiritual awakening, infused with the comic and tragic by turns. And the blurring of fiction and real: the real-life and almost-real-life places, people, and events scattered throughout.

In short, *Olenka* was unusual—*is* unusual, by all metrics, back then and today, in Indonesia and beyond. It certainly succeeded in turning heads on the literary prize scene, placing first in the 1980 Jakarta Arts Council competition for unpublished novel manuscripts, winning the Jakarta Arts Council Literary Award (*Hadiah Dewan Kesenian Jakarta*) after its publication in 1983, and receiving a S.E.A. Write Award in 1984. Reviewing the book for the newspaper *Sinar Harapan*, the writer and journalist Satyagraha Hoerip predicted it would prove to be the best literary novel released that year and applauded it for being "richly experimental and innovative."[i]

But experimentation and innovation start somewhere. And as Budi Darma himself observed in the afterword, "Everything that winds up in my work has had a very long running start."[ii] Beyond a chance encounter in an elevator, how did *Olenka* come to take the particular form it did?

* * *

The fact that Budi Darma wrote something experimental wasn't necessarily surprising. Well before he embarked on his studies abroad, Budi Darma had made a name for himself as a writer of experimental short fiction of the absurdist variety—"absurdism" in the Indonesian context referring to works that diverged from mainstream realist modes of storytelling and style, featuring bizarre characters and circumstances. By the early 1970s, he had already developed a reputation for writing stories of a certain type. The phrase "Kafkaesque" springs to mind, and indeed, in an interview published in a 1974 issue of *Horison*, he said that Franz Kafka had left the deepest impression of all the writers he had read.[iii] In the same issue, a special one devoted to Budi Darma's short fiction, Harry Aveling described the world of Budi Darma's stories as "extremely cruel, bereft of humanity, and altogether unconcerned with logic . . . A dark world, with no place in it for God, myth, society, family, or friend."[iv] Korrie Layun Rampan, writing anonymously in 1981, would use similar words: "To Budi Darma, human beings are a strange lot. So hard and cruel, so inhumane, and devoid of conventional logic."[v] "In general, his short stories are very hard and cold, seemingly indifferent to societal moral values as they stand," wrote the writer and critic Ajip Rosidi.[vi]

But Budi Darma's time in Bloomington was to usher in a new phase in his fiction-writing career. There, away from the numerous duties and tasks he was usually saddled with in his capacity as a lecturer and administrator at the State University of Surabaya (Universitas Negeri Surabaya), he found the time and space he needed to write. “I had myself felt out of breath in Indonesia from the thousand and one affairs that kept me busy in addition to my writing, and it so happened that I found myself abroad, which is why *Olenka* is not about Indonesians,” he would reflect a few years after returning from the United States.[vii] In the same essay, adapted from a lecture delivered earlier that year, he remarked, “If I hadn’t gone to America, I probably would have never written a novel, for, truly, a writer needs privacy, concentration, and intensity of focus.”[viii]

Indeed, his last year in Bloomington—1979—would prove an exceptionally fertile one. It was during this period, as his dissertation was being finalized and his academic workload had lessened, that he would write the remaining five of the seven stories that would be compiled and published the following year as *People from Bloomington* (*Orang-Orang Bloomington*). He would write a short story inspired in part by Nathaniel Hawthorne’s “Young Goodman Brown.” And he would write *Olenka*.

Set in America and peopled with American characters, *People from Bloomington* and *Olenka* were both a departure from Budi Darma’s usual subject matter.[ix] But their American content was a byproduct of a deeper shift away from the overt absurdism that was, up to that point, his hallmark. It was only because he was writing about real life, inspired by the people, places, and events around him, that he began writing about Americans at all. “These stories just happen to be set in Bloomington,” he wrote in the preface to *People from Bloomington*. “If I had been living in Surabaya or Paris or Dublin at the time, I would likely have ended up writing *People from Surabaya*, *People from Paris*, or *People from Dublin*.”[x]

In light of this movement toward realism, the nonfiction elements of *Olenka* read as an almost logical next step—one-upping the stories of *People from Bloomington*, if you will, with the inclusion of documentary evidence from newspapers and magazines and the incorporation of real-life and near-real-life places, people, and events. How much more realistic could fiction get?

Olenka also marked the first time in Budi Darma's literary career that his fiction bore marks of the other kind of writing for which he was known: literary criticism. A well-read and prolific critic with strong views on literary aesthetics, the distinct role of literature in society, and what constituted "good" and "bad" literature, Budi Darma arrived in IU Bloomington's English graduate studies program already exceptionally knowledgeable and articulate about both Indonesian and world literature. If his new surroundings compelled him to try his hand in an extended way at realism, then perhaps the scholarly research and writing he was undertaking for his doctorate inspired him to lift the boundaries separating his criticism from his creative work—to incorporate into his fiction allusions and references and quotes from the realms of literature, film, and visual art in a way he had never done before.

The result was a hybrid entity—realistic characters acting in absurd ways, navigating realistic but absurd circumstances; a work of metafictional fiction with scholarly nonfiction elements. Real yet unreal. Fictional yet factual. At one point in *Olenka*, the narrator, Fanton Drummond, stands naked before his bedroom mirror and scrutinizes himself: "In the wet mirror, my body looked misshapen and warped."[xi] One might describe *Olenka* in the same way—a distorted reflection.

But when you look into a mirror and see a flaw, is the mirror flawed, or are you?

* * *

In the closing paragraphs of *Olenka*'s afterword, Budi Darma likens *Olenka* to a looking glass—a very special one, with the power to reveal to its reader the true self that lies within:

> I have never encouraged anyone to be a narcissist. A narcissist always sees himself as handsome, with no awareness of the disease lurking within. In my writing, I seek to testify to the human condition, that we are creatures, wretched and covered in sores, though glorious and graceful too. Examine for yourself every

line of every page of literature's most monumental works. Every word bears testimony: human beings are not agreeable creatures.

Indeed, if we want to see ourselves for who we really are, narcissism will not serve us. Fancying ourselves heroes of the dime-novel variety will not help us if we aspire to become nobler than we are. As the ancient Greeks would say, what we need is "catharsis," brought on by a revulsion at one's very self. Roquentin in Sartre's novel *La Nausée* experiences a *suprême dégoût de moi*, as does Fanton Drummond at the end of *Olenka*. Their gaze penetrates their bodies, through to that which rages within.[xii]

Olenka offers no flattering reflection—no likeness of ourselves worth falling in love with, as with Narcissus. No hero's mettle or sculpted body. Instead, its X-ray vision reveals our true condition, diseased and pitiful, alongside what grace and glory we do possess. Like the mirror Fanton Drummond stands naked before, only to see a warped version of himself, *Olenka* reflects back a distorted version of ourselves, which its author asserts is no distortion but the unpleasant truth.

The idea of literature as a mirror appears elsewhere in Budi Darma's writing from this period, specifically, in a piece titled "Moral dalam Sastra" ("Morals in Literature"), delivered as a lecture in December 1981 and published as a two-part essay in *Basis* magazine the following year, when he composed *Olenka*'s afterword. Odds are, he drew on this piece to write the afterword—for there we find a few lines almost identical to the ones above about narcissists and humans being flawed yet glorious—and also, a more direct statement about literature functioning as a mirror: "An essential quality of literature . . . is that it depicts human beings as they are. A good literary work will invite the reader to regard it as a reflection of himself."[xiii]

When the novel is read as a mirror, *Olenka*'s unusual attributes take on different meaning. Its deeply flawed and often ridiculous characters, struggling to find purpose and fulfillment in life, are none other than ourselves. The Javaneseinflected language spoken by its American characters: a foreign yet familiar counterpart to Budi Darma's readers and himself. Its preponderance of allusions and references: signs pointing the way to reflections scattered across time and space, similar iterations of the same characters, events, and circumstances. The accompanying images from newspapers and magazines: not meant to dupe the reader into mistaking fiction for fact, but to emphasize the factuality of the fiction before the reader's eyes. Or as the writer Sapardi Djoko Damono put it in his review of *Olenka* for *Tempo* magazine, "By colliding [fiction and fact], Budi Darma is trying to force us to acknowledge the reality of his fiction. Or, that there is no difference between fiction and fact."[xiv]

Fitting, then, that the narrative is filled with mirrors. Of all kinds. From literal mirrors, like the ones in which Fanton Drummond examines himself, to the pervasive sense throughout the narrative that the characters and their situations are distorted mirror versions of each other. Fanton Drummond thinks himself the opposite of Olenka's awful, cowardly, and selfish husband, Wayne Danton, and so do we, until, over time, both he and we realize that scarcely a letter's breadth separates Fanton from Danton after all.

In fact, once one starts seeing reflections in *Olenka*, it's hard to stop. It becomes a veritable mirror maze: Olenka and the Olenka of Wayne's short story "Olenka"; the two Marys—Mary Carson and Mary Bentley, nicknamed MC and MB. And of course, when Fanton orders pizza, one of the delivery women turns out to be named Mary Carson too. There are Janes in triplicate: the Jane of *Jane Eyre* (which the narrative quotes and references often and at length); the Jane who inherits Olenka's job at the nightclub; the Janet who, with Mary, delivers pizza to Fanton ("Janet" in *Jane Eyre*, lest we forget, is one of Rochester's pet names for Jane).

Characters' circumstances, too, repeat and mirror each other. Fanton himself realizes, when forced to spend the night in Indianapolis, that "the bus station was a lot like my everyday life: wandering here and there, looking for ways to pass the time, with no real purpose. It was the same out there, every day."[xv] Fanton finds himself "rolling" ("*menggelinding*") off to Kentucky, Illinois, and Pennsylvania, and later discovers that his movements have repeated Olenka's movements, and those of her father, and those of Abraham Lincoln and Lincoln's father as well.

Fanton finds another mirror image in another unexpected place: the mute peddlers in the bus station in Indianapolis, who initially remind him of Wayne but who, he then realizes, are more akin to him. But he, Fanton, suffers from a far worse condition—not loss of speech, but a "leprosy of the soul."[xvi] He comes to this realization when he discovers an unflattering fictional mute version of himself in a story Wayne has written: "The writer's skill was such that I found myself despising the Mute. He had to be banished from society, not because he was mute, but because he harbored an extremely dangerous psychological illness that might easily spread."[xvii] So, within the story of *Olenka*, we find a story enacting what *Olenka* itself is meant to enact: reflecting the reader's self to the reader, revealing the spiritual sickness therein, the story within the bigger story reflecting in miniature what the bigger story is meant to do.

And indeed Wayne, with all his pretentious and insufferable writerly airs, turns out to be a reflection of another author: Budi Darma himself. "My mind was assailed by an overpowering urge to keep writing, until I was left with no time to attend to any other tasks," recounts Budi Darma in the afterword—very Wayne-like behavior, as we learn from Fanton: "As long as the desire to write held out, he would keep at it, omitting, if necessary, to eat or sleep."[xviii] "As a writer, I resemble Sisyphus," remarked Budi Darma in a 1982 essay titled "Confession" ("Pengakuan").[xix] "I turned into Sisyphus," Wayne admits to Fanton, of his obsessive writing ways.[xx] Even as Budi Darma, through *Olenka*, asks readers to peer into their true selves, he submits to a dose of his own medicine. The result: a self-portrait of the writer as an obnoxious man. And when, in the coda, Fanton takes on the role of author, referring to the pen he has used to write the narrative we have been reading, the reflection is doubled: the irresponsible, self-centered Fanton Drummond is a version of the author Budi Darma too.

The preponderance of allusions and references to external texts, films, artworks, and events extends the work's mirror-maze quality. For wherever the characters go, whatever they do, whatever they think, they are not original at all—simply reflections, repetitions, iterations of other characters elsewhere. Fanton, variously, becomes the narrator of Roop Katthak's "Manu," the speaker in Chairil Anwar's poems, Santiago from *The Old Man and the Sea*, Roquentin from Jean-Paul Sartre's *La Nausée*, Michel from André Gide's *L'Immoraliste*, among others. Even when he asserts his difference from others—say, Madame Sosostris from *The Waste Land*, or an orphan in Victorian England—contrast is merely a form of comparison, and the ultimate effect is similar: his thoughts and actions are not unique, are at most variations on themes that have come before.

Similarly, Olenka is an iteration of Manu from Roop Katthak's story, of Jane Eyre, of Ursula from *The Rainbow*, of Olenka from Anton Chekhov's "The Darling," of the real-life Margaret Trudeau. Even in her artistic prowess and ambition, which promises to set her apart, she becomes Andrea del Sarto, as rendered by Robert Browning in his eponymous poem, her work "flawless" but lacking what it takes to be truly great.[xxi] Her fate is sealed when she turns to art forgery to make a living, her art, like her person, an imitation—a mirror image of others' art. MC's disability turns her into Elizabeth Barrett Browning and Jill Kinmont—not even quite the real-life Barrett Browning, imply the footnotes, but the film version, adapted from the stage play *The Barretts of Wimpole Street*, and not the real-life Kinmont either, but the version from the biopic *The Other Side of the Mountain*, based on a biography of Kinmont's life.

The novel's major themes—the monotony of day-to-day existence; the meaninglessness of life's activities and people's ambitions; the sameness of individuals across time and geography and space—extend to our world, rendering utter fiction all in which we place our own purpose and hope. Earlier, I said there was no escape for *Olenka*'s characters from the mirror maze. There would appear to be no escape for us either.

If it weren't for the coda, that is.

* * *

In the coda, the final part of the novel's narrative portion, Fanton Drummond submits to God. Invoking the Quran, which he has glanced through in the library, and, unconsciously, Chairil Anwar's poem "Doa" ("Prayer"), he acknowledges God's sovereignty and his own sin. This is not the first time he has called on God—he has done so at certain times before, kneeling and pressing his forehead to the earth, facing various directions, in a semblance of the Islamic practice, muttering the odd prayer. But each of these times, he has felt "something was missing." Though whether he succeeds this time is left open-ended, the finality of the act—and its being the final act in the narrative—suggests it is. That he finally sees himself for what he is: flawed and helpless. And, in the words of the afterword, not the architect of his body and soul.

This is Fanton's way out of the mirror maze—and by implication, our way as well. For if we are indeed, like Fanton, fictional creations existing only on the page, then the only escape is to be found in the truly real, our Creator.

Is it a satisfying conclusion? Interestingly enough, the text itself informs us, from the standpoint of literary aesthetics, it is not. In fact, Fanton, the author of the coda, explicitly says that if he were Wayne, with Wayne's inerrant literary instincts, there would be no coda at all:

> If I were Wayne, after writing the line *I, too, longed to shatter into pieces, to lose all form*, I would stop. The story would end there. I would be careful, knowing exactly where to begin and where to end. I would avoid the nonsensical and insignificant. But I'm not Wayne.[xxii]

The implication is that the coda is aesthetically displeasing. And indeed, one does have the strong sense that it would have been more "literary" for the narrative to have concluded where Part IV leaves it: Fanton wandering Washington, D.C., beset by nausea, realizing how thoroughly disgusted and disillusioned he is with everything and everyone, including Olenka, unconsciously thinking to himself the lines from Chairil Anwar's poem, *I, too, long to shatter into pieces, to lose all form.*

And yet the coda exists. As if merely thinking the lines of Chairil Anwar's poetic crying out to God is, like all of Fanton's previous gestures at turning to God, insufficient, missing something. He must write it out: "My God, in my utter despair, I still call on You." For true moral cleansing to happen, catharsis can't stop at nausea; the individual must purge.

This explicitly religious conclusion to the narrative portion of the novel was, like the realist and heavily intertextual aspects of *Olenka*, a marked change from his pre-Bloomington work, which, as I've previously mentioned, was seen by critics as "cruel," "cold," "indifferent," "inhumane," and "with no place for God." In fact, Budi Darma himself had often expressed the belief that overt moral messaging compromised the literary quality of a work. For example, in a 1973 essay, he criticized writers who set out to "instruct the reader" via their fiction, remarking snidely of two novels by Iwan Simatupang and Sutan Takdir Alisjahbana, respectively, that reading them "feels like listening to a speech."[xxiii] "Doctrinaire concepts also lessen the sublimity of a literary work," he asserted in a lecture delivered toward the end of 1982, the year before the publication of his own arguably "doctrinaire" novel.[xxiv]

The two-part "Morals in Literature" essay of 1982 provides what is perhaps the most extended and relevant articulation of his belief that moral education and literary quality were often at odds with each other. In the essay's second installment, we find remarks such as "Rhetorical concerns may not align with moral ones, the latter sometimes sacrificed for the sake of the former, and so that which makes a work interesting is its aesthetic appeal, not its moral aspects. What is morally beneficial may be distorted by the acrobatics a writer performs."[xxv] Citing the example of Jane Austen as a writer struggling to find a balance between morality and rhetoric, he observes, "In reality, many matters that are, in fact, at odds with moral concerns have been slipped into, or form a key part of, great literary works."[xxvi]

Indeed, there are a few scenes in *Olenka* that, in their descriptiveness, might have especially offended the moral sensibilities of readers, especially Fanton and Olenka having sex in all positions everywhere in Fanton's apartment and the steamy descriptions of Olenka and Winifred's same-sex love affair ("We were still kissing fiercely, even as she started the engine. When we got to her apartment, we took off our clothes. She pulled me into the bathroom, turned on the hot water, and we bathed together in the same tub [. . .] I had never experienced such enjoyment, such satisfaction").[xxvii] But if Fanton's guilt over their adulterous affair and Olenka's guilt over hers are insufficient to nullify the sensuality of the images that linger in the reader's head, then the coda would appear to be a definitive attempt. The Indonesian literary critic Tirto Suwondo has observed that by *Olenka*'s close, the polyphony of different voices is shut down by their incorporation into the author's voice, the dialogic aspects of the novel giving way to the monologic.[xxviii] Arguably, this applies to the novel's moral aspects as well: any moral ambiguity regarding the characters' deeds, thoughts, and actions are shut down by Fanton repenting and turning to God.

So what could have motivated Budi Darma to incorporate a religious message into his novel, despite his belief that doing so could have a potentially deleterious and unaesthetic effect? As with his shift toward realism and the incorporation of scholarly elements into his fiction, the answer may partly lie with his circumstances at the time. *Olenka* was written as Budi Darma was finishing up his dissertation on character and moral judgment in Jane Austen's novels—specifically, the predicament Austen faced in balancing her moral sensibilities and her artistic ones. "The balance is delicate indeed," he wrote. "If she surrenders her impulse as a novelist to her moral principles, her characters will more or less act as her moral mouthpiece [. . .] If she surrenders her moral principles to the requirements of her art or craft, the functions of her characters as moral agents may become blurred."[xxix] He concluded the dissertation by observing that Austen's later novels were able to strike a balance with some success by deploying the narratorial voice in a subtler manner, "us[ing] the narrator not as a means of instruction but as a vehicle of the reader's perception."[xxx] Certainly, Budi Darma creates for himself a similar dilemma in *Olenka*—and his use of Fanton Drummond's personal repentance and submission to God in the coda in order to guide our perceptions as readers seems a page out of Austen's playbook, as interpreted by him.

In thus deliberately opting to balance morals and aesthetics, rather than avoid the balancing act altogether, it seems that Budi Darma set himself a literary challenge. Deploying the narratorial voice à la Austen was one method of meeting it. His decision to create a coda, thus separating the overt religious message from the rest of the narrative with its subtler religious messaging, might be seen as another clever tactic. In this, he effectively creates two endings, one aesthetically pleasing, one morally satisfying—having one's cake and eating it too.

One might see Budi Darma as following in the footsteps of other great authors before him who sought to channel and articulate the divine and the divine order in their writing, and whose works are mentioned in *Olenka* by name: the poetry of Indonesia's revolutionary poet Chairil Anwar; Alexander Pope's *An Essay on Man*, from which *Olenka*'s epigraph is drawn; Charlotte Brontë's *Jane Eyre*; Nathaniel Hawthorne's "Young Goodman Brown"; John Donne's poetry. Just as these authors grappled with God and faith through their work, so does Budi Darma through *Olenka*. And although, by *Olenka*'s own admission, such an enterprise risks compromising the novel's aesthetic appeal, the act is also a liberating one. Wayne Danton, consumed only with producing writing worthy of worldly praise, remains enslaved. It is Fanton Drummond who ultimately walks free.

* * *

If I may, I would like to reflect a little on the experience of translating Budi Darma's *Olenka* in comparison to translating his short-story collection *People from Bloomington*. I had the joy and privilege of corresponding with Budi Darma on the latter before he passed away in August 2021, a few months before Penguin Classics' publication of the work. I did not realize how much I would miss his keen insight, his sharp memory, his humor, and his willingness to help in all matters. Translating *Olenka* has been a much more solitary endeavor, needless to say, and I often found myself recalling the many conversations over WhatsApp that we had during that very surreal Covid pandemic period.

My special thanks to the National Library of Australia and the University of Sydney Library for their assistance and for having such extensive holdings of Indonesian-language material. To the State Library of New South Wales, which, fortunately, happened to have several of the books mentioned in *Olenka* among their collections. A warm thank-you to the staff at the IU Bloomington Archives, who fielded and answered all my queries (including a difficult one regarding the circulation figures for the *Indiana Daily Student* newspaper in 1979). And to Larry Lockridge for his willingness to field questions about the house and sundial belonging to his father, Ross Lockridge Jr., which is mentioned in Part IV, Chapter 10.

TIFFANY TSAO

NOTES

i. "novel yang kaya eksperimen maupun pembaharuan"; "dan boleh diramalkan sebagai novel sastra terbaik terbitan 1983": Satayagraha Hoerip, "Kesanggupan Mengebor Sukma," *Sinar Harapan*, March 2, 1984, 7.

ii. "segala sesuatu yang masuk ke dalam tulisan saya sudah menempuh ancang-ancang yang amat jauh": Budi Darma, *Olenka* (Balai Pustaka, 1983), 221.

iii. Budi Darma, "Wawancara Tertulis Dengan Budi Darma," interview by Sapardi Djoko Damono, *Horison*, April 1974, 127.

iv. "sangat kejam, tanpa kemanusiaan dan samasekali tidak mementingkan logika [. . .] Dunia gelap, tanpa tempat bagi Tuhan, mite, masyarakat, teman atau keluarga": Harry Aveling, "Dunia Yang Jungkir Balik Budi Darma," *Horison,* April 1974, 100.

v. "Pada Budi Darma manusia itu serba aneh. Manusia begitu keras keras dan kejam; tak berperikemanusiaan dan padanya tak ada logika konvensional": "Dalam Lintasan Sejarah Sastra Indonesia," *Horison,* July 1981, 225. Although no name was attached to the essay as it appeared in *Horison*, the same piece appeared the following year in a collection of essays by Korrie Layun Rampan about the contemporary Indonesian short story, titled *Cerita Pendek Indonesia Mutakhir.*

vi. "Cerita pendeknya pada umumnya terasa sangat keras dan dingin, seakan-akan tidak menghiraukan nilai moral kemasyarakatan yang ada": Ajip Rosidi, *Laut Biru Langit Biru* (Pustaka Jaya, 1982), 387.

vii. "Dan saya sendiri merasa tersengal-sengal di Indonesia oleh seribu satu macam kesibukan di luar kepengarangan saya, dan kebetulan berhasil tinggal di negeri orang, dan karena itu novel *Olenka* bukan mengenai manusia Indonesia": Budi Darma, "Novel Indonesia adalah Dunia Melodrama," *Horison,* September 1983, 384.

viii. "Andaikata saya tidak pernah tinggal di Amerika, mungkin juga saya tidak akan pernah menulis novel. Memang pengarang memerlukan *privacy*, konsentrasi, dan intensitas": Budi Darma, "Novel Indonesia adalah Dunia Melodrama," 391.

ix. It should be noted that Budi Darma was not the first to write about foreign characters in foreign climes, though doing so was still highly unusual. Some of the stories in Umar Kayam's *Seribu Kunang-Kunang di Manhattan* (Pustaka Jaya, 1972) were about Americans in America. Nh. Dini was another author who made use of a foreign setting and foreign characters for *Namaku Hiroko* (Pustaka Jaya, 1977), set in Japan.

x. "Andaikata pada waktu itu saya tinggal di Surabaya, atau Paris, atau Dublin, mungkin juga saya menulis *Orang-Orang Surabaya*, *Orang-Orang Paris*, atau *Orang-Orang Dublin*": Budi Darma, "Prakata: Mula-mula adalah Tema," in *Orang-Orang Bloomington* (Sinar Harapan, 1980), xvi.

xi. "Di dalam cermin yang masih basah tubuh saya nampak bengkak-bengkok": Budi Darma, *Olenka*, 76.

xii. "[. . .] saya tidak pernah mengundang siapa pun untuk menjadi narkisus. Narkisus selalu melihat dirinya sebagai tampan, tanpa merasa mengantongi penyakit. Dalam menulis saya selalu mengaku, bahwa manusia adalah makhluk yang penuh luka, hina-dina, dan sekaligus agung dan anggun. Baca jugalah setiap jengkal halaman karya sastra yang menumental [*sic*]. Kata demi kata adalah pengakuan bahwa manusia bukanlah makhluk yang enak. Memang untuk dapat melihat diri kita sendiri dengan benar kita tidak selayaknya menjadi narkisus. Untuk menjadi lebih agung, kita tidak perlu menonton diri kita sebagai jagoan dalam novel-novel picisan. Seperti yang dikatakan oleh orang-orang Yunani Kuno, kita memerlukan 'catharsis,' yaitu rasa mual terhadap diri kita sendiri. Roquentin dalam novel Sartre *La Nausée* juga merasakan *suprême dégoût de moi*, demikian juga Fanton Drummond menjelang akhir novel *Olenka*. Mata mereka menembus tubuh mereka, dan mereka tahu apa yang berkecamuk di dalamnya": Budi Darma, *Olenka*, 223–24. Budi Darma's understanding of catharsis relies on a popular interpretation of it that emphasized catharsis's morally cleansing aspects, in addition to its emotionally cleansing ones. See Budi Darma's description of the mechanism by which such catharsis works in the first installment of his essay "Moral dalam Sastra," published in the February 1982 issue of *Basis*.

xiii. "Salah satu hakekat sastra [. . .] adalah menggambarkan manusia sebagaimana adanya. Karya sastra yang baik akan mengajak pembaca melihat karya tersebut sebagai cermin dirinya sendiri": Budi Darma, "Moral dalam Sastra," *Basis*, February 1982, 46.

xiv. "Dengan membenturkan keduanya, Budi Darma berusaha memaksa kita mengakui bahwa fiksinya realitas. Atau, bahwa tidak ada perbedaan antara fiksi dan fakta": Sapardi Djoko Damono, "Catatan Kaki Si Tukang Ejek," *Tempo*, February 25, 1984, 30.

xv. "Setasiun bis mirip benar dengan dunia saya sehari-hari, berjalan kesana-sini, iseng, tanpa tujuan": Budi Darma, *Olenka*, 117.

xvi. " 'orang yang jiwanya menderita penyakit lepra' ": Budi Darma, *Olenka*, 119.

xvii. "Oleh pengarang saya diajak untuk membenci Si Bisu, seolah-olah dia harus dikucilkan bukan karena bisu, akan tetapi karena mempunyai penyakit jiwa yang sangat berbahaya dan cepat menular": Budi Darma, *Olenka*, 119.

xviii. "Otak saya diserbu oleh desakan-desakan hebat untuk terus menulis, sampai-sampai waktu saya untuk keperluan-keperluan lain banyak terampas"; "Selama seleranya untuk menulis belum longsor, dia menulis terus, kalau perlu melupakan makan dan tidur": Budi Darma, *Olenka*, 117, 86.

xix. "Sebagai pengarang, saya seperti Sisipus": Budi Darma, "Pengakuan," *Horison,* May/June 1982, 125.

xx. "saya menjadi Sisipus": Budi Darma, *Olenka*, 85.

xxi. " 'Pelukis Tanpa Kesalahan' ": Budi Darma, *Olenka*, 157.

xxii. "Andaikata saya Wayne, maka setelah menulis 'Saya juga ingin remuk dan hilang bentuk,' saya berhenti. Cerita berakhir di sini. Saya harus hati-hati, tahu dengan pasti di mana mulai dan di mana berhenti. Yang bukan-bukan dan tidak berarti harus saya hindari. Tetapi saya bukan Wayne": Budi Darma, *Olenka*, 214.

xxiii. "mengajari pembaca"; "kita merasa mendengar pidato": Budi Darma, "Tak Lain dan Tak Bukan," *Horison,* December 1973, 360.

xxiv. "Dan konsep pengarang yang doktriner mengurangi suasana sublimitas": Budi Darma, "Beberapa Gejala dalam Penulisan Prosa," *Horison,* January 1983, 15. This piece was originally delivered as a lecture on November 7, 1982.

xxv. "Kepentingan retorika dapat juga tidak sejalan dengan kepentingan moral. Kepentingan moral kadang-kadang dikorbankan untuk kepentingan retorika, sehingga yang menarik adalah daya tariknya, dan bukannya moralnya. Distorsi kepentingan moral dapat terjadi dalam akrobat pengarangnya": Budi Darma, "Moral dalam Sastra," *Basis,* March 1982, 9.

xxvi. "dalam kenyataannya, banyak hal-hal yang justru bertentangan dengan kepentingan moral terselip, atau bahkan menjadi bagian yang pokok, dalam karya-karya sastra monumental": Budi Darma, "Moral dalam Sastra," *Basis,* March 1982, 112.

xxvii. "Sebelum mobil berjalan, kami masih bercium-ciuman ganas. Begitu masuk apartmentnya, kami sama-sama melepas pakaian. Winifred menarik saya ke kamar-mandi. Kemudian dia menyetel kran panas, dan mandi satu bak dengan saya [. . .] Sebelumnya saya tidak pernah menikmati kepuasan sebesar ini": Budi Darma, *Olenka*, 159.

xxviii. Tirto Suwondo, *Membaca* Olenka *dalam Perspektif Bakhtin* (Penerbit BRIN, 2022), 124. The book also provides a useful summary of Indonesian-language literary criticism on *Olenka*, and is a revised version of an earlier work by Suwondo: *Suara-Suara yang Terbungkam:* Olenka *dalam Perspektif Dialogis* (Gama Media, 2001).

xxix. Budi Darma, "Character and Moral Judgment in Jane Austen's Novels," (PhD diss., Indiana University, 1980), 331.

xxx. Budi Darma, "Jane Austen's Novels," 334.

Bibliography

Aveling, Harry. "Dunia Yang Jungkir Balik Budi Darma." *Horison* (April 1974): 100–102.

Damono, Sapardi Djoko. "Catatan Kaki Si Tukang Ejek," *Tempo*, February 25, 1984.

Darma, Budi. "Beberapa Gejala dalam Penulisan Prosa." *Horison* (January 1983): 5–17.

———. "Character and Moral Judgment in Jane Austen's Novels." PhD diss., Indiana University, 1980. ProQuest Dissertations & Theses Global.

———. "Moral dalam Sastra." Part 1 of 2. *Basis* (February 1982): 42–50.

———. "Moral dalam Sastra." Part 2 of 2. *Basis* (March 1982): 109–20.

———. "Novel Indonesia adalah Dunia Melodrama." *Horison* (September 1983): 376–92.

———. *Olenka*. Balai Pustaka: 1983.

———. "Pengakuan." *Horison* (May/June 1982): 124–26.

———. "Prakata: Mula-mula adalah Tema." In *Orang-Orang Bloomington*. Sinar Harapan, 1980.

———. "Tak Lain dan Tak Bukan." *Horison* (December 1973): 359–60.

———. "Wawancara Tertulis Dengan Budi Darma." Interview by Sapardi Djoko Damono. *Horison* (April 1974): 127.

Hoerip, Satayagraha. "Kesanggupan Mengebor Sukma." *Sinar Harapan*, March 2, 1984.

[Rampan, Korrie Layun]. "Dalam Lintasan Sejarah Sastra Indonesia." *Horison* (July 1981): 224–25, 238.

Rosidi, Ajip. *Laut Biru Langit Biru*. Pustaka Jaya, 1982.

Suwondo, Tirto. *Membaca* Olenka *dalam Perspektif Bakhtin*. Penerbit BRIN, 2022.

———. *Suara-Suara yang Terbungkam:* Olenka *dalam Perspektif Dialogis*. Gama Media, 2001.

Suggestions for Further Reading

PRIMARY WORKS BY BUDI DARMA

Darma, Budi. "Bambang Subali Budiman." *Horison* (October 1981): 332–42, 359.
———. *Kritikus Adinan*. Bentang Pustaka, 2017.
———. "Mulai dari Tengah." In *Proses Kreatif: Mengapa dan Bagaimana Saya Mengarang*. Edited by Pamusuk Eneste. Penerbit PT Gramedia, 1982.
———. *Orang-Orang Bloomington*. Sinar Harapan, 1980.
———. *People from Bloomington*. Translated by Tiffany Tsao. Penguin Classics, 2022.
———. *Sejumlah Esei Sastra*. PT. Karya Unipress, 1984.
———. *Solilokui: Kumpulan Esai Sastra*. Penerbit PT Gramedia, 1983.

ESSAYS, BIOGRAPHIES, AND CRITICISM

Hoerip, Satayagraha. "Beberapa Catatan Mengenai '*OLENKA*' Karya Budi Darma." *Horison* (June 1986): 195–97.
Paramaditha, Intan. "Foreword." In *People from Bloomington*, by Budi Darma. Translated by Tiffany Tsao. Penguin Classics, 2022.
Pinurbo, Joko. "*Orang-Orang Bloomington*: Potret Manusia Aneh." *Basis* (October 1989): 379–90.
Saraswati, Asri. "Mad in Indiana: Disability as Dissent in Budi Darma's *The Bloomington People*." In *Cold War Mobilities: Indonesian Sojourning Writers, Neoliberalism, and Cultural Politics*. PhD diss., State University of New York at Buffalo, 2019. UBIR Repository.
Siswanto, Wahyudi. *Budi Darma: Karya dan Dunianya*. Grasindo, 2005.

Tsao, Tiffany. "Introduction." In *People from Bloomington*, by Budi Darma. Translated by Tiffany Tsao. Penguin Classics, 2022.

———. "When We Became the People from Bloomington." *Sydney Review of Books*. February 7, 2023, sydneyreviewofbooks.com/essays/when-we-became-the-people-from-bloomington.

A Note on the Text

For this translation, I consulted the original edition of *Olenka*, published by Balai Pustaka in 1983, with occasional reference to the 2018 edition published by Noura Books when further clarification was required. Any errors that were clearly typographical or unintentional have been corrected.

Instances of "Skokane" have been changed to "Skokie"—in line with what Budi Darma and I agreed on during our discussions for my translation of his short-story collection *People from Bloomington* (Penguin Classics, 2022).

In some cases, in the narrative portion of the novel (parts I through V), I have removed or shortened explanatory details meant specifically for an Indonesian audience (for example, a parenthetical note that pumpkins and squash are popular crops around Halloween time).

As with *People from Bloomington*, *Olenka* blends the factual with the fictional. There are many details—places, people, events—that correspond to real life. But there are also many details that, purposely, don't.

Unfortunately, it was not possible to include here the images that accompanied the text in the original edition. To replicate the effect of these as best as possible, I have translated these images into descriptive text.

The reader may notice that my own notes on Budi Darma's text and endnotes are extensive. I feel this is in line with the annotative, multiplicitous spirit of the original text. My notes appear with roman numerals in the text. Budi Darma's notes appear with Arabic numerals.

There are two features that I especially regret not being able to capture in this English edition: (1) the Javanese words sprinkled throughout the text, particularly the usage of "*sampean*" for "you," and (2) how the original Indonesian text displays Budi Darma's great skill as a literary translator—for the quotes he included from various non-Indonesian literary works are almost always accompanied by his rendering of them into Indonesian for his readership.

Olenka

For my late father and my mother

The proper study of mankind is man.

—Alexander Pope, *An Essay on Man*

PART I

CHAPTER 1

THREE SCRUFFY CHILDREN

When I first met her, the woman I would later come to know as Olenka, it was purely by chance. I was taking the elevator up to the fifteenth floor. She was in the elevator, too, with three scruffy children who looked around the ages of six, five, and four. At a glance, apart from their ragged clothes and the dirt on their skin, they looked like Olenka. All their noses had a detachable quality to them, as if you could pull them right off, and they had oval faces and ocean-blue eyes.

When the oldest child jumped to press the ninth-floor button because it was too high, Olenka did nothing. I couldn't help but assume that she would get off at the ninth floor too. Meanwhile, I pressed the button for level fifteen, and she still did nothing. So of course it didn't occur to me that she might be heading to the fifteenth floor as well.

But when the three scruffy children got out on level nine and she didn't, I asked, "Aren't you getting out?"

She shook her head.

I really should have kept quiet, or merely made some inoffensive remark. But for some reason, I asked, "Aren't they yours?"

She shook her head again. I should have stopped there or apologized, but I assaulted her with yet another remark. "Oh, I thought they must be yours. Funny, they look like you."

Only then did I realize that I was probably making her uncomfortable.

Indeed, she had taken offense. This time, she didn't shake her head but snapped fiercely, "They're not mine!"

She proceeded to tell me who they were and I discovered

that the object of her wrath wasn't me but the children's mother. She said about ten days ago, without any explanation, their mother had left.

"Why?" I asked.

"How should I know?"

She told me their father started work every day at eight and came back only at half past five.

"No wonder they're in such a state," she said.

She went on to criticize their mother, calling the woman "irresponsible" and "lacking any sense of humanity."

"A mother should raise her children properly," she added. The way she said it suggested her frustration at not having any kids herself.

I didn't verify whether this assumption was correct.

She and I got out on the fifteenth floor. She turned left and I turned right. Before parting ways, she asked which apartment I lived in. I should have asked her the same thing, but for some reason, what came out of my mouth was "I didn't know you live here too!"

How stupid I sounded. And stupider still, I didn't make any attempt to catch her name. It turned out to be Olenka, which I discovered only after meeting her a few more times.

After that day, I'd often see her, waiting for the bus, sitting in the park, lying in the grass. She always had a book in her hand. As she read, she always munched on something—nuts, cake, a sandwich, an apple. Sometimes she would even be chewing on a blade of grass, or on her own nails. She never looked up, so I never dared disturb her. When the bus came, she would immediately shut the book and get on board. And once inside, she would continue reading. Even if I did get the chance to strike up a conversation, she probably wouldn't remember me. From the way she acted, I concluded that she'd forgotten who I was.

The more I saw of her, the more she possessed me, filling my mind. I would see someone else and think it was her when it wasn't. Not infrequently, I felt as if she were sitting at my side. Also not infrequently, I sensed her hiding beneath the table or dashing behind a pillar. I would have the impression that she was running across the grass, or leaping from tree to tree. Sometimes, I felt her pulling at my clothes, tugging my ear, breathing down the back of my neck. I even felt, from time to time, as if she had slipped beneath my blanket and was tickling me. If I got up, she would run away, beckoning me to give chase.[1] The only way to free myself from these imagined Olenkas, I thought to myself, was to avoid her entirely. But in this, I failed. Practically every time I went to the bus stop, she would be there as well. Whenever I took a walk in the park, she would happen to be on a bench I passed. And whenever I went jogging and cut across the grassy field, there she was, lying in the sun. What puzzled me was why I never saw her again in our apartment building—Tulip Tree, massive, with hundreds of units, including hers and mine. I would see her at the bus stop in front of the building, but I never saw her coming or going from Tulip Tree itself.

Was she a student? Or did she work for the university? Or was she someone's wife? I had no idea. Her reading choices were eclectic. Sometimes she read fiction and sometimes textbooks. I couldn't tell for sure, but even the textbooks were never the same ones. The way she held her books as she read suggested that she was trying to avoid attracting attention. Maybe she wasn't a university employee after all. She'd never be able to fritter away her time like that if she were. She was probably a student. But a student of what, I couldn't guess either. She was always getting off the bus at different stops. In front of the liberal arts building. Or at the school of economics. I even saw her get off the bus and hurry toward the law school complex several times. And she often alighted at other places across the college campus as well.

She was probably married to someone, but I never saw her with any man. And I couldn't tell what kind of ring she was wearing. Maybe it was a wedding band. But maybe not.

The only conclusion I could draw was that she lived in her own world. And in this world, she never spoke with other people—had no desire to disturb nor be disturbed. Such was Olenka in public. How she was in private, I didn't know.

In the meantime, I would look out my window and see those

three scruffy children playing on the playground to pass the time. I must have seen them around before I'd met Olenka, but I noticed them only now. They seemed to be keenly aware of their place and kept their distance from the other kids. They behaved meekly and would merely look on while the others had fun, for they had no toys of their own. As such, they only played in ways that didn't require anything extra: like swinging on the swings, or running in and out of the tunnel. I was still of the opinion that they had Olenka's eyes.

CHAPTER 2

WAYNE AND STEVEN

I spent so much time observing the three scruffy children that I ended up noticing someone else as well. I must have seen him around before, but as with them, I hadn't paid any attention until now. He was lanky with thinning hair. Both his clothes and his person had a grubbiness about them. He looked perpetually insecure, afraid to face anyone, and was always glancing furtively about. He always had a boy with him, who looked around four years old. Up to this point, the boy had escaped my attention too.

But over time, I did recall having seen them in various places around Tulip Tree. They would hang around the parking lot, and also the grassy field, which separated Tulip Tree from the other large buildings. They also liked to take walks in the tulip garden, about a quarter mile away. Like the trio of scruffy children, they kept to themselves. But they seemed to prefer quiet places, as if they felt the playground wasn't the best place to pass the time.

Eventually I began focusing more on the child. I would later learn his name was Steven. It was as if he'd been trained to be submissive, to make no demands, to never associate with anyone besides the man. Gradually, I learned the man's name too: Wayne Danton.

Steven intrigued me because I had come to realize that his manner and person resembled those of Olenka. In fact, the similarities between Steven and Olenka were far more striking than those between her and those three scruffy kids. The differences between the boy and Olenka had nothing to do with appearance but rather circumstance. Olenka was free to determine her own movements and thus had her own world, whereas Steven had no choice but to submit. He was scared of everyone and everything.

One day I saw Wayne and Steven walking in the direction of the tulip garden. In order to confirm my suspicion that Steven was Olenka's child, I tailed them. I'd prepared some candy bars for the occasion, but I made as if I were simply out for a walk, with no particular destination in mind. Wayne seemed to sense that I was following them, and his movements became uncertain.

In the customary manner of someone starting a conversation, I said, "What fine weather we're having today! I hope it doesn't rain tomorrow. If I'm not wrong, I heard on the radio that it'll be clear for at least another three days."

Wayne merely nodded away, like someone who had lost his wits. He didn't say anything to Steven, but I knew that Steven, too, was surprised. They were acting like two thieves who'd been caught red-handed. Especially Wayne.

Just as I'd suspected, winning Steven over wasn't easy. He was silent, but I sensed he suspected me of evil intent. *So you think you can bribe me with chocolate?* seemed to be the thought running through his head. And this manner of thinking must have been instilled in him by Wayne.

Only then did I see it, the similarity between Steven's features and Wayne's, especially in the suspicious look I received for my gesture of goodwill. From this I put two and two together: Wayne must be Olenka's husband.

After fishing around using various tactics, I learned that I was right. Wayne and Olenka were indeed husband and wife. About one and a half years into their marriage, Steven had been born.

This was the story as Wayne told it: when he'd first met Olenka, he'd already been living in Skokie, Illinois, for a while. He had badly wanted to become a writer and, in fact, had already written several things. But they'd all been rejected by editors and publishers. In the meantime, he had bided his time, searching for like-minded friends. Eventually, he met a Ronald

Mitchell, who had himself long harbored dreams of being a writer but had since conceded total defeat. Mitchell had become a reporter for a local paper, the *Skokie Review*, instead. It was due to their shared literary ambitions that they became friends, and Wayne would often drop by Mitchell's office to visit.

Around the same time, there happened to be a new employee at Mitchell's workplace. Olenka was her name. Mitchell apparently sensed that she and Wayne would be a good match. He deployed various methods to draw them together. His efforts succeeded. Wayne and Olenka began spending a lot of time with each other.

Olenka knew that Wayne possessed a seed of writerly talent, and it was to this seed that Olenka was drawn. At Olenka's encouragement, Wayne wrote a short story, and this story wound up getting published in a well-known literary magazine, *The Kenyon Review*. Not only that, but in a letter to Wayne, the editor had declared the piece outstanding and worthy of inclusion in the *O. Henry Prize Stories* annual anthology.[2]

And that's what happened. Wayne's story was included in the anthology. Of course, no one in Skokie knew anything about literary magazines. And they didn't care whether a story made it into an anthology, much less which anthology it was.

But not Mitchell. As far as he was concerned, Wayne was God's gift to Skokie. He insisted that he wasn't going to let Wayne be ignored. He interviewed Wayne for the paper and wrote him up in glowing terms. He didn't stop there either. He brought in the mayor, informing him proudly that a bona fide writer called this town home.

Mitchell was like a machine gun, riddling the mayor with high praise for his friend. The mayor called Wayne in for a chat. Through all this, Mitchell never left Wayne's side. A few days later, the mayor held an official ceremony in Wayne's honor. The local newspaper, radio, and TV stations all covered the event.

Soon afterward, Wayne and Olenka were wed. Their marriage started well but went downhill fast. By the time Steven was due to be born, things were already dire, and eventually, their marriage broke down, though they never got divorced. According to Wayne, there was one simple reason why their marriage had failed. "Deep down, I'm a writer," he told me. What he meant, I had no idea.

Understanding Wayne's story was no easy business. Telling any story was a great struggle for him, and he had a complicated way of speaking, exacerbated by his confusion when it came to stringing together sentences, or a clear narrative arc. After saying, "My marriage failed for one simple reason," he didn't go on to explain what the reason was. He leaped abruptly to another matter: "Deep down, I'm a writer." He would use the wrong words. For example, he said he'd received an "envelope" from the mayor, though what he meant was a "letter." He himself was aware of these shortcomings. As such, he'd often pause and think before giving a bovine bellow of frustration, saying, "Point is, you know what I mean, don't you?"

There were other issues too. The more I genuinely tried to listen, the more he suspected that I was merely pretending to listen, and that I thought his story was made-up. Every now and then I sensed he thought I was only listening to him to make him happy. And also that I was only feigning listening in order to mock him. The look in his eyes suggested, also, that he thought I was putting him to the test, to ascertain whether his story was actually true.

If you ask me, he suffered from a strong subconscious, against which his much weaker conscious mind was no match. He processed and expressed ideas more on an intuitive level than a logical one. He wasn't necessarily wrong, but he often made errors. His subconscious knew he meant "letter," but his conscious mind would utter "envelope" instead. His subconscious knew precisely the sequence in which he wanted to recount his experiences, but his conscious mind would struggle to keep up.

He was better suited for a world where there was no need to communicate with others. But because he did have to communicate, it had eroded his self-confidence. Writing freed him to communicate only with himself, and ignore the readers whom he would never have to meet face-to-face. He could spend more time putting forth ideas and correcting errors without worrying whether people thought him stupid. And I was sure he wasn't as dim-witted as he looked. If he were given the chance to observe a matter from a distance, his observations were likely to be purer than those of someone else—of someone ruled more by their conscious mind and cleverer at articulating their opinions, however unsound those opinions actually were.

CHAPTER 3

THE OLENKA OF THE STORY

The next day, I went straight to the library. I rummaged through the card catalog until I found the anthology Wayne had been telling me about.

His short story was titled "Olenka." My supposition about Wayne had proven correct. In telling the story, he was talking to himself. For him the reader's world didn't exist, and if it did, then the reader was him.

I couldn't tell whether the story had been completed on the first pass or revised several times. A few of the words weren't quite right and the narrative arc wasn't very clear, but the story had a fullness to it, reflecting a first-class mind. His observations were keen and his insight strong, though the details were muddled. I was impressed.

The Olenka of the story was a girl of about twelve. Her family, the Albrights, lived on the Illinois plains. Just how many generations had lived there before them, even Albright himself didn't know. Their source of livelihood was that of their forebears, that is, a stone dam for trapping fish. Family lore had it that the dam had been built by Native Americans. They'd already received several notices from the sheriff's office ordering them to destroy the dam, but since the sheriff's office was about fifteen miles away, they could never do much. Anyhow, the sheriffs came and went, and they were all soft at heart. They would issue reminders, but never did anything more.

But then John Albirkin became sheriff. The first thing he did was examine the records. Unlike his predecessors, Albirkin was fiery and unyielding. He went on the offensive, but Albright went into hiding and Albright's wife pretended not to know what was going on.

The only one strong enough to stand up to the sheriff was Olenka. She looked adorable, but she was tough. Olenka proved too much for him and he was forced to retreat.

A few days later, Albirkin returned, breathing murderous threats. And it went on like this for some time. Albright kept hiding, his wife kept playing dumb, and Olenka kept bravely refusing to give Albirkin any ground. Finally, Albirkin could contain his wrath no longer. He brought dynamite with him, and after a short scuffle with Olenka, he destroyed the dam. It was blown to smithereens. Olenka quivered with rage and ground her teeth, but managed to keep her cool.

Olenka's father was beside himself. Hearing the explosions from his hiding place, he felt as if his own heart had been blown to bits. Olenka's mother had only been playing the idiot, but now she really turned into one. She roared and ran about, helpless to do anything more.

Meanwhile, Olenka calmly went and got a rifle. She ran behind a rock and secretly watched her brazen adversary from there. Satisfied with his handiwork, Albirkin mounted his horse and was about to ride back. Still calm, Olenka took aim. The rifle went off, the bullet whizzing over Albirkin's bald head. But Albirkin remained serenely seated in his saddle. The horse, too, remained steady on its feet without faltering or freezing in fear.

Again Olenka took aim, and again she fired. The same thing happened. And again with the third shot. Coolly, Albirkin dismounted. He lit a cigarette and walked over to Olenka. Equally unruffled, Olenka waited for him.

"Trying to kill me, you pesky little girl?" he yelled.

Olenka spat at him before replying. "Kill you, you crazy sheriff? No way. Not that I'm scared of going to jail. I just don't want to waste good bullets on something so worthless. I was just trying to scare your horse. If I were really out to kill you, I would've laid a trap between those two big rocks. Those ones, see? Over there. Then, once I'd caught you, I would've put a hole in your bald head. One should act only if it's worthwhile, don't you think? You've set an example for me yourself—you thought it worthwhile to blow up our dam. This dam once belonged to Indians, and they handed it down to my family generations ago."

Thus went Wayne's story. As I read it, my thoughts flew to Wayne's wife, whom I would only learn later was named Olenka. It felt as if the young Olenka of the story was an incarnation of the older Olenka, whom I knew only as "Wayne's wife." Her eyes, her detachable nose, all reminded me of her. As did her form, and the way she walked and lay on the grass and spoke and sat and did as she pleased.

Since Wayne wrote mostly from his subconscious, what I gathered about the Olenka in the story was merely implied by the story as a whole. This was Wayne's unique gift—his writing was more an act of suggestion than a statement of facts. He left things up to the reader's imagination. The story felt more like poetry than prose. As such, the Olenka of the story could live on in the mind, spectral, untouchable. Wherever I ran, she pursued me, and wherever I pursued her, she fled.

My relationship with the Olenka of the story was truly like my relationship with Olenka, Wayne's wife. I could never get close to her, could only gaze at her as if from afar, yet she never vanished from my thoughts. Sometimes I sensed her squatting at my feet, offering to slip off my shoes. I'd even feel as if she were running far ahead of me, goading me to chase after her. Silently, birdlike, lust descended on me, an urge to plunder Wayne's hidden treasure—the Olenka of the story and the Olenka who was his wife.

CHAPTER 4

IN OLENKA'S SHADOW

When I expressed my admiration for his story, Wayne looked doubtful. He didn't seem to believe that my praise was genuine. Then he acted as if I hadn't truly understood the story and was praising it only to make him happy. But when I went into detail, telling him my thoughts on the language he'd used and his turn of phrase—then his eyes shone like stars. He, in turn, praised my good taste.

He went on to confess that "Olenka" was the only short story he'd ever published. The rest had been rejected wholesale. Most editors had no taste, he said. And the few editors whose taste couldn't be faulted hadn't been able to publish his stories, deluged as they were by the sheer quantity of good stories written by others. They were too numerous to count.

"That's the problem with being a writer," he told me. Writers couldn't kill each other to get rid of the competition, so they just had to keep on writing. As such, even their best-quality works were regarded as if they were mass-produced. Supposing only one or two individuals had a monopoly over production. Then the public might value what they were producing. But if the masses were producing en masse, why, then the products might as well have come off an assembly line.

What Wayne meant by this, I didn't really know. And whether this was his actual opinion or he was using the wrong words again—like when he said "envelope" when he meant "letter"—I couldn't really tell. But he said it all in a matter-of-fact tone.

He had also written a few novels, but no one had wanted to publish them.

"If that's the case, then save your manuscripts for later," I said. "Who knows? Maybe you'll find a publisher one day."

"That I cannot do," he said, looking and sounding downright pitiful.

"Why?" I asked.

He refused to reply.

"And now I can't write anymore," he complained.

I wasn't sure what he meant. Had his talent dried up, or his energy given out, or were his hands tied in some other way? He wouldn't explain.

In the meantime, Olenka stopped waiting at the bus stop. And sitting in the park and lying in the field. I didn't know where she'd gone.

As usual, Wayne bummed around Tulip Tree with his son. Almost always, they walked silently, hand in hand. They seemed to communicate wholly through hand gestures. Naturally, I watched silently and never dared to ask, "Hey, Steven the Kid! Where's your mom?" Nor did I dare call out, "Hey, Wayne Danton the Writer! Where's your wife?"

Sometimes, Wayne's insecurity annoyed me. As did the way he would look around, stealing furtive glances, like a slave about to run away. My annoyance made me want to call the police. "There's this guy who's been lurking about," I'd report. "He doesn't seem dangerous but he's not quite right. Can you come and arrest him? He's spoiling the view." I wanted to watch them truss him up and kick him in the rear.

But once in a while, I felt sorry for him and thought of asking about the state of his marriage. Who knew? Maybe I could help lighten his load.

Back when he'd told me about getting married, all he'd said about his wife was the following: "If you ever see a woman gliding as if she's walking on air, like a fairy, then that's my wife. There's always a small bag slung over her left shoulder and an open book in her left hand. In her right hand, she carries something to snack on. Her mouth is always making slow chewing motions, as if she's uttering a prayer. That's my wife, all right. It can't be anyone else. Of course, you know what I mean, don't you?"

For a passing moment, I had thought he was joking. But from his tone, I realized the heaviness, the torment in his words.

And so I said nothing.

Then one day he told me how his wife was often to be found waiting for the bus, sitting in the park, lying in the field. He spoke piteously, as if he didn't approve of what his wife did but had to put up with it to avoid losing her. I surmised that, to him, his wife was no less a shadowy, spectral figure. She haunted his mind yet existed beyond the reach of physical touch.

Then he told me in a weepy voice about how their marriage had come to break down. I kept quiet, having no heart to comment, though, frankly, I desired to plunder his wife. I wanted to tell him, "Hey, Wayne Danton the Writer! I have something to say. At some point, I want to see your wife dressed in a sari from India. Then, someday, I want to see her in Persian garb like in *A Thousand and One Nights*. Then like a cowboy. And after that, like a female Tarzan. And oh, let's not forget: I want to see your wife dressed like Cleopatra. After that, I want to see her in a swimsuit. And last of all, I want to see her completely naked. That's what I want, Wayne Danton the Writer."

Indeed, whenever Olenka had been lying on the grass, she had been wearing a swimsuit. But she would cover herself with a blanket when anyone had passed by, including me. Her actions had suggested that she regarded people as if they were flies, buzzing around her, waiting for their chance to land. Accordingly, I put a great deal of brainpower into imagining how Olenka looked in that bathing suit.

Sometimes I found myself yearning to treat her body like a map. Given the chance, I would roll her up, then unfurl her on a bed or table, on the floor or a grassy field. If I had to, I'd hang her on a wall and point at parts of her body like a geography teacher pointing to cities. I would trace the roads connecting one city to another, one lake to another, one hill to another, one forest to another, one lowland to another, before shouting, "Hey, look! Here's the road to paradise!"

Meanwhile, fleeting shadows of Olenka refused to dislodge themselves from my mind. When I showered, she offered to scrub me, then pout for me to scrub her in return. But the real Olenka, who used to wait for the bus, sit in the park, and lie in the grass, I never saw.

I'd often take walks to drive out those apparitions, hoping to meet Olenka in the flesh. Nearly every day, I'd trace the places she used to visit. I even went on expeditions—a great many bus stops, a great many large parks, a great many grassy fields, all of which, as far as I could tell, she'd never visited at all. Yet Olenka was nowhere to be found.

Sometimes I'd stroll around the woods in the heart of the campus. There I would sit beneath a tree, or on a stone bench, or I'd rest awhile in the guard house. I'd also pass the time by watching the squirrels leap and run and eat acorns. Not infrequently, I'd even go up to the many sculptures scattered throughout the woods and stroke them with my hands. I'd even soak my feet in the river dividing the campus in two, which the locals dubbed the Jordan. They'd come up with a whole story, too, about Joshua's ghost crossing it one night.

In the middle of the forest I'd often see drama students rehearsing, yelling out their lines, as if performing a play were merely a matter of quarrels and shrieks. Their voices would reverberate, leaping from tree to tree. Meanwhile, the squirrels, chipmunks, birds, and other creatures calmly went about their business.

I often saw art students, too, sketching away—at trees, bridges, sculptures, big leaves, the guard house. A few works were very good, enough to elicit admiration. Even so, deep down in my heart I sneered. To me they were nothing but two-bit artists. They treated what they drew as if they were inanimate things rather than a joining together of subject and object as one. If only they could unify the two—then their work would possess spirit. And joy and sorrow, envy and rage, compassion and love.

The way they treated the objects they sketched was nothing like how I treated Olenka in my head or all the things Olenka had once touched. I would stare at the bus stop bench and the tree providing shelter overhead, at various spots in the park and the grass in the field and the footpath that Olenka had once trod, and they would become living creatures to me. The sight of them made me miss Olenka, made me angry at myself, made me laugh at myself—wasn't I tired of thinking about her?

If I were an artist, I would treat whatever I drew or painted as if it were my beloved, someone with whom I could converse and quarrel, whose faithfulness I could put to the test. These art students were no better than gamblers, pitting their skills against each other. Their artistic souls and visions were withering away, approaching zero. If they were orators, the equivalent would have been devising empty arguments and sparring with words. Like it or not, I had to admire Wayne Danton. He was the opposite of these so-called artists.

Sometimes, on the edge of the woods, I would listen in passing to a street preacher. He didn't have a loudspeaker but was determined to bellow out his sermon anyway. How shrill his voice was. He sounded angry, accusing and shouting and screaming away. And sure enough, some of the young people there did feel he was yelling at them, so they in turn yelled back. There were also those who egged him on, which caused the listeners to roar with laughter. Like many of the others, I thought his sermons were a joke.[3] Even so, something he said did leave an impression on me. "Thou shalt not covet what is not yours!" he boomed. And there I stood, longing to plunder Olenka.

A black-and-white news clipping from an issue of the *Indiana Daily Student*, published on Thursday, October 4, 1979, in Bloomington, Indiana. Below the newspaper logo, title, and date is a photo of a fair-skinned, portly, balding middle-aged man wearing sunglasses and a suit and tie. He brandishes a Bible in his right hand, and his left hand is gesturing, a blur of motion. He is arguing with a young dark-skinned man with a mustache who is wearing a white collared shirt and a sweater. The dark-skinned man holds a sheaf of typewritten pages in his left hand and points at the other man with his right hand as he speaks to him. In the background stand other young men watching intently, one of them laughing and motioning to his neighbor.

The text at the photo's bottom right corner attributes the picture to the staff photographer Brad Johns.

The photo's caption is titled "Just a minute" and reads as follows: *Max Kalumba, an African graduate student in philosophy, shakes a finger at evangelist Max Lynch during a short confrontation behind Woodburn Hall Wednesday afternoon. Lynch was delivering a sermon on the end of the world. Kalumba became upset when the preacher referred to Ethiopia in a derogatory manner. He said the evangelist was unqualified to speak about Africa.*

The street preacher being heckled by listeners. Fanton Drummond would often witness such scenes during his walks near the edge of the woods.

CHAPTER 5

I MEET OLENKA

One night, Bloomington was buffeted by strong winds. A good part of the city lost power for almost half an hour. Reportedly, "very few" people got trapped inside elevators, but the university and downtown area suffered considerable damage.

The next day, I went walking in the woods. Fallen trees lay here and there, casualties of the windstorm from the previous night. I saw students sketching them and felt angry for the same reason as before: they were treating the fallen trees as lifeless, inanimate objects.

I walked on, into the heart of the woods. Eventually, I reached a small hill. From there, I had a good view of my surroundings. The wind had toppled many trees there as well.

And then I saw something I hadn't noticed before. A woman with a large clipboard sketching a tree that had fallen onto a wooden bridge. Her back was to me, so I couldn't be sure of her identity, but it was entirely possible that she was Wayne's wife. So I approached her—from behind, of course.

Apart from my interest in the person herself, I was impressed by what she had chosen to draw and how she had positioned herself. From these things alone, I could tell she had artistic sensibilities. And when I saw her work, I was even more in awe. It was as if the storm were raging before my eyes, and the tree, overcome, was keeling over and falling onto the bridge, and the bridge itself was now suffering, wounded. A simple sketch, yet it implied the entire progression of events, the falling of the tree, the wounding of the bridge.

"Fanton Drummond!" she called out. She must have looked

up my apartment number in the residents' directory and found my name. "I knew you would show up at just the right time."

She didn't turn her head. And I didn't know why, but I drew still closer.

"Fanton," she said, still not looking at me. "Sit here, Drummond. Guard this drawing. I'll only be a minute, Drummond."

She stood and ran over to the bridge, studied it awhile, walked back and forth a few times, then returned. Not once did she glance my way.

"Fanton, I knew you would come. Now sit here, Drummond. Near me, Fanton."

I obeyed.

As she examined her work, she asked, "Fanton, why are you following Wayne around? Answer me, Drummond!"

I replied that I wasn't following him around. "We just happen to bump into each other. Then we start chatting," I said.

"Fanton, I know what you two have been chatting about. Drummond, you were talking about his short stories. Isn't that right, Fanton?"

I didn't deny it.

She spoke scornfully. "Wayne must have told you all about *The Kenyon Review*. And bragged about his story getting into that anthology. He must have run out of breath telling you about Mitchell and the mayor and the official ceremony and being in the news, and everything else. Come on, Drummond, admit it. It's true, Fanton, isn't it?"

I didn't argue.

She continued, "I bet he told you all about when Steven was born. I bet he was shameless enough to tell you about our marriage breaking down. Come on, Fanton, be straight with me. Isn't that what he did, Fanton?"

Again, I didn't argue.

Then she told me to copy what she had just done—stand up, run to the bridge, study it for a little, then pace back and forth for a few seconds examining the tree before returning where we were.

When I did, she issued more instructions. "Hey, Drummond. Go back to the bridge and walk back and forth again."

I obeyed.

She said, in order to draw an object well, she had to study all the movements around it. If she paid attention only to the object itself, it would become a mere thing, devoid of life. She found it easier to draw something if it was surrounded by movement.

"An object must be the motion, must be the connections it forms with everything around it," she said.

Then she told me that not paying attention to the object itself was to commit a great error. "True, one doesn't need to draw every detail. But if one doesn't master all the details of an object, one won't be able to draw it well."

From her manner of speaking, you would think we had known each other for a long time.

"I know you've been watching me, Drummond. Fanton, do you hear? I know that my movements have been etched into your brain. And I knew you would show up because I *felt* that you've been looking for me. And also, I *felt* it was high time you found me, Fanton."

Then she openly admitted that she had been watching me too. She said she *felt* she'd seen me somewhere before, though she didn't know where or when or on what occasion.

"Even before I asked you about those three scruffy kids who live on the ninth floor of Tulip Tree?" I asked.

"Yes, Fanton. *Before* you asked about them, Drummond. *Before* I moved into Tulip Tree. *Before* I moved to Bloomington. Now, Fanton, listen. I feel I know you from somewhere—from even *before* I got married. Do you believe me, Drummond? Before any of this, Fanton."

I laughed.

"Have you ever been to Chicago, Fanton?"

"No."

"How about Rockfield, Illinois, Fanton Drummond?"

"No."

"Peoria, Fanton?"

"No."

"Springfield, Drummond Fanton?"

"No."

"Hmph. Well, in that case, how about Urbana-Champaign, Fanton Drummond? Hold on a second. Is your name Fanton Drummond or Drummond Fanton?"

"Fanton Drummond."

"Ever been to Urbana-Champaign, Fanton Drummond?"

"Almost, but I didn't end up going."

"Oh, in that case, it must have been someone else, or a few other people, who looked like you. I saw you in all those places, *before* I moved to Skokie, Illinois. That's why when I saw you in Tulip Tree, I thought, 'Ah, here he is. That same guy. He must be following me again. Just wait and see. He's biding his time, waiting for the right moment.' "

CHAPTER 6

THE MEETINGS THAT FOLLOWED

Olenka and I met often. Anyone watching would have thought that our meetings were purely by chance. Olenka was wonderfully clever in setting a time and place, then acting as if she'd run into me without intending to do so. I was merely Olenka's object. She determined the schedule and location, and I bowed to her will. Where we would go and what we did at our meetings were also up to her.

All the scheduling was done without taking Wayne into account. She chose places far from Tulip Tree not because she was scared or intimidated by Wayne but because meeting near her apartment wouldn't be enjoyable.

"It would spoil the mood," she said. If Wayne did ever happen to catch us during one of our meetings, "then I could plausibly say that we met by coincidence," she reasoned.

"Won't Wayne know you're making things up?" I asked. The little Olenka of his story popped into my mind.

"He'll know I'm lying, but he won't know if his suspicion that I'm lying is correct."

She then told me that Wayne was genuinely stupid, though admittedly, his powers of perception were very strong.

"He's a casualty of the struggle between intuition and logic, Fanton. It's why he's always confused, frightened, and insecure, Drummond."

She confessed that she loved Wayne because there was something primitive about him, but that she also hated and despised him for his stupidity. "No wonder he always has such a tough time with everything," she said.

She had her own faults too. "I don't always think about where my actions will take me," she said. "And I've suffered a great deal as a result."

When she was younger, for example, there had been a football player who'd liked her. "As heaven and earth are my witness, I love you, Olenka," he'd declared.

His sweet-talking and being nice to her was enough to get her knocked up. As luck would have it, after the football player retracted his declaration of love, calling her a "slut," the pregnancy miscarried on its own.

She would find herself reading books that she admired initially, but which would turn out to be awful. The reverse happened too. And sometimes, she had no idea whether a film she was watching was good or bad. Only when someone else declared it good did she know that it was. Then she could argue in the film's defense. The same if someone declared it bad.

She felt Wayne was the opposite. Wayne knew immediately whether the thing before him was good or bad without being told. But if contradicted, he'd get confused.

His powers of imagination were also first-rate and very strong. Believe it or not, Wayne's conjectures would sometimes come true. For example, one day, when they were still living in Skokie, Wayne saw a helicopter land in a field near their apartment building. It wasn't long before the helicopter attracted a small crowd. The helicopter then began giving rides. After circling a few times, the helicopter landed and took different passengers on board, and on it went. The crowd got bigger. People were lining up.

Out of the blue, Wayne remarked, "Imagine if the pilot just got his flying license. The helicopter might crash."

After taking off and landing several times, the helicopter took four children on board. They looked like they were siblings.

Wayne remarked, "Imagine if their father were only buying life insurance for them today. There'd be problems, then."

Soon afterward, the helicopter crashed in a vineyard. The

pilot sustained serious injuries. His four small passengers winged their way to heaven, leaving the pilot to suffer his misfortune alone. What Wayne imagined came true: the insurance company refused to pay compensation for the snuffing out of the four children's souls. They said the accident had occurred mere minutes before the father had bought the insurance. Furthermore, the accident could have been avoided because everyone should have known better—the pilot had only gotten his flying license the day before. The case ended up in court. What happened afterward, Olenka didn't know.

According to Olenka, Wayne had written a short story based on these events, and it had been even more powerful than the events themselves. He'd used the helicopter crash as inspiration, but his own imagination had provided the rest. That was how strong Wayne's imagination was. "And I'm willing to bet that anyone who read Wayne's story and happened to know about the incident would never guess the two were related," said Olenka.

I asked whether the story had gotten published.

"No," she replied.

"Why?"

"There are lots of equally powerful stories out there."

Then she repeated what Wayne had said about how good writing became a mass-produced item if there were more than one or two people writing to that standard.

"Those are Wayne's words," she continued, "and he really means them. Or rather, that's partly what he means. But what is true—and this is what Wayne actually wants to articulate but can't—is that under the circumstances, Fanton, a writer needs to be better than the average writer, all of whom are good. And he's failed to become a better good writer than all the other good writers. Like I said, Drummond. Logic's not his strong suit."

CHAPTER 7

THE NEW ENGLAND MIND

Olenka and I weren't as intimate with each other as I'd initially hoped. During the coincidental meetings she scheduled, she'd fall into old habits. She'd go on living in her own world, reading and chewing away. If I greeted her, she would utter a "hello" before returning to her world.

One day she was waiting for the bus in such a manner. When the bus came, she boarded it without so much as an upward glance. I deliberately sat next to her. She didn't acknowledge my presence at all, as if I were merely part of the seat.

She got off near Ballantine Hall without saying a word to me. Actually, I wanted to get off and follow her but felt shy about doing so. So I stayed on the bus. All I knew was that she'd been reading *The New England Mind: The Seventeenth Century*, by Perry Miller.[4] The pages she'd been reading were about how the Puritans in seventeenth-century New England dealt conceptually with matters of destiny and free will. They saw both destiny and free will as God-given. The distinction between them wasn't at all clear. Anyone who used their free will to become lawless and immoral must have been already destined to do so. Unfortunately, this meant that self-righteous individuals considered themselves "destined" by God to lead those "not destined to lead." Over time, they began to lord it over those they considered unrighteous, who therefore needed to be set on the right path.

The topic reminded me of the arguments between the street preacher and his onlookers. The preacher had once yelled, "God sent me to rouse you all from the filth of your sins!"

Mockingly, an onlooker had yelled back, "What gives you the right to say you've been sent by God?"

Another onlooker had sneered, "What gives you the right to accuse me of being filthy with sin?"

At this, the people in attendance had cheered.

But back to this book—no wonder then, said Miller, that some writers took up their pens to accuse the Puritan leaders of being the devil's agents. They were abusing their authority. Ironically, in the extreme measures they had taken to flee the devil, evil desires had taken hold of them instead.

CHAPTER 8

THE ELBERHART BELL TOWER

In the following meetings she scheduled, Olenka began acting more warmly, her every action inviting me to trace her every curve, inside and out. Every gesture of hers showed, too, a desire to dive into my own depths, body and soul.

Once, as we were leaving the woods and approaching Ballantine Hall, I heard the cries of students taunting the street preacher. Olenka called him a "phony." As such, she approved of the measures taken by local authorities in Terre Haute, Ellettsville, and Morgantown to ban such preachers from sermonizing at will. She concurred that such people shouldn't be allowed to go around yelling anywhere and everywhere. They should keep to their own buildings, where they could bellow away as much as they pleased. She felt such people were too full of themselves. They believed themselves sent by God without even batting an eye, and they took anyone who happened to be nearby for a sinner without thinking twice either.

Following Olenka's lead, we walked toward the Elberhart Bell Tower, situated on a small hill about two miles from Tulip Tree. She expressed her regret at choosing an apartment overlooking the state road instead of the grassy field. As a result, she couldn't see the bell tower from her window. How happy it would make her, she told me, to go up to the top one day and look out over the whole of Bloomington.

Then she brought me up to the ninth floor. A sign there read: *Special permission required to access floors beyond this level. Call: 812-339-6651.* There was a pay phone next to the sign.

Two young people happened to be there too—a couple.

"I wish I could go to the top," said the girl. If I'm not mistaken, her name was Alice.

"I went up there once," said the boy. If I'm not mistaken, his name was Cody.

"How did it feel?" asked Alice.

"Terrifying," said Cody. "Just picture it. Every building in Bloomington spread out before you, with only one of them standing out—the proudest, the noblest, the most intimidating of them all. Though, it's not even that big or that tall, compared to the rest of them."

"And which building is that?" asked Alice.

"The hospital," Cody replied.

As Olenka listened to their conversation, I saw her eyes glisten with emotion. What was it about what they had said, I had no idea. On our way back down, I told her that the tower had been built by a doctor named Elberhart in memory of those who had died from cancer.[i] In life, Dr. Elberhart had spent almost all his time and energy waging war against that cursed disease. His failure must have irritated him, so he'd donated nearly everything he had to the Institute for Cancer Research. A portion of the money was used to erect this tower.

"And what happened to Dr. Elberhart?"

"Suicide. People say he got cancer in the end too. The consequences of his failure, I guess."

Then Olenka repeated the word over and over—"suicide"—in a peculiar tone.

"It's a shame that someone like him died by suicide."

Then, shyly, Olenka took out her folder and showed me a drawing of the bell tower. I was astonished. It was like the other drawing I'd seen. I could feel the wind blow and the swooping of the birds.

"It's a shame I didn't know the story behind the bell tower before drawing it, Fanton. If I did, Drummond, it would have turned out different."

Once again she expressed her desire to climb to the top, so she could draw it accurately.

"Not now, but maybe someday," she said.

She spoke uncertainly, as if her mind had flown far away, who knew where. Unusually for her, her palms were sweaty.

When it was time for us to part, she didn't say anything about our next appointment. Even when I asked, she wasn't willing to answer. Then she held my hand and expressed her desire to extend our present session by a few minutes more.

After some silence, with an air of regret, she said that Wayne had been out of a job for too long and that she wanted to start working again. It would be ideal if she could get a job at a nightclub. There, she'd be able to study all sorts of faces—the lonely, the downhearted, the idle, the foolish, the drunk, and the like.

CHAPTER 9

OLENKA'S PHONE CALL

Two months later, I received a phone call from Olenka. She said she'd recently started working five days a week as a cashier at Nick's English Hut, a nightclub on Kirkwood Avenue.

Once I learned this, I'd amble over to Kirkwood Avenue every night. I'd stop outside on the sidewalk and watch the back of Olenka's head through the window. I would never go in.

At first it didn't bother me, but over time I grew jealous. My attempts to run into her by chance never worked. Meanwhile, I would still see Wayne and Steven from my apartment window as they hung around Tulip Tree, killing time. I felt sorry for Wayne but not jealous. I saved that for the men who would visit Olenka's nightclub—men sporting beards and sideburns and wide-brimmed hats and colorful clothes and who smoked. True, I only ever watched the back of her head, but I got a good view of their heads, too, because they were always swarming in and out of the club, often stopping to strike up long conversations with her. From the movements of her head, I was sure that Olenka was pleased at being thronged by so many men.

One night my phone rang. Olenka said that she had sent Wayne and Steven on a vacation to Stoneville, Illinois. She invited me over so I could see they were really gone.

"I'm taking tonight off work, Drummond Fanton, oh, Fanton Drummond."

A grainy black-and-white photo clipped from the *Indiana Daily Student* newspaper dated November 15, 1979. A stout fair-skinned man with light hair, dressed in a dark long-sleeve top and jacket, stands smiling in front of a row of stores at night. Pinned to his chest is a large circular badge. The text on it is difficult to make out, but the large number 30 is discernible. The storefront behind him has a Tudor-cottage-style appearance to it, with a scalloped overhang and lattice-pane windows. The sign above the door reads, in large Old English font, *Nick's English Hut.* Above the door to the establishment is the Indiana University trident. The photographer's name is printed at the bottom right corner of the photo: David R. Lutman.

The accompanying text below the photo reads: *When Dick Barnes was a business student at I.U., he put himself through college by working in a local clothing store on Kirkwood Avenue. After work, he'd ramble down the street to relax over a beer at Nick Hrisomalos' tavern, and Barnes and the old Greek developed a friendship. After he graduated, Barnes spent an unsuccessful year job hunting. He returned to Bloomington in 1953 and opened another local legend—Cafe Pizzaria—just down the street from his old haunt. Upon his friend Hrisomalos' death, Barnes bought the tavern and has been supervising it ever since. (Photo taken with 16mm fisheye lens.)*

Nick's English Hut, the nightclub where Olenka worked.

On the way to her apartment, the street preacher's words rang in my ears. If he knew what I was doing, he'd declare without a doubt that I belonged in hell. But I wanted to see Olenka in a thousand different costumes. I wanted to see her in an Indian one, and a Japanese one, and a Chinese one, and a thousand-and-one-nights one, and an American Indian one. Then I wanted to view her in her swimsuit. I wanted to roll her up like a map and sling her over my shoulder and unfurl her, on table, floor, or bed. If I had to, I'd hang her on the wall and play geography teacher, tracing cities and rivers, roads and railways and hills on my map.

Upon entering her apartment, I found her already in her swimsuit.

"I *knew* you wanted me to wear this. I've *felt* you whispering, telling me to do so, oh Fanton, my Drummond."

After that evening, she'd invite me to go swimming at different pools around town. Sometimes she'd drag me to the various lakes surrounding Bloomington. Unsatisfied with the job I'd do toweling her off, she'd invite me to do it over, but with my bare hands. She said my touch was warm, enjoyable, intense.

The street preacher must have been ordered to move on from the first place, because he relocated his practice to South Tenth Street, near the public pool. This was the one Olenka and I visited the most, so I often heard him hollering outside.

Apparently, the street preacher wasn't satisfied with his solo efforts. He'd found two cronies to take turns. If there were too many people laughing at them, they would advance in a line. Together the three of them would screech at the top of their lungs and brandish their fists for good measure. The more people who viewed them as a laughingstock, the louder their voices, and the clearer their shouting could be heard from the pool. The content of the shouting must have seeped into my heart. When Olenka and I parted ways this time, I made the decision not to see her again.

Three meeting times passed and I avoided Olenka. I felt that, until now, I'd focused only on the listeners who mocked the street preacher. Yet I knew that among the many clustered around him, there were those who truly listened and nodded earnestly along. Some of them even had tears in their eyes.

But all this time, I'd simply ignored them. Sometimes I'd see one or two young people chasing after him on his way home—to inquire about issues pertaining to this world and the hereafter. One night I even saw someone greet him cheerfully: "Hello, Mr. Street Preacher! How are you?" They went on to discuss the sermon the preacher had given. One time I even saw him at the post office standing in line to buy stamps, and a number of people greeted him warmly and chatted with him for a bit.

A black-and-white advertisement from an issue of the *Indiana Daily Student* dated Tuesday, November 13, 1979. In the upper left corner is a photo of a dark storefront bearing the sign *Nick's English Hut* in white letters. Visible at the photo's edges are part of a car and a streetlamp. To the right of the photo is text, reading: *Draft Beer Specials!! Come down to Nick's and help Celebrate Ruth's 30th anniversary of serving IU Students, Wednesday, Nov. 14*. Below both the photo and this text is a separate box of text that reads, *Nick's English Hut, 423 E. Kirkwood, "An IU Tradition for Over 4 Decades."* Each word in *Nick's English Hut* is in a different font: *Nick's* and *English* in Old English style fonts, and *Hut* in all capital letters and a more modern-looking font.

The nightclub, Nick's English Hut, in the early forties, before Olenka was born.

CHAPTER 10

WAYNE'S WRITING METHOD

I should have thought to probe more into Olenka, Wayne, and Steven's relationship from the start. This whole time, I'd regarded Wayne and Steven merely as Olenka's backdrop, without any curiosity about how their lives had come to be the way they were. From the beginning, I should have lent a hand in bringing about reconciliation. And I wondered at my past actions—how, whenever Olenka had made fun of Wayne, I had deemed it a sound thing to do, earnestly joining in. Even when we were in Olenka's apartment and she'd shown me Wayne's manuscripts, I considered what she had done to them a clever joke.

According to Olenka, there was a Russian writer whose method of working Wayne greatly admired. Wayne himself had forgotten the name of the writer—he'd read him in translation as a child. According to the translator, this writer had a certain habit: he would take walks every day. Sometimes, during these walks, wonderful words would pop into his head. The writer would jot the words down and affix them to the wall of his study. Using them as a springboard, he would then begin to write. The words would open up new horizons in his mind, which he required in order to complete his works.[5]

Wayne had started imitating the writer. At first, it was the walls of his study that were covered with words. He forbade Olenka from entering. But once the study walls were full, Wayne covered the kitchen in wonderful words too. He forbade Olenka from taking them down. Finally, Wayne moved on to the bedroom. That was why even the walls of their bedroom were filled with notes.

Wayne would wake up in the middle of the night and order

Olenka to leave the room. He'd say inspiration had struck and he wanted to use some of the wonderful words as his springboard. He claimed that if he didn't start writing immediately, his inspiration would vanish without a trace. And Wayne had kept up with this method, from those early days until now.

Besides all this, Wayne refused to find work. He said it would disturb the flow of his craft. As a result, Olenka was saddled with the burden of supporting the family. Olenka was patient at first. Eventually, she suggested Wayne adopt a different method. He refused. Olenka proposed that Wayne get a job and write in his spare time. Wayne replied that the Russian writer he admired had never had a job. Yes, but he was a feudal lord, said Olenka. Over time, Olenka got fed up. Even so, she left Wayne's manuscripts alone.

It was only when Olenka couldn't bear her suffering any longer that she took his manuscripts—every one that received a rejection from a publisher or magazine—and scattered them, and stuck their pages all over the walls.

Indeed, upon entering Olenka's apartment for the first time, these wall decorations had astonished me. After hearing Olenka's story, I joined her in having a good laugh. Some pages had been posted upside down, some askew, and some straight. A few sheets had holes in the middle and a few had been folded into paper kites. Some bore labels: *Tolstoy's third-rate writing*, *One of Dostoyevsky's major works*, *An unpublished Pushkin*, *A note from Solzhenitsyn*, *From the Guggenheim Museum archives in New York*, *A lost manuscript by an unknown writer*, and the like. All the labels had a mocking, disdainful tone. I had added my own comments. I now regretted doing that.

Nevertheless, almost every night I went walking on Kirkwood Avenue. As before, I would stare at the back of Olenka's head. And as before, I would be jealous. And as before, whenever I saw Wayne, I felt no jealousy at all.

One day I found several drawings that had been slipped under my apartment door. They were all scenes of nightclubs. And as with Olenka's other drawings, they seemed to breathe, demanding to be treated as living things. From one glance I could feel the nightclub's hustle and bustle, its clamor and commotion. There was a waitress carrying a tray, a man drunkenly pinching the waitress's bottom, men and women roaring with laughter, and other similar scenes.

It puzzled me that Olenka drew only for her amusement. She was genuinely gifted, and if she wanted, she could sell her art at a good price.

On the back of one drawing was a message: *I'm* not *mad at you for feeling how you do. I've* always known *that you'd end up avoiding me someday. But give me one more chance to meet you again. It's important. Meeting me openly would be better than standing on Kirkwood Avenue spying on the back of my head.*

I decided to ignore her message. And I resolved never to go to Kirkwood Avenue again. In Tulip Tree, I never used the elevator in the middle of the building—the one closest to her apartment—for fear she might spot me. Better to use the elevator on the south side, even though it was a little farther away. I also tried to avoid seeing Wayne, stopped taking walks in the woods, and steered clear of the bus stop and park as much as I could. I wanted to rid myself of anything to do with Olenka. Yet I couldn't help but wonder why Olenka drew only for fun.

Unexpectedly, as I was reading the notice board near the journalism school, Olenka came up and pinched my bottom. I couldn't run now. She dragged me to the basement level of the journalism school and took me to the vending machines to buy drinks and nuts.

"I'm low on cash," she said.

Then she told me Wayne was still unemployed—a parasite in his own home. True, he'd gotten a job at a burger joint, but only for two days. After that he'd gone on strike. Not only had he given the same old excuse, namely, being unable to write whenever his attention was divided, he'd also accused Olenka of being "a useless woman—incapable of even looking after her own child."

"If I got a job, what would you do with Steven?" Wayne had asked, according to Olenka. Though she also admitted that, in this matter, Wayne had been right. But there's a story behind everything, and Olenka's tone was merely explanatory without being defensive or hostile toward Wayne. I wanted to know the backstory but kept quiet instead.

She told me that she really did enjoy working at the nightclub. The pay was good and the work was fairly easy. With three mouths to feed, of course, it simply wasn't enough. She was now planning to buy or rent a place where she could live, on Bloomington's west side—it could double as a studio, so she could sell her art. Meanwhile, she'd keep working at the nightclub. She was willing to keep paying for the apartment in Tulip Tree, as well as for Wayne's and Steven's expenses.

I wondered silently where she would get that kind of money, but I didn't ask out loud. Truth be told, I'd never had any reason to think that she had any problems when it came to funds. She always wore nice clothes, even though I knew she hadn't worked for a long time before getting the nightclub job.

Unasked, she explained that she had once attended the School of Art & Design at the University of Illinois Urbana-Champaign. But she'd gotten discouraged when she'd realized that her professors weren't as good as her. She had also once lived with some other artists in Chicago and had held a few exhibitions. A lot of people had looked around, complimented her on her work, and then gone home without buying anything.

"I think I was too earnest, Fanton. I wanted to be original. As a result, Drummond, no one wanted to buy my art."

I praised the works of hers that I'd seen. Modestly, she laughed.

Then she said, "When I make art for fun, Fanton, it ends up turning out good. If I do get my own studio, Drummond, I'll probably try to have the same attitude. I exhibited once in San Francisco. I sold almost eighty percent of my works, Fanton. They fetched good prices too."

CHAPTER 11

THE FLEA

Olenka and I continued to meet at set times. In every encounter, we couldn't help ourselves—we turned into animals. She felt freer coming to my apartment than if I went over to hers. She said walking into my apartment was like walking into heaven—a fresh, beautiful paradise where she could be content, body and soul. To further enhance the paradisical mood, she bought me a lot of potted plants. Meanwhile, her own apartment was left to languish and gather dust.

As usual, I used Olenka's body as I would a map of the world. I committed every curve to memory. I could have recognized even the beating of her heart. I'd place her on the bed, then move her to the desk, and then to the bathtub, and on to the sofa, the rug, the kitchen counter, and even the dresser. Sometimes, when I placed her on the dresser, she would fall asleep.

The air in my apartment was often very dry, which irritated my skin, especially my cheeks, hands, and lips. To counter the dryness, I would open all the windows. And little creatures would jump in—they'd been crawling around outside on the building walls.

One day, Olenka fell asleep after I'd placed her on the dresser. Then I myself fell asleep, on the rug.

Suddenly, I felt something hot on my arm, and I woke up. There was a red dot there, and Olenka was already awake. She chuckled and compared my arm with hers, also speckled with red.

Then I spied a flea crawling around, its body swollen, filled with blood. This, of course, was the creature to blame for Olenka's red spots and mine.

I was about to kill the flea, but Olenka wouldn't let me. She ran to the bookcase to get out a collection of poems. After searching the index, she read me a poem by John Donne. I thought the poem awful. Perhaps I lacked taste. Notwithstanding, the poem had survived, all the way from the seventeenth century, when it was written, to the present day. Many people even considered it good:

Mark but this flea, and mark in this
How little that which thou deniest me is;
It sucked me first, and now sucks thee,
And in this flea our two bloods mingled be;
Thou know'st that this cannot be said
A sin, nor shame, nor loss of maidenhead.[6]

In the poem, a flea bites two lovers. Naturally, their blood is united in the flea's body, like Olenka's blood and mine.

As in his other poems, John Donne was emphasizing the symbolic importance of physical union in representing the unity of spirit, world, and afterlife. It wasn't just about union on a spiritual level.

Olenka and I laughed.

"He took something common, repulsive even, and turned it into a good poem," she observed.

Then she complained about the difficulty she encountered when trying to transform simple objects into good art. She also complained how hard it was to kill the artist part of her brain. She might be waiting for the bus, or people-watching, or she might look up at the sky to see two birds falling as if they'd been shot, and she'd be overcome with the urge to channel these things into art. But then she'd feel too embarrassed to try. She was sure she would fail. So she tried to forget that she was an artist at all. Even as her hands itched to make art, her brain would order her hands to suppress their desire to do so. A tremendous struggle.

As she talked, I turned back to studying Donne's poem.

When she was done, I pronounced the poem bad. Even in light of the fact that it had been composed in the seventeenth century, this poem wasn't worthy of praise. A flea was a flea. Nothing more. Not like the phoenix in another one of Donne's poems, where the phoenix dissolves into ashes, and from those ashes a new phoenix is born. "There's regeneration there," I said. "Spiritual and physical love, this world and the next, are like the phoenix, turning to ash one minute, and the next, transformed into new, fresher love."[i]

Olenka agreed, saying she also had trouble assigning her objects roles beyond their physical ones. This was what killed art, she said. Accordingly, the artist's great challenge was to infuse their objects with other elements. Only in this way could the object function as a symbol and, at the same time, a mystery. Only in this way, too, could an artwork invite the viewer to continually ponder an object, and therefore, never get bored. The more people looked, the more they'd want to keep on looking, unsatisfied by their attempts to penetrate the object's mystery. A good painting must be something familiar to the viewer, inviting them to enter the object's world, even though no one ever could. In order to accomplish this, many artists had looked to mythology for their objects. She gave several examples, adding, "John Donne too. He took the phoenix from an ancient Greek myth."

I agreed. Even so, most mysteries had now become mundanities. Even the old myths were now obsolete. Once people made it to the top of Mount Olympus and found nothing there, the very fundament of ancient Greek mythology crumbled. No kingly Zeus, no heroic Hercules, no childlike gods who treated human beings like flies.[ii] The phoenix, too, was nothing but nonsense, as were Donne's ideas concerning heaven:

> *Is the Pacific Sea my home? Or are*
> *The eastern riches? Is Jerusalem?*[iii]

In this poem, Donne ponders where his soul is headed. To heaven, of course. But where was heaven? This is the matter raised by Donne. To make things easier for the reader, he says perhaps it's in the Pacific Ocean, or the exotic East, or perhaps even in Jerusalem. In the seventeenth century, these places were still a mystery. But once people could travel there with ease, the mystique surrounding the splendor of these sites was gone. No longer could anyone believe that heaven might be somewhere there. On a similar note, there were some Polish schoolchildren in the early twentieth century for whom America was a mystery. Their teacher told them that America was located on the other side of the world—meaning, of course, the opposite side of the world from Poland. So they thought people in America must walk upside down, with their heads below and their feet above.

In that case, observed Olenka, what about when Copernicus proposed his theory about the earth being round and orbited by the moon? And the earth and other planets orbiting the sun? That must have put an end to all notion of heaven being above, since the very nature of the mystery concerning what was "above" had changed in itself.

"I suppose," I said.

For some reason, Olenka switched topics—to a famous story from the nineteenth century called "Young Goodman Brown" by the eminent short-story writer Nathaniel Hawthorne. Once upon a time, so the story goes, some centuries back, a young goodman named Brown lived in New England. And at the time, New England was governed by Puritans, who strove to shun all devilish influences in order to keep themselves pure. As a young goodman, naturally, Brown keeps all the Puritan customs and laws. He is devout to a tee and his actions are faultless. As with the rest of society at the time, Brown's one and only goal in life is to prepare himself in the present to enter everlasting life in heaven.

But for some reason, there are nights when he hears laughter—long, drawn-out howls, which conjure up images of a pack of dogs convening to worship the devil. And he can't figure out why, every time he hears the commotion, he feels a pull, a compulsion to dash outside and join the fiendish howls. Of course, as a good, devout young man, Brown is resolved to not leave the house and to turn his back on the howls that make his very hair stand on end. He prays and tries his best not to quake in fear.

But Brown is no hero. He can battle the influence of that fiendish howling for only so long, and eventually, he leaps up and runs outside. A great force compels him to find out where the howls are coming from. Naturally, he feels great remorse. His conscience curses him for leaving the house, even as he races in search of the source of the howls.

As he goes, cursing each step, he looks up to the sky. In agony, hot groans fill his heart, and he wonders, "Will I still go there—to heaven above?" He tries to turn back, but a great force drives him onward, to a place beyond anything he's ever dreamed.

That is, the very heart of the wild woods. There, he beholds a multitude of people conducting a ritual, laughing as one, pledging their allegiance to the devil himself. Many of them turn out to be respected figures, as well as people known for their piety—and in fact, the loudest, shrillest peals of laughter come from these.

At a pause in the shrieking, someone leaps onto a large rock and confesses to one and all his true way of life. In the same way, several people come forward one by one. They reveal their secret, that the only way to remain good in one's everyday life is to submit to the devil at night. Everyone has their flaws, and in order to purge them, a person must unleash their devilry every now and then.

Brown even sees that his own wife—known, like him, for her piety, sense, and virtue—has already plunged herself into the howling rites. And as for himself, Brown still feels the urge to look up at the sky. He believes that heaven lies above and that he has now been shut out.[7, iv]

"Actually," said Olenka, "he shouldn't feel the need to look up at the sky. All he needs to do is examine his own conscience."

Olenka told me that she'd been examining her own conscience and mulling over our relationship for some time now. Even before this, long before we met, she would always rely on her conscience to mull matters over. That was why she considered the street preacher "a public nuisance."

Olenka said that her relationship with God was her own affair. She was a human being, possessing reason, morals, and animal desires in combination; as such, she felt it was up to her to settle her own affairs. "Human beings have been endowed with both good and bad qualities, and they're answerable for whichever side they choose." Consequently, if our relationship really was a sin, she would take responsibility for it.

"The time will come when we must part," she said.

CHAPTER 12

OLENKA LEAVES ME

Wayne's habit of glancing around furtively, like a slave about to run away, and the fact that he suspected everyone of trying to belittle him and wanting to give him a good swift kick in the rear—this was his own business. Frankly, I didn't care. But I remained curious about him nonetheless, mainly because he would shoot his mouth off about being a writer to anyone who happened to be nearby.

I found this out by chance. I was laying out a picnic blanket behind a large rock in a corner of the tulip garden. The weather was good, and I knew Olenka never came here. I wanted to forget about her.

Suddenly, I heard Wayne's voice. There he was, ambling along, informing someone that he was a writer. He'd written seven novels. Number three was the longest, seven hundred pages thick. The shortest was number seven, about three hundred pages in length. He spoke as if he were merely providing objective information. Then he went on to say, self-effacingly, that the publishers had rejected them all.

Eventually, I learned that the person listening to him had just moved to Tulip Tree and lived in the apartment across from me.

A few days later, as I waited with some other people for the elevator, Wayne walked by. Someone greeted him. "How are you, Wayne?"

Wayne replied, in the same explanatory tone as before, that he'd been suffering from writer's block for a few days now. He didn't speak in a conceited way, but I was annoyed at how he could be so loose-lipped. Especially when I saw him talking so much about his writerly affairs. I inferred that he wanted people to see him as a writer. It didn't matter if it was as a good writer, being regarded as a failed writer was sufficient too. As long as everyone knew that he was a writer first and foremost. If I were a woman and were married to Wayne, I would have been fed up with him by now.

Olenka actually had the right to call herself an artist. But she tried hard to think of herself as nothing special instead. She kept some paper and drawing pencils, nothing else. When she drew, the only equipment she ever used was a clipboard, which she would place on her lap. I only ever saw her use a large clipboard once—when I met her for the first time in the woods. I never saw that clipboard again. And her room was never streaked with paint, nor her hands, nor her clothes.

Supposing Wayne had a talent for art like Olenka. He would have carried paints and a giant clipboard everywhere and announced that he was an artist to everyone. His hands would be covered in paint, and his clothes. Just look at Wayne's room: papers strewn everywhere, books scattered about, the chair overturned, and his desk—pens and pencils crowding, jostling for space. Not to mention all the books that had been left open, and the magazines, and the other reading materials. He even had multiple typewriters, all of them covered in dust.

"What if I want to continue this piece where I left off? And this piece didn't turn out, but what if I use it as a springboard for something else?" This was what Wayne would say, according to Olenka.

Not infrequently, Wayne would lose his temper trying to find items buried beneath the chaos of all the other items in the room. Other areas in the apartment had been invaded, too, a mass of papers, typewriters, and books left open and scattered about. In contrast, Olenka would simply throw all her art away. I'd seen her rip up her drawings as if they were nothing but old paper bags.

Both she and I had often said, "The time will come when we must part." We had also made other decisions together—that "we must end it properly, not for made-up reasons or under forced circumstances." Yet we still met often. And we turned into animals every time we did.

Olenka told me that even now she had no intention of getting a divorce. And she didn't want to marry me even if she did. Her reason was simple. She could love me because it was "easy but difficult" to have a relationship with me. If this weren't the case, I'd be nothing but a second Wayne.

I agreed. I wasn't willing to marry her either. My desire to play the geography teacher to her map would vanish if she were my wife. No longer would I see every inch of her body as *terra incognita*.

And so, she and I kept up our regular meetings. One day, bored by a soap opera on TV, Olenka took up a paper and pen. She drew a caricature. In no time at all, she had completed three of them.

"Remind you of anything, Fanton?" she asked.

They did, but I couldn't place them. I had seen similar ones before, in multiple newspapers, magazines, and books.

When I gave up, Olenka added a signature to each one. Only then did I recall.

The first was in the style of Herblock, a cartoonist who had won the Pulitzer three times. The second was after the caricaturist David Low, famous for his cartoons about World War II and the tensions between America and Russia during the Cold War in the early fifties. I'd seen the style of the third one before, in books about nineteenth-century British literature. If I wasn't mistaken, his name was Robert Seymour, a caricaturist born in a village near London in 1798. I faintly recalled reading about him once, when I'd had nothing better to do.

I was surprised at the speed and accuracy with which Olenka imitated their style. I complimented her. What a difference from Wayne, she told me—who was always putting her down.

"If I didn't like doodling so much," she said, "I'd never have ended up marrying Wayne."

She told me how she'd spent ages drifting around, made penniless by her artistic ambitions. Finally, she decided to move out of the big city in order to find some peace. That was how she wound up in Skokie, a little town in another part of the state, quiet and clean. She'd seen photos of it in a Chicago newspaper. "One of the prettiest towns in Illinois," the paper had said.

Her first job had been at an ice-cream parlor. Even at work, she'd make sketches of this or that. Then she applied to be an illustrator at the *Skokie Review*. She got the job, and she saw Mitchell bringing Wayne into his office a few times. Even when Mitchell introduced her and Wayne to each other, Wayne had already started presenting himself as a writer who had produced a lot of work but hadn't published anything.

So began her interest in Wayne. She concluded that Wayne had primitive instincts, a keen sense of perception, and was a bit of an idiot. Wayne told her she had an utterly serene constitution, able to face life's trials and tribulations with a smile on her face and a steady heart. And that she had the potential to be coarse, wicked, and cruel—not only toward herself but others as well. And also that she was capable of doing amazing things. It seemed that Mitchell sensed which way the wind was blowing. Using various ploys, he would maneuver Wayne into chatting with Olenka alone. In nearly every exchange, Wayne complained about how difficult it was for him to write and get his work published. Then, in a short space of time, Wayne got a short story accepted. He was happy beyond all belief.

Olenka told me that, character-wise, Wayne was like a beggar who'd been given a soft bed to sleep in. If left alone, he wouldn't have dared do anything, and if beaten, he'd have run away in fright. And if treated with compassion, he would become rude and overbearing.

And so, once he had been received favorably by Olenka, Wayne had the gall to accuse Olenka of being a trade artist, not a proper one. He complimented her abilities—as a trade artist. But being one was hardly exceptional. "Only real artists are worthy of respect," Wayne had said, according to her. The vast majority of Olenka's drawings he dismissed as "trash," "unoriginal," "devoid of individuality," "commercial"—"only someone with no artistic sensibility would want to waste time drawing stuff like that."

Olenka told me that after she'd started working at the newspaper, their circulation numbers had increased. Where other newspapers used photographs, the newspaper she worked at would use her drawings. Court proceedings, city council debates, suicides, fires, football matches, et cetera, were often accompanied by Olenka's illustrations. Even so, Wayne continued to insist that Olenka's work was nothing but "trash."

After disparaging Wayne, Olenka performed another astonishing feat. In no time at all, she drew a woman in the nude, reclining on a sofa. She asked whether I'd seen a similar painting before. I was sure I had, but I couldn't remember where.

"Keep thinking," she said.

I kept trying to recall. She rose and came back with a book on art history by Germain Bazin. She flipped through the index, turned to a page, and showed it to me. A painting by Goya.[i] Now I remembered. I felt embarrassed—I'd bought the book a long time ago but never really devoted any attention to it.

Again in the manner of a magician, she replicated other famous artworks, from the Baroque period to the Cubists.

Suddenly she began to cry. I didn't know why, and I didn't have the heart to ask. She told me her life had been nothing but torment. It wasn't just her marriage that was in ruins but her entire life. She wished she'd died in infancy, or at least in childhood—when she wouldn't have been able to reflect on the matter so much. Now it was too late and she was too afraid to die. She tarried on, her life a deferral of defeat—no, not merely defeat but destruction—until the day she would finally succumb.[8]

After a while, she asked if I loved her.

"Yes," I said.

"Do you want to make me happy?" she asked.

"With all my heart," I replied.

Her request was this: that I let her bite me and suck my blood. She would trace every part of my body, kiss every part, inch by inch, leaving none of me untouched. It was then that I feared it, that the time had nearly come for us to part.

Sure enough, after I fell asleep, she disappeared without leaving so much as a note.

I woke up to a commotion outside. Wondering what it could be, I went downstairs.

People were abuzz about the DaVinci TransAmerica balloon. It was crossing over Bloomington and, at that very moment, was directly above Tulip Tree. I recalled hearing about the balloon before, but I hadn't paid it much attention at all.

Six days ago—according to some people gathered on the Tulip Tree lawn—the DaVinci had struck out for Virginia from Oregon. The first TransAmerica balloon flight in history, they said.

A newspaper article printed in four columns—the first, third, and fourth columns contain the text of the article; the second column contains a simple black-and-white illustration of a hot-air balloon. The article's headline is not included, and the very top of the balloon illustration is cut off.

We can see, however, that the article was written by Seth Eisenberg and Andy Hall, credited as staff writers. The article text is follows:

> A shimmering, tear-shaped balloon soared four miles above Bloomington Monday evening, just 40 miles ahead of turbulent weather that threatened to end an attempt to make the first non-stop piloted balloon crossing of the United States.
>
> And as twilight was replaced by darkness, the helium-filled balloon's windswept odyssey, that had begun Wednesday in Oregon, threatened to end abruptly, in rain and lightning in Ohio.
>
> The 10-story DaVinci TransAmerica, being chased by weather that led to a statewide tornado watch in Indiana, was encountering snow in its lofty flight above Ohio, said a spokeswoman at the DaVinci Control Center in St. Louis. She said if the balloon is not forced down, it could land in Southern Virginia or the Carolinas as early as this afternoon. Its approximate speed is 40 mph.
>
> Brad Vrcek, supervisory meteorologist for the National Weather Service in Indianapolis, said the weather "definitely could affect the balloon. The balloon wouldn't try to outrun this."
>
> The spokeswoman at the balloon's control center said crew members Monday night were determined to try to avoid the storms, by changing course. She said crew members were reporting the turbulence was dissipating.
>
> "No way," said a meteorologist at the Federal Aviation Administration's Aircraft Control Center in Indianapolis, adding the storm heading southeast was not weakening.

Bob Williams, assistant chief at the FAA's control center, said it appeared the balloon was being overtaken by the storm system.

Craig Edwards, a weather service official, said the balloon was running into a squall line and being chased by stormy weather. He predicted the squall line, a band of showers and thunderstorms west of the balloon, probably would force the craft to land.

"I really think the thing is going to come down (tonight)," said Jerry Thacker, an Indianapolis ham radio operator who talked with the balloon crew several times Monday. A communications failure plagued the craft throughout much of Monday night, and Thacker was sometimes the only person capable of contacting the crew.

Trailed by a storm system, the balloonists had dumped ballast most of Sunday night as they struggled to outrun a storm.

Thacker said, "I would feel awfully good if they would just put the balloon down."

By late Monday, the DaVinci had traveled more than 1,800 miles. The crew members, who last Friday broke a long distance mark for ballooning in the U.S., was to break the all-time balloon endurance record at 4:23 a.m. today, surpassing the record of 137 hours and six minutes.

The record was set last August by the three-man crew of the Double Eagle II, which flew 3,150 miles from Maine to France in the first successful manned crossing of the Atlantic Ocean.

The balloon is piloted by Vera Simons, of McLean, Va., a contemporary artist specializing in helium mobiles. Also aboard the craft are Rudolph Engelmann, project director, who is collecting bacteria samples to determine what disease-causing organisms are entering the atmosphere from urban areas; Dr. Fred Hyde, a Kansas City ophthalmological surgeon and veteran of 1,000 balloon flights; and Randy Birch, an NBC photographer/reporter.

Below the article appear the newspaper name and edition details, cut out and pasted, as follows: *Indiana Daily Student.* Bloomington Ind. Tuesday Oct. 2 1979. Two sections. 48 pages. 20 cents.

Shortly after the DaVinci TransAmerica balloon passed over Tulip Tree, Olenka left Fanton Drummond for good.

CHAPTER 13

OLENKA, ACCORDING TO WAYNE

Wayne carried on as usual. He'd always been this way. Whether his wife had a job or not, and where she worked, it was all the same to him. Whether his wife slept at home or elsewhere made no difference to him either. And whether she came home in the middle of the day or night, he didn't care. He would keep living in his own little world, along with Steven, suspecting everyone around him of mocking him and seeking his ruin.

When I pretended to run into him by chance and asked how he was, he complained of the trouble he was having writing.

"Why?" I asked.

"No reason, most likely. My brain's just stopped working, that's all. Or maybe my brain has stopped working and there's a good reason why."

"What could be the reason—if there were one?" I asked.

He puffed out his cheeks, tried to open his lips, and moved his head forward and back. But he didn't answer. His expression was one of agony, probably from all the emotions pent up inside him, which he was trying to find words for.

To keep him from clamming up, I resorted to asking for his thoughts on the weather. Then I told him about the tiny creatures coming in through my window. He still couldn't find the words to express himself, so I changed the subject and talked about the plans to repair the railway tracks near Tulip Tree. As a last measure, I recited some news I'd heard in passing on the radio about the DaVinci balloon. According to estimates, the balloon was now crossing eastern Pennsylvania.

At long last, he said, in imprecise words and rather convoluted sentences, that he was currently experiencing a colossal setback. He'd always been stupid when it came to matters of logic, but now he found himself stupid in all respects. His perception, his intuition, his imagination—they were all on the brink of death. For example—three days ago, he'd read a short story. Even now, he couldn't tell if it had been good or bad, and whether the writer had found it difficult to compose.

"Now, see those cars?" he said, pointing at the traffic on State Road 46. He used to be able to look at them and sense exactly the feelings of one or two of the passengers inside. And now he couldn't. His ability to take real-life facts and turn them into a story was also spent.

"How about me, Wayne? Can you tell what I'm feeling?" I asked.

He laughed, and the tone of it was mocking and vindictive. As if he'd actually been baiting me all along so I would ask him that very question.

"Yes, I can. You're like a lot of other men. You're attracted to my wife. Don't think I can't see the elephant in the room."

Then he said that he may be stupid, but he wasn't as stupid as everyone thought. Especially when it came to his wife. He knew her every movement. Smugly, he claimed to know his wife like the back of his hand.

"A lot of men have fallen for her. She's serviced them all. You'd think it was her sole duty in life—servicing men, as long as she drew breath. So, pal, don't feel too pleased with yourself at becoming my wife's plaything. She changes them like changing outfits, wearing them a few times, then tossing them before they wear out. But don't worry, pal. I'm past the point of being jealous. She'll come back to me when the time comes. And as usual, I won't treat her like my wife when she comes back. How will I treat her? Wanna know, pal? I'll treat her like a slave!"

There was a note of pride in his voice. And also mockery—not just of me but Olenka. Unlike before, his words flowed smoothly and articulately, as if he'd been waiting to say them for some time.

He said even before they got married, he could tell Olenka wouldn't make a good wife. Her way of walking, like a fairy, or sometimes like a harem girl; the look in her eyes, wild and piercing; the shape of her body, like an instrument waiting to be strummed—they were all signs that she was and would only ever be a wanton woman, a slave to her passions.

Yet, despite all this, he was grateful to Olenka. "If it wasn't for her, I would never have gotten anything published at all. Thanks to her, my story appeared in a well-known magazine and a respected anthology."

Once it became apparent that no other publications were forthcoming, Olenka had promised him the freedom to write full time, regardless of failure, no strings attached. And he held this promise of Olenka's in high regard.

Even so, continued Wayne, humans are human. He knew why Olenka had wanted to marry him. She'd said it herself: his "instincts, sense of perception, and intuition were keen." According to her, the power of his imagination was undeniable. And the short story that had been published proved just how wild his imagination could be. Olenka had declared herself profoundly in awe of his story in this respect.

Olenka had initially believed that Wayne was bound to become a writer—a true writer. He would go on to publish many works, all of excellent quality. Her promise to give him the freedom to write, regardless of failure or success, had been premised on the assumption that he wouldn't fail. Olenka had married him in the full faith that he was a primitive genius, his raw talent buried under a large rock, waiting to be set free. Because she believed this, Olenka used to buy him great works of world literature. She would read them to him as he lay next to her, or sat, or stroked her back. In return, he used to feel free to treat her however he wanted, and for whatever purpose he saw fit.

Olenka really had been willing to serve him hand and foot, at first. But over time, it got old, and she realized he wasn't going to become a true writer after all. In the meantime, Wayne

A black-and-white photo from an issue of the *Indiana Daily Student*, published August 23, 1977. The photo is of a stretch of road completely backed up with traffic, a long line of cars stretching into the distance. Behind the cars looms a large, flat, wide rectangular building. A sign in the foreground points the way to various residence halls on the Indiana University Bloomington campus. At the bottom right corner of the photo is the photographer's name: Don Winslow. Below the photo is the following text: *Ind. 46 Bypass traffic was backed up at the 10th Street intersection Sunday afternoon as students and parents crowded into Bloomington in anticipation of the new school year. The I.U. Police Department said it would be lenient about ticketing unregistered cars parked in red and black zones this week only.*

The traffic behind Tulip Tree. According to Wayne, he used to be able to look at the cars and tell what one or two passengers were feeling. He said this ability to sense people's feelings had vanished.

himself had taken the opportunity to turn Olenka into his slave. "Olenka, I'm thirsty. Get me some apple cider." "Olenka, my brain's not working. Read me the first page of the book with the red cover—the one I bought from Caveat Emptor about a month ago. Come on, you know—the one I marked up in red pencil. Don't get it mixed up with the one I marked up in pen, okay? Come on! Let's get moving! One . . . two . . . three . . . go!" "Olenka, I've been typing the whole day and have nothing to show for it. If I keep on like this, I'll die, my muscles are so sore. Can you massage my hands?"

By his own admission, he often asked Olenka to help with this or that, at all hours of the day. He didn't care if Olenka was sleeping or not. Even if Olenka were sick with diarrhea and hurrying to the bathroom, he would ask her to locate the scattered pages of a short-story manuscript from two or three weeks before; or to find a red pencil—one that had been sharpened on both ends; or to hunt for a book he'd bought seven months ago, and so on. He said inspiration could strike at any moment, regardless of time. Hence, he needed Olenka to be on hand at any given moment as well.

Naturally, Olenka was willing to be a slave for only so long. The more certain she grew that Wayne wasn't going to become a true writer, the greater her urge to mock, belittle, and play pranks on him. She would scrawl all over his manuscripts, adorn them with obscene pictures, cut them to pieces. All to drive home that he wasn't a true writer at all.

Wayne told me that Olenka would fool around with any man who was willing to be the object of her affection. Even so, Wayne was grateful to her because no matter what, Olenka would always eventually return. And she would be willing to bathe him, massage him, fetch him drinks in the middle of the night, and whatever else he wanted. When she was in the right mood for it, she found it heavenly to serve him like a slave waiting on her master.

"I may be stupid and pathetic and an easy target for jokes," said Wayne, "but there's something special about me, and no one on this green earth can take it away. Neither she nor I knows exactly what it is, but I don't think she realizes just how much she depends on me. Naturally, every time she asks for a divorce, I say yes right away. And just as I suspect, once she has my permission, she doesn't follow through. She goes back to singing my praises and begging me, her master, to give her a good plowing."

Wayne spoke with great pride, his words flowing smooth and clear.

He didn't seem to perceive Olenka as any sort of enigma. Then again, to him, Olenka wasn't where the mystery lay at all. To him, it was more of a puzzle to properly recount being interviewed by Mitchell, invited by the mayor, being made an honored guest. His heart quickened when he talked about these experiences—a quickening that wasn't apparent when he spoke about her. Sometimes I even detected a certain disgust in his tone, as if Olenka were a corpse, or an infectious disease, or moldy leftovers.

"Just look at her armpits," he said. "They're cute when she shaves them, but repulsive when she leaves them alone."

Perhaps he considered it a great honor to be a writer, which was why speaking of his writerly ways excited him. And even though he knew he'd failed as a writer, he still wanted to be treated as someone exceptional. Maybe he thought it was better to be a writer like him than to not be a writer at all. Not everyone had his talent.

It baffled me why both Wayne and Olenka acted as if Steven didn't exist. They never spoke about him. It was as if it made no difference to them whether he was dead or alive. He did seem to have a very good relationship with Wayne, but it was clear that the boy needed Wayne far more than Wayne needed him. And it wasn't just that the boy was still young, or withdrawn, or unable to socialize. There was something else that gave the impression that Wayne was Steven's whole world. What that something else was, I wasn't sure. He relied on Wayne not like a boy on his father, or an animal on its trainer, but as someone blind might depend on a cane.

In the meantime, Steven seemed to change, to withdraw. He used to regard the world with fear, as if people would get angry if he did anything, or so much as moved. But, gradually, it was as if the boy's mind had become empty, as if his spirit had been snuffed out, as if he were paralyzed, with no ability to respond at all.

Unlike the three scruffy kids, who no longer interested me much, Steven never spoke or moved. They were the reverse, constantly reacting. They kept away from other children because they lacked confidence, yet they would rise up as one to defend their honor whenever they felt insulted.

Steven continued to be a great puzzle to me. Yet I never tried to get Wayne to tell me more about him.

CHAPTER 14

ANOTHER GLIMPSE OF OLENKA

Wayne had kept boasting that Olenka was sure to return. I was the opposite. I had a feeling that she was never coming back. She'd left in a way that signaled she was going for good. She'd run off when I was asleep and taken all her belongings with her—things she usually left in my apartment. She knew I enjoyed stroking these objects in her absence, and it was as if she'd tried to erase all trace of herself.

Old habits returned with a vengeance. Like a grief-stricken dog, I followed her trail. Unlike before, it was only traces I sought now, not her in the flesh, because I was sure she was never coming back. I passed by the nightclub on Kirkwood a lot. The cashier was another woman now—a brunette.

One night, following her trail led me to the ninth floor of the Elberhart Bell Tower. It was stone silent up there.

I went to the pay phone, put in two dimes, and dialed 339-6651. The phone rang for a good while.

Then someone picked up.

"Hello?" he said. He sounded elderly and like he'd just woken up. "Elberhart Bell Tower caretaker."

"Can I go up to the top?" I asked.

"What? Now?"

"Yes," I said.

"You must be drunk."

"No," I replied.

"If you're not drunk, then you're out of your mind."

"I'm not. I want to go up right now."

"Are you nuts? It's nearly three in the morning!"

"Sorry, what time did you say it was?"

"Nearly three in the morning, you nut!"

He hung up.

I went back down and walked a little ways off to take a look at the clock face on the tower. It really was nearly three in the morning.

I broke into a run across the field. It was one and a half miles to Tulip Tree. The wind was blowing strong. Fall was nearly here. My bones began to ache with cold. I realized my jacket was too thin. And that all the lights in Tulip Tree were off, except for the outdoor security lamps and the red glow of the television antenna on the roof.

Suddenly, in the middle of the field, I caught a fleeting glimpse of Olenka. I shouted her name, and she shouted mine. The echoes of her voice and mine filled the air. Olenka wanted me, I was sure of it. But then why was she rushing away?

She came to an abrupt stop near a tree, as if unsure of where to go. She seemed divided—the Campus View building or Eigenmann Hall? But she wasn't heading for Tulip Tree, that was for sure. Suddenly, she flashed by again, even faster than before. Her white scarf fluttered to the ground, not far from the tree where she had stood.

I picked it up. To my surprise, what I'd mistaken for a scarf was nothing but an ordinary piece of paper. Then a fierce gust blew the sheet out of my hands, up and away. And then—the roaring wind in the cold night.

CHAPTER 15

LET US POSSESS ONE WORLD

In the middle of that enormous field, I felt the sudden urge to kneel. Who knew why. Then I looked up to the sky and prayed, asking forgiveness for all my sins and errors. I forgot all about my assertion about the sky being devoid of mystery since Copernicus declared the earth round, not flat. I forgot what I'd said about how looking up at the sky and pleading was no guarantee of reaching one's intended audience since no one knew whether God actually lived there. I even forgot how I'd once asserted that my conscience, and my conscience alone, served as my guide.

But now I felt, or realized, or acknowledged, that my conscience wasn't enough. There was something else—higher, grander, purer—and I didn't know where it was to be found. But it felt easier to search for it if I knelt and looked up. I did this reflexively, in surrendering myself, in pleading for forgiveness, in pleading for help. I felt small, meaningless, powerless.

Who knew why, but I felt this still wasn't enough. I longed to submit, to surrender myself completely, but I felt something inside me wasn't ready yet. The act of kneeling and raising my head still felt insufficient. Compelled by a desire to acknowledge my insignificance, to be at peace and submit, there, on my knees, I bowed and pressed my forehead to the grassy earth. A lightness stole into my heart, even as I felt immense guilt. Something wasn't quite right. As if I were driving a car and couldn't get the gas and clutch to work in sync when shifting gears. I also felt a wrenching sensation in my heart. If I were a car and kept on like this, the gears would come loose and break apart.

I felt something urging me to reorient myself. So I tried facing different directions, all the while pressing my forehead to the ground. Something was still missing. But what it was, I had no idea. Perhaps I had committed too many sins, too many errors, and God wasn't ready to forgive me yet. Or perhaps I wasn't approaching God in the right way.

Suddenly, I was reminded of something that Cardinal Terence Cooke said once, in Harlem, New York. Pope John Paul II had visited his church ten days prior, and Cooke said, "Prayer has power insofar as it is accompanied by good works in one's everyday life."[9]

I had done no good works.

I brought this feeling—that I had no good works to my name—back to my apartment. All the while, thoughts of Olenka returned, flooding my mind. I even resorted to flipping through all the poetry anthologies that Olenka used to flip through. I found a poem by John Donne that Olenka would often read:

Let us possess one world; each hath one, and is one.

Such was John Donne's invitation to his wife to think of each of their bodies as a globe. To join themselves in union was to merge these globes, which Donne equated with the act of worshipping God. And Donne was thankful for this graciousness on God's part—that such union could be achieved through the merging of two globes into one.

CHAPTER 16

I WANT TO HAVE CHILDREN

Even if Wayne really was telling the truth about Olenka's many lovers, I wasn't jealous. I loved her. And only now did I realize that I wanted to marry her. If she agreed, and if a divorce could be arranged, and if Steven could remain in Wayne's custody, I'd take her to Oregon. I'd transform her into a good wife; we'd have two or three kids and live quietly in a small town. I wanted my children to grow up loving nature as much as they loved themselves, and as much as they loved their parents—that is, Olenka and me.

Why Oregon specifically sprang to mind, I couldn't really say. Perhaps it was its connection to a personally significant event in our relationship. I'd tell my children the story when they were old enough to start going to school: "You know something, kids? Back when your mother and I were dating, the first TransAmerica balloon crossed over Bloomington, Indiana. Do you know where the balloon began its journey? From right here, in Oregon." I would express my hope that they would one day demonstrate the same initiative and strength of character as the crew members piloting the balloon. The crew had been accomplished scientists, bravely venturing forth for the good of mankind. "Follow their example, my children, and be like them."

I hoped they wouldn't follow in my footsteps, living with no more purpose than an animal or plant. Day to day, I thought only of my own enjoyment and never made any bigger plans. I'd only scramble in search of work when I was about to run out of money. Looking back on my life, all I saw was a void. I'd never had any grand ambitions. I'd never reflected on who I was, except in the literal sense—an orphan from birth, lacking even a last name. I'd been plucked from the orphanage by a couple named Drummond, who died when a giant truck smashed into their car. I'd survived because they had used their bodies to shield mine. They and the car were destroyed, while I sustained only minor wounds.

When this happened, I was sent back to the orphanage, which was in Kentucky, in a small town. The local government sent me to kindergarten, then elementary school. I graduated and went on to middle school, working at the same time as a cleaner in the dorms. After graduating from high school, I got a job painting buildings for a year, then for a little less than a year, I worked at a hamburger joint. I worked all kinds of jobs until, eventually, I got a scholarship to go to college. I continued working in my spare time. I got a two-year degree and worked as a clerk for the Freshman Advisory Board. Then I got another scholarship to get my bachelor's degree. And once I graduated, I moved around until I ended up in Bloomington. I hoped my children wouldn't live as aimlessly as I did.

Olenka had brains. And I could have made something of myself if I'd wanted. But we each lived as aimlessly as an animal or plant, and accordingly, it was possible that our children might be similarly cursed. Armed with this knowledge, I would try hard not to pass on my vague attitude toward life. I was sure that if I set a good example, they would avoid inheriting our bad dispositions.

I had only ever been responsible for my own self. Whenever I was employed, I had formal duties and obligations, but I'd leave them behind upon leaving the job. For the greater part of my life, I had always been my own master, never feeling the need to be answerable to anyone. But once I had a wife and children, I would be mindful of how my actions affected them, and it was they who would enable me to restrain myself from doing whatever I pleased. Only I could make myself into a responsible person. And the only way to do it was to marry and have kids. And marriage couldn't be taken lightly. Fortunately, I already had someone I loved—Olenka.

Strange that Olenka should be the one to pave this path for

me. After all, she would leave her husband whenever she felt like it, and she neglected her child. She had turned me into an animal, and yet, because of her, I didn't want to be an animal anymore.

Until now, my relationship with her had been nothing but an outlet for my lustful passions. But if I did end up marrying her, our relationship would be transformed into an act of worship, a tribute to God's goodness. The curves of her body would be a God-given blessing for me to enjoy, and her wild ways a God-given challenge for me to overcome.

If a louse bit her and then bit me, I would no longer worry whether enjoying her body was a sin. I would no longer feel ashamed. In the words of John Donne, "this cannot be said / A sin, nor shame." No longer would the mingling of our blood be sinful or shameful. John Donne said so himself.

CHAPTER 17

JEALOUSY

Olenka never came back. Even Wayne got anxious in the end. Unusually for her, Olenka showed no sign of returning. Ordinarily, she would send a message, but he hadn't received a single word.

Given the tenuous situation, Wayne began to consider searching for employment. If he got a job, he would put Steven in daycare. He cursed Olenka, yet he still felt indebted to her. Wayne filled me in on the background details: before getting married, he'd had a job. He hadn't earned much, but then again, he'd never wanted to make a lot of money.

"I had enough to eat, to pay rent, to buy something now and then. Why work more? It was better to use the time to write," he said.

After they got married, Wayne had wanted to earn more money. He wanted to rent a bigger, more suitable apartment and start having kids. Olenka was in agreement on one of these matters: renting a bigger, better apartment, so Wayne could write in peace. Then Olenka told him that he should go ahead and keep working if he wanted to, but that he shouldn't increase his hours. She was happy as long as he made enough to pay the rent. Olenka would take care of everything else. Wayne agreed. So Wayne paid around a quarter of their expenses, and Olenka saw to the rest.

Because she wanted to save up, and in order to do so, to work as much as possible, Olenka rejected the idea of having children right away. Wayne had never liked working, so he was happy to acquiesce. He stayed at home as much as possible, and Olenka poured all her mental and physical strength into increasing their income.

But humans are human, sighed Wayne as he told me how he began to rather like staying at home. As time went on, he worked less and less, until at last, he handed the entire burden of providing for the family to Olenka. Initially, Olenka didn't say anything about it. Then she grew sarcastic. And finally, angry.

"The more convinced of my failure she was, the more glaring her bad attitude and disposition. She began treating me like a parasite and a bum."

And now that he had an inkling that Olenka might not be coming back, or at least wasn't coming home any time soon like she usually did, he had no choice. He had to find work. He ended up getting a job at a gas station on South Tenth Street called Glandy's, not far from Fess Avenue. A lot of the traffic in Bloomington passed through that area.

I would take walks over there—at first merely to trace Olenka's footsteps, then, increasingly, to see Wayne. As I'd suspected, Wayne had an awkward way of working, as if he couldn't strike a balance between what he wanted to do and what he actually did. He often looked bewildered. What came first? A tune-up? Or should he wipe the windows? Or go straight to pumping gas? He could never decide right away. Sometimes I saw him start pumping before inserting the nozzle into the tank. Or the gas would still be flowing when he pulled out the nozzle. I even saw him fill the tank before the window cleaning was done. The more mistakes he made, the more jittery he looked.

But over time, I grew jealous. Not like, *Hmph, how did a guy like that wind up with someone like Olenka. Poor her. No wonder she took off.* Nothing like that. I became jealous of his physique, which I'd never noticed before. I watched him move around and stand still, bend over and straighten, walk thither, come hither, and jog around tending to all the cars—and it was this that caused the true beauty of his body to shine through.

I once had the impression that he had a lousy physique—as rotten as the rotting soul inside. Now I realized how rash my prior assessment had been. And this was what turned me green with envy. Don't tell me that, apart from falling in love with his primitive nature and writerly airs, Olenka had fallen for his body as well! And if so, how often must she have kissed it, tracing every part, inch by inch, leaving nothing untouched! How often must she have bitten his skin and sucked his blood!

These jealous suspicions grew fiercer by the day. And one day, after yet another round of Wayne-watching, I returned home, heart aflame. Upon entering the apartment, I stripped off my clothes, got into the bathtub, and turned on the hot water, letting the steam turn into a thick fog. I was angry at Wayne and Olenka. The fog darkened the bathroom. The hot water made my skin feel as if it were about to peel right off.

It was too much. I leaped out of the bathtub and opened the door. The steam, too, drifted out. Some of it followed me to the bedroom and clouded up the large mirror near the bed. I was unable to see my body's reflection, even though, for the first time, I wished to examine every curve.[10] Before, when Olenka had tended to my body, I hadn't felt the need to verify whether her opinion of it was correct. Only after I wiped off the condensation with my towel was I able to see my reflection. In the wet mirror, my body looked misshapen and warped.

It reminded me of a book that Olenka had once read out to me—*The Rainbow*, by D. H. Lawrence, about two characters of Polish descent, living in England, named Anton Skrebensky and Ursula. In the novel, Skrebensky wants to marry Ursula, but Ursula keeps stalling for time. They end up having to part. Skrebensky is deployed to India. Before his departure, he still takes the time to write to Ursula. With a happy heart and a quick hand, Ursula dashes off a reply. Olenka admired Ursula's response very much. It went like this: "I love you very much. I love your body. It is so clear and fine. I am glad you do not go naked, or all the women would fall in love with you. I am very jealous of it, I love it so much."[11]

"I bet you've got better curves than Skrebensky, Fanton,"

Olenka had said one day after reading Ursula's letter aloud for the umpteenth time. She continued, "Still, if you ever proposed to me, I'd say no, just like Ursula." Then she had praised Ursula for not tying herself down to Skrebensky. At the time, I, too, had been happy to follow Ursula's example.

Indeed, I'd once had no intention of marrying Olenka. But now, I pleaded for God to deliver her to me as my mate. I also knew why I'd suddenly felt compelled to pray after seeing Olenka rush past in the middle of that field. I'd felt filthy, covered in sin, unfit to go back to thinking myself a good person. Someone as sin-encrusted as I had no right to marry anyone, much less someone else like me, equally covered in mud. God was the only one who could forgive me—that is, if my sins weren't unforgivable. And only God could make Olenka my wife, if a pair as polluted as us could ever be established as husband and wife.

Once again, when I looked skyward, something was missing and not quite right. But what was missing, what was not quite right, I couldn't articulate—as if there were an obstruction of some kind in my heart.

I was resolved to marry Olenka. Nothing could dissuade me. I wanted to have two or three children with her. I would watch them grow, and every night I would read them children's books before they went to bed. I'd select only the finest, most interesting, most educational stories. I would tell them why God created human beings and why people were accountable for all their actions, not just privately or before their fellow men, but before God. I would teach them to respect their elders, to fight for the common good, and to shun the devil and other bad influences.

I would work hard and pay for my children's education so they could make something of themselves. They would become skilled doctors, able to help others; capable lawyers who would stand up for what was right; formidable politicians who would defend the poor and the helpless.

How happy I would be if my children were, like the pilots of the DaVinci TransAmerica balloon, to submit themselves in the service of mankind. I would say repeatedly and emphatically, "Children! Look at your father! He didn't amount to a hill of beans. Set your sights as high as the sky and work as hard as you can in the honest pursuit of your ambitions. Don't make the same mistakes as I did. Make something of yourself and I'll be able to die in peace."

The days rolled on without any resolution.

CHAPTER 18

MUTE

I ran into Wayne one afternoon. He complained that he was having a hard time finding a job that would be a good fit for him. Ideally, it would be somewhere he could work on his own, without constant supervision and without having to deal with the general public. He could rest easy if he found such employment.

By coincidence, I'd been thinking the very same thing. I myself had been mulling over what job would suit Wayne best. I knew he was incapable of working with other people. They made him too nervous. He must be given the opportunity to work by himself.

Just as he was griping about it, a brilliant idea suddenly popped into my head. He should get a job at the university library, shelving books. To show how pleased he was at my suggestion, he shook my hand.

The next day, he put in an application, and a few days later, he got a phone call. He took the job. In addition to telling me how happy he was, he also expressed his gratitude.

"I won't have much interaction with other people," he said, "but I'll show them all that I'm a good worker."

Let's hope so, I thought.

I began making frequent trips to the library to take a look at him. It was indeed light work. He pushed a cart around, removed books from the shelves, then put them back. He said it was peaceful and enjoyable, not to mention easy as pie.

Upon arrival, he would head to the staff room on the fourth floor and use his time card to punch in. Then he would ride the elevator to the other levels, collect the books strewn around the tables, load them onto his cart, and return them to the shelves. When it was break time, he'd return to the fourth floor and punch out and, afterward, come back in and work some more before punching out again and, finally, going home. And on it went.

He hadn't had the job for ten days before he began to grumble. He said there were too many people who needed help looking up books. They would pummel him with all kinds of questions.

"I get too nervous around them," he told me.

I knew how he felt. Furthermore, I knew how hard it was to locate the book you wanted when there were millions of them spread out across dozens of levels. I myself had often asked the staff for help. I had to think of some way to help Wayne.

I couldn't sleep all night. It was only the next morning that I came up with an idea. Wayne should pretend he was mute, so no one would ask him anything.

Wayne thought this a good plan. And he did a good job pulling it off. Whenever someone approached him to ask about this or that call number, he began pointing here and there. Eventually, they'd leave and ask someone else. He was happy. And I was happy too.

There were other aspects of the job he still enjoyed. There, in the midst of thousands of shelves housing millions of books, Wayne felt small, as if he were of no significance. Yet it was in this state of smallness that he felt his individuality become even more concrete.

I enjoyed it too. For, among so many shelves and books, the beauty of his body was no longer apparent. This was what made me happy. I had no reason to envy him anymore.

CHAPTER 19

SETTING OFF FOR KENTUCKY

There was still no sign of Olenka. Wayne wasn't particularly anxious. He said he could carry on without her, though barely. From the way he talked, you'd think she was a source of income and nothing more. He showed no sign of missing or loving her, unlike me. My attitude toward her absence was the exact opposite of Wayne's.

I persisted in visiting the places Olenka once went. And I began trying to find out where she might be now. I would travel to west Bloomington, hoping fervently to run into her. I distinctly remembered her saying that she wanted to rent or buy a place over there. I'd visit the branch offices of various banks, where there were real estate ads on display—houses, empty lots, and apartments for sale or for rent. Using them as leads, I'd try to track her down.

My hopes dimmed as the days went on. I felt like an aimless, wandering creature. I would shout her name, even though I knew the world would be loath to reply.[12] With no clear destination in mind, I hitched a ride on an eighteen-wheeler heading south on 46. After changing trucks a few times, I decided to head for Kentucky. I even found my way to the orphanage where I grew up. The buildings had been cleared to make way for farmland. The town of Brackford was dead, its activity shifted west. There were no more inhabitants. Just a few old houses, left to rot.

I spent the night in a tiny town, about ten miles from where Abraham Lincoln had been born, and thought about how he was shot after the Civil War. This town, too, smelled of farm and field. I took a short walk before going up to my room. To my surprise, there was Olenka, sitting on the windowsill. The sight of me startled her, too, and she jumped out the window, calling my name as she disappeared into the dark night.

I'd been haunted by apparitions of Olenka even before we'd started seeing each other. And since we'd parted ways, I'd glimpsed her three more times, each encounter stranger than the last. The first was in the field, as I was coming back from the Elberhart Bell Tower. The second was when I crossed the Indiana-Kentucky border. And now a third time, in this room.

When crossing the border into Kentucky, I had spied her in the passenger seat of a truck heading into Indiana. I was the only one who saw her. Duncan Mundir, the driver giving me a lift, swore he "didn't see a thing."

"But I wasn't paying close attention," he told me. "Doesn't mean you're not right. A lot of drivers pick up lady travelers." His tone was neutral, but his choice of words caused me pain—as if, without meaning to, he'd called her a whore.

On this trip, I attempted to reconstruct my childhood. But I was unsuccessful—most likely due to how barren that time in my life had been. The orphanage had been my entire world. I hadn't felt any deep connection with the other children. The same went for the staff. And when I started working there myself, I still felt no warmth for anyone else. I never knew what it was like to be part of a family, to have relationships that transcended one's role as playmate, coworker, employee.

There was a time when, after getting my two-year degree, I was hospitalized for pneumonia. I remembered thinking how being in the hospital was a lot like being in the orphanage. There had been kindnesses, yes, but they'd been doled out as a matter of duty. Even events that should have been happy—school breaks, puppet shows, picnics, and the like—I didn't remember as such.

Once I was free, released from the orphanage, able to eat, sleep, and arrange my schedule as I liked, I looked back on my time there and felt that even eating had been a chore. And sleeping and dreaming too.

"Good night, children. Sweet dreams," the superintendent would say each night. If I did manage to have sweet dreams, and reported as much the next day, the superintendent would commend me: I was a good child, a worthy recipient of a pleasant dream. But if I had a bad dream, she would instruct me to be a good child so I'd be rewarded with pleasant ones. And like the other children, I reported my dreams out of obligation. Prayer became a duty too.

Life in the orphanage was uninteresting. Nothing about it was especially stirring, or thrilling, inspiring of awe. I wonder if it would have been more interesting if there had been more of us—to the point of national crisis. True, one could find orphans anywhere, in the care of various governmental, church, and charitable organizations, but our numbers were nothing spectacular. Also, the people who worked at the orphanage were just trying to earn a living; they didn't pretend to have noble aims about shaping our character. The chaplains and teachers were also there to make a living, though they had a sense of calling as well.

Not only that, the chaplains were open-minded people and didn't regard religion as the only guiding principle for this life and the next. So there weren't any dramatic exchanges of the kind you got in orphanages in nineteenth-century England—exchanges that went something like this:

"Do you say your prayers night and morning?"

"Yes, sir."

"Do you read your Bible?"

"Sometimes."

"With pleasure? Are you fond of it?"

"I like Revelations, and the book of Daniel, and Genesis and Samuel, and a little bit of Exodus, and some parts of Kings and Chronicles, and Job and Jonah."

"And the Psalms?"

"No, sir."

"No? Oh, shocking! I have a little boy, younger than you, who knows six Psalms by heart: and when you ask him which he would rather have, a gingerbread-nut to eat or a verse of a

Psalm to learn, he says: 'Oh! The verse of a Psalm! Angels sing Psalms'; says he, 'I wish to be a little angel here below'; he then gets two nuts in recompense for his infant piety."

"Psalms are not interesting."

"That proves you have a wicked heart; and you must pray to God to change it: to give you a new and clean one: to take away your heart of stone and give you a heart of flesh . . . Do you know where the wicked go after death?"

"They go to hell."

"And what is hell? Can you tell me that?"

"A pit full of fire."

"And should you like to fall into that pit, and to be burning there for ever?"

"No, sir."

"What must you do to avoid it?"

"I must keep in good health, and not die."[13]

When it came to religion, no one bullied or frightened children anymore. So no one had to pretend to enjoy reading the Bible in order to get some gingerbread. Nowadays, children were rewarded for other things, like solving crossword puzzles or answering geography questions, doing algebra or keeping their bedroom tidy, weeding the lawn or cleaning the bathroom. Children were healthy and well-fed. They took it for granted that they wouldn't die young. They didn't need to come up with such answers: to avoid going to hell, one shouldn't die.

Child pickpockets, or runaways, or troublemakers weren't a problem either. They weren't a category unto themselves or a pressing social issue that had to be dealt with. There was no need to build special factories to put such children to work. Members of Congress didn't have to worry about passing laws about how to treat them. And such children didn't need to drift from one family to another, being exploited, or demeaned, or indulged.

Yet at the same time, the love of a family—which I'd read about in books—never graced my own life. Nor was I lavished with compassion because of my orphaned state. My childhood had been governed by schedules and duties. And at the time, I had yearned to be free.

CHAPTER 20

THREE LETTERS FOR WAYNE

A few days after I came back from Kentucky, I saw Wayne. He was hastening toward me.

"Important news!" he gasped. "Most important! All-important!"

I had the sense that he'd already prepared what he had to say and was now ready to fire it off. His breath came in short, shallow puffs. The words that followed were disjointed and choppy. His sentences were a jumble. In the end, even he seemed confused about what he wanted to tell me.

Eventually, he produced three letters from his pocket—which he appeared to have prepared in advance too. He told me all three had arrived on the same day. He was immensely pleased. He even confessed to having kissed the letters multiple times.

"Here! And here! And here! See my lip marks?" he managed to stutter.

His hands were shaking.

The three letters were from the editors of three magazines, respectively—*The New Yorker*, *The Saratoga Review*, and *The Atlantic Review*. Each editor had written to accept a short story of Wayne's. "The Mute and the Books" would go to *The New Yorker* for the sum of five thousand dollars. This was a big deal—and they said there was a good chance of them including it in their anthology of best short stories for 1979, for the same amount. "The Whore and Her Hoodlum" was to go to *The Saratoga Review* for two and a half thousand dollars. Additionally, this magazine promised to recommend that the Viking Press include it in a short-fiction anthology coming out in the fall. And *The Atlantic Review* was to publish "Green Fields, Grass, and Grasshoppers" for four thousand dollars. Each editor congratulated Wayne, saying they had found his submission "wonderful, interesting, and a pleasure to read."

Wayne was happy, and I was too. So I tried to shake him by the hand. But before I could, I found he'd already taken my hand in his. And before I could clap him on the back to show how happy I was, his hand was already on my back, clapping away. He regarded me with awe, as if I were the one for whom the stars had aligned. Indeed, he took my hand and, pumping hard, said, "Congratulations, congratulations, congratulations!" Moments later, he picked up where he'd left off, saying, "Isn't it wonderful? Isn't it fantastic? Isn't it amazing?"

He explained that the three stories were ones that he'd written only recently. Unlike other times, he'd encountered no difficulties at all. The writing had flowed quickly, smoothly, assuredly. Upon finishing the three stories, and making barely any corrections, he'd sent them off to those magazines. And before long, he'd received their replies. He praised the three editors for their "excellent taste" and the soundness of the decisions they'd made.

After telling me about the stories, he jumped to talking about Olenka. He sang her praises. She had once cared for him, and to encourage his writerly ambitions, she had lavished him with love and other means of support. Case in point: the story "Olenka."

There was a time when Olenka would read over his work and make comments.

"Her feedback was always excellent," he said.

Olenka would retype his manuscripts as well.

"If I'd done it myself, I would have kept making changes. It would never have ended."

Regarding all of Olenka's efforts, he told me, "I'm in her debt. She did all that for me, and I turned into Sisyphus.[14] I spent every day turning over stones in search of my hidden talent. I know how disappointed she was in the end, though she tried to pretend everything was okay."

Wayne even proclaimed Olenka's most recent act "admirable." If Olenka hadn't up and left, his mind would still be in a muddle—just like his papers and books.

I was startled by the manner in which he spoke. He referred to the state of his apartment and his habit of leaving his writing materials around as if he knew how familiar I was with his home. Every now and then, his tone suggested he was trying to trick me into admitting my act of trespass.

He continued. Like it or not, now he had to make a living and work according to a schedule. Not like before, writing whenever the mood struck, until his whole life had been engulfed in chaos. There had been no schedule at all. Sometimes, he could hardly tell whether it was day or night. As long as the desire to write held out, he would keep at it, omitting, if necessary, to eat or sleep. The end result: he'd wasted away, his thinking became hazy, his energy levels wavered. But that was before. Not anymore.

He proceeded to tell me, "I see it now. To be any good, I have to become a machine."

The world wasn't likely to shatter to pieces, he observed, or stray from its orbit around the sun, or pass a whole year without heavy rain. Why? Precisely because it operated like a machine.

The alternation of seasons, of day and night, and other cyclical aspects of the natural world confirmed all the more that he must live according to a fixed schedule.

He kept repeating it over and over: "To be any good, I have to become a machine."

Then, after singing Olenka's praises over and over again, he reflected, looked bewildered for a while, and corrected himself.

"Maybe 'becoming a machine' isn't quite what I mean."

What he meant, he said, was that one had to live like a machine, without becoming a machine, in order to cross the sea. Every night, before going to bed, he would give himself a talking-to: "Wayne. Tonight, you didn't even finish page nine. When you get home from work tomorrow evening, you have to do X and Y. Then, at the very least, you have to write until page fourteen."

Before bidding me farewell, he sang Olenka's praises once

more and concluded by saying, "May the name of Olenka be praised. Amen."

A few days later, I ran into him again. He was back to complaining.

"Thanks to Olenka running away, I improved. Now that she won't come back, I'm a wreck. That whore."

"Why?" I asked.

"I need oiling. Olenka's my oil. Why won't she come back? Damn whore."

He told me his muscles were all knotted up, and flesh and bone he was stiff and sore.

"Look here. Even my ears are hard. Like a cast-iron boner. The screws need oiling."

I burned with anger. And besides that, jealousy. He seemed to perceive how I felt. His tone was triumphant and mocking and disdainful and cursing as he said, "I just know she'll come back. *To me.*"

Any day now, he said, Olenka would read one of his stories and come running. She'd wash his feet and lick his soles and say, "Oh Wayne. My pride and joy. Oh Danton."

Luckily, someone else happened to be passing by. If not, I would have punched him in the mouth.

CHAPTER 21

WAYNE QUITS

I began to feel more unsure of myself. And I became increasingly anxious. I started to feel more uncertain about the way I interacted with others as well. Until now I organized the people I knew into fixed categories: people I worked with, people I knew, and people who needed my help or whom I required help from. I traveled through life like a car along a highway. I stopped at red lights and went at green lights and when approaching a crossing I would slow down. If my car got hit, I'd report it to the police, and if I was the one who hit someone else, I'd compensate them for any damage, and if my engine stalled, I'd pull over and stop. And so it went.

I'd exchange greetings with a few people each day: "Hello, how are you?" "I'm good, thanks. And you?" Sometimes we'd talk a little longer, about the weather, or football, or the rising price of gas, or other such things. If I had a leaky faucet, I'd call the Tulip Tree management office. If my jacket got dirty, I'd take it to the cleaners, chat awhile, then leave. And if my hair got too long, I'd go to the barber and we'd converse as he cut my hair. If I saw a kid fall off his bike, I'd help, and if I saw a car crash, I'd call the police. Such was my life.

Only after I became emotionally invested in my relationship with Olenka did it dawn on me that I had a desire to procreate, to revisit my childhood, to peer into the emptiness of my past. And this awareness became all the more acute whenever I felt anger or jealousy toward Wayne.

I felt I was nothing but a symptom. On my own, I had no meaning, no function, no existence. Amid the busy traffic of the highway, I was a passive sort of symptom—an object. I never drove too fast, or too far over, or ran a red light because I didn't want to crash. On the other hand, if someone crashed into me, I never got out of the car to punch the driver who'd hit me. That would complicate the situation even further. Anyway, the police were there to handle things. All I had to do was follow official protocol.

My relationship with Olenka had transformed me into an active symptom. I was no longer merely an object. I had options. I could go looking for Olenka, I could break up her relationship with Wayne, I could take Olenka to be my wife. I might not succeed, but even so, I had a chance to exercise my freedom of choice.

I was aware that things between Wayne and myself had already escalated to Cold War levels. As such, I was determined to learn more about him and Olenka, for the sake of better understanding myself. With this, I could bend them to my will. Knowing why Olenka was so eager to make herself Wayne's slave, and why she didn't want to marry me if they got divorced—the answer to these riddles lay not just with them but me as well. Wayne was thwarting me by his mere presence, standing in the way of my natural instinct to sire children and father them well.

With these thoughts in my head, I set off for the library. I wanted some peace and quiet. There I would sit on the floor amid the many rows of book-lined shelves and breathe in their bookish scent. I would shut my eyes, reflect and ponder, and flip idly through books. Who knew—maybe I'd get a clearer sense of who I was.

But this objective of mine melted away the instant I set foot on the library's grounds. Instead, I had the urge to see Wayne. And I was unable to hold myself back. I wanted to see him mute and insignificant among all the millions of books. Starting at level one, I leaped from floor to floor in search of him. But he was nowhere to be found.

On the seventeenth floor, I ran into Galpin Danzig, a former coworker of mine. Two or three years ago we worked together at the same advertising agency. He told me he preferred shelving books to making deceitful ads. One time, for one of our TV commercials, he had played the role of John, a lover of Crawley's Cakes. He'd sung and sliced a cake and given some to his neighbor, James Gilpur, who had sung along. They ate cake together—"Nom nom nom"—then together they danced, singing songs of praise about how wonderful Crawley's Cakes were. The director of the commercial had been none other than myself. Once we'd wrapped up the scene, Galpin wanted to talk to me. He informed me he intended to quit and find a more honest, decent line of work. Everyone at the agency knew that Crawley's Cakes weren't actually easy to slice—especially if the person slicing it was busy singing and on the verge of doing a dance. At the time, I'd deliberated at length with the technical crew about how to keep the cake from falling apart when John cut it. In the end, we decided to use a fake cake. Galpin's decision to quit made me ashamed of myself. I had ended up quitting too.

When I asked Galpin about Wayne, he said, "You mean the Mute? Geez, what a joke."

Then he told me what kind of worker Wayne was—"inconsiderate, irresponsible, lazy. Always trying to foist his work onto others. Insufferable to anyone who helped him out or tried to be kind."

I knew Galpin to be an honest and open sort of person. And he had sound judgment. So I took him at his word and shook my head at how Wayne had behaved.

Galpin went on to tell me that Wayne had quit a few days before. Wayne said the working conditions at the library were exploitative—there was no freedom, the work was hard, and even dockworkers got paid more.

"People rummage through the books as they please, and I'm the one who has to deal with the fallout," Wayne had said.

He had also said that he was looked down on for being a book-shelver. If the patrons had any respect, Galpin told me Wayne had told him, then they wouldn't strew books all over the tables and carrels, the smoking room, the restrooms, the seminar rooms, and the other locations too numerous to be mentioned one by one.

In halting speech, imprecise language, and convoluted sentences, he'd informed Galpin of his intention to quit. Wayne had said he had "no regrets" quitting because he had another job where he was highly respected and made a lot of money.

"What job is that?" I asked.

"He said he was a writer," replied Galpin.

The day Wayne had left the library, Galpin told me, he'd acted "arrogant and conceited. Unwilling to give anyone the time of day." And that he'd "behaved as if working here was disgusting, no better than garbage."

Galpin said it was time for his break. He invited me to go down to the fourth floor with him to get his time card and punch out. On the way down, he told me Wayne would often take breaks without punching his card. Time theft. He told me, at first, Wayne had been humble, accommodating, and pleasant. It was only after he began to feel he was "way too good for this job"—so Wayne had said, according to Galpin—that Wayne had begun to act up.

I accompanied Galpin down to the cafeteria in the basement to get some coffee and cake. When he picked up the cake, it fell apart.

"Must be from Crawley's Cakes," I remarked.

Galpin laughed.

"Good thing that damn ad isn't in circulation anymore," he said.

"But other damn ads are."

"It's all right, Fanton. The main thing is, we're not part of it anymore."

Galpin informed me he was getting married soon and moving into a new apartment. He would have two or three kids and bring them up and put them through school.

"Sure," I said. "But tell me, do you think you'll regret it someday? Watching your children grow up and become independent? Watching them go to school and eventually leave? Someday, do you think you'll feel like they've cast you off? That in the end, you'll feel like you've lost them?"

At least, that's what I wondered in my own heart. Back when I was little, my heart never said anything at all. My childhood had borne an uncanny resemblance to the cars coming and going on the highway—held together by official regulations, everything in order, with no emotions involved.

"Why must children grow up?" I wondered sadly. "Why do they have to leave their parents? And why do they have to go off and get married someday?"

CHAPTER 22

THE WEATHER AND THE WORMS

I returned home by way of the footpath near the Campus View building. But first, I stopped by Crosstown to buy some popcorn. I sat down on a rock near a small bridge and rested awhile.

A few mourning doves descended nearby. Before long they would fly away, who knew where, before returning when the weather started warming up. I threw some popcorn at them. They fluttered into the air. The beating of their wings made a lovely sound. Then they returned to the ground and began pecking at the popcorn.

Soon other birds would arrive. And all winter long there would only be those black birds—the ones that resembled little eagles, whatever they were called. In the meantime, the rabbits, worms, crickets, and other small creatures would disappear and go into hiding underground.

And then spring would come, coinciding with the rain. Time for all the worms to come crawling out and everywhere, even onto the pavement. If the sun was hot and they lost their way, they'd die drenched in sunlight, or they'd be trampled underfoot or run over by cars.

Time, also, for the robins to come flocking in, followed by the blue jays. A feast awaited them: worms, ready to eat. All the birds had to do was scoop up the worms and fly them away, before pecking them to death and gobbling them down.

And when spring was about to give way to summer, the birds would peck the worms to death to feed them to their young. By the time the offspring were able to fly, summer would be nearly over, on the brink of giving way to fall.

Then when it got too cold for them, the birds would fly off again to who knew where. Meanwhile, the surviving worms would breed, preparing to return underground to await the arrival of spring.

Then the time would come for them to reemerge—to be trampled underfoot, run over by cars, and feasted on by birds.

People said worms didn't have brains. Still, I thought, they must be able to feel fear. Sure, they ended up all over the place because they couldn't tell safe spaces from dangerous ones. But if a worm was in danger and had the chance to escape, it was sure to try to save itself.

I had once seen a robin advancing on a worm. The worm had tried to quicken its pace. But by nature's decree, worms move slowly not swiftly, and despite its best efforts at speed, it lost to the robin, who gobbled it up. Even as the robin gripped it in its beak, the wretched worm thrashed about. The harder it thrashed, the more gleeful the robin, who, indeed, had a nature-given mandate to fill its stomach with worms. Why it was the lot of some creatures to be worms, and others to be robins, I had no idea.

Two or three years ago, when I was still working for the advertising agency, I'd witnessed a blue jay cruelly tormenting a worm. I gathered it was schooling its child, a fledgling, in the art of worm catching. The worm was left to go on its way, at first. But then the birds closed in. The prospective victim seemed to sense it was in danger, so it began crawling faster. Then the blue jay began pecking at its victim—leisurely. The worm writhed about. The bird pecked at it again, driving it toward its child. The child drew closer as the worm's writhing became more frantic. Then both birds began pecking their victim with merriment and delight.

The sight of such tyranny made me livid. I picked up a stone and, without pausing to take aim, threw it at the mother. I missed and was promptly attacked by another blue jay. It must have been the father, who'd been watching from a large tree as his family enjoyed itself.

When his attack proved unsuccessful, the female took a turn. Luckily, she failed too. Then they took turns attacking me from different angles. I knew what they were aiming at: my eyes. Fortunately, I managed to shoo them away. Actually, if I'd wanted, I could have killed their child. But instead I let them all go and left their family intact.

I hadn't thought about it at the time—that if I had a child, I, too, would attack whoever might cause him or her harm. In hindsight, I felt their attacks on me were worthy not of censure but praise.

It was getting cold. The stream burbled on. I saw a small sharp stone lying on its banks, cast ashore by the water's flow.[15] I picked it up, feeling its heft. Near the railroad tracks, a rabbit emerged from a wild thicket. It glanced left and right before hopping toward me. Then it hesitated and stopped. Its eyes were large and round. Again it looked left and right, before staring at me. I felt insulted. It had been heading in my direction and changed its mind, and its air of defiance reminded me of Wayne. Just look at its expression—meek, and at the same time, arrogant. Self-important. Conceited. Bigheaded, just like Wayne. I felt rage.

Reflexively, I hurled the pebble at its head. *Thwack!* The rabbit fell backward. After a moment, it got back on its feet and hopped left and right in confusion before darting into the thicket again. *Oh Wayne*, I thought to myself. And then I thought, *Isn't this where I helped two kids a week ago, when they slipped at this very same spot? And here I am now, committing a bad deed. But why?*

Before long, a loud clanging came from the direction of Campus View Road, signaling the approach of a train. The clickety-clack of wheels followed. And soon, I could feel a faint tremor beneath my feet. Several rabbits dashed out of the thicket, springing every which way.

It wasn't long before the train engine came into view, boxcars trailing behind. It chugged along the spine of the long, narrow hill between the Campus View and Eigenmann buildings. The engineer tipped his hat and waved at me. He shouted (I think), "Howdy, buddy!" "Goody, buddy!" I shouted back.

I took the trouble to count the boxcars and occasionally took note of the writing printed on the sides. *Pacific Railway Track. Southern Illinois Railways. Conrail. Beppo Kentucky Indiana. Olenka and Olenka, Inc.*

I was stunned. A coincidence I'd never noticed before. I lost track of the boxcars altogether.

At the very end of the train was a red caboose. The brakeman looked my way. I waved and shouted, "Howdy, buddy!"

"Goody, buddy!" (I think) he replied.

I'd once worked as a railroad hand. This was how they greeted each other.

My hopes faded when I didn't see Olenka waving from any of the cars. I was suddenly sure of one thing: that the three times I'd seen Olenka's fleeting form—in the middle of a field, at the Kentucky border, in the village not far from Lincoln's birthplace—were none other than a manifestation of our desire to see each other. It was what was called a "spiritual affinity."

I learned about spiritual affinities a while back when Olenka had told me about Charlotte Brontë's novel *Jane Eyre*. Jane Eyre is an orphan. She is raised by an aunt who treats her cruelly and spends every waking moment thinking of how to torment Jane. And so, Jane must suffer. But she is a brave, stubborn child, and she rebels.

For her rebellious ways, Jane is sent to an orphanage. There, she suffers still more. Disease, mental anguish, the corrupt ways of the orphanage staff—all this the orphans must endure. A great number of them perish. But eventually, improvements are made. Jane grows up, graduates from the orphanage school, and is permitted to become a teacher there herself.

Then her close friend, her former teacher, moves away to join the man she will marry. Jane grows lonely and disconsolate. She looks for other jobs and becomes a governess to the daughter of one Edward Rochester, an older man, handsome but fierce.

Jane experiences a new kind of suffering. She falls in love with her employer, who seems to grow fiercer by the day and is probably the same age as her late father. Rochester, too, falls in love with Jane and vows he will give her everything—his riches, his body, his soul. So they prepare to wed.

Mere seconds before the priest pronounces them husband and wife, someone exposes Rochester's deception, that he already has a wife and has imprisoned her in the attic. Sure enough, he is married to a beautiful woman who went mad and has a compulsion to burn and destroy. And so Jane's marriage to the man she idolizes is called off. She runs away in the dead of night, leaving Rochester with his wife. Where should she go? She herself has no idea. She surrenders herself wholly to her fate, even as Rochester remains firmly in her heart.

One night, Rochester's wife flies into a rage. She lights a fire and burns down the whole house with everything inside. She herself ends up trapped by the flames. In a failed attempt to save his wife, Rochester is injured and sustains damage to his eyes. It is in this blind state that Jane's face appears to him in his mind.

Meanwhile, an unwelcome suitor proposes to Jane. She keeps saying no, but at last, she gives in. Just as she is about to accept, Rochester sees her image flash before his eyes. At that same moment, she hears Rochester calling her name. Jane and Rochester share a spiritual affinity.

"Look at Jane," said Olenka in wonder. "Neither angels nor demons, nor any power in heaven or earth could have ever predicted that Jane and Rochester could love each other so, even when the two of them were miles apart. After enduring so much intimidation and hardship, Jane nearly gave in and became the minister's wife. But no sooner than Jane was about to say, 'Yes, St. John Rivers. I agree to take you as my husband. My very life and death are now in your hands,' did John Rochester—blind, broken, lonely—have a vision of Jane. Rochester tried to call out to her, but his voice caught in his throat. Rochester *never uttered* a sound. Yet the vibrations of his heart leaped from hill to hill, piercing the darkness, shaking all the trees. How fine-tuned were nature's senses, to detect the tremblings of one pursued by love, and how capable of speech, to carry them to Jane's ear! She heard Rochester calling—only Jane heard him, not Rivers. She cried out, shaking herself free of the minister's grip, rushing into the wild expanse of the night. 'I am coming! Wait for me!' she cries.[16] And once more, Rochester sees Jane flash before his eyes."

CHAPTER 23

I ASSAULT WAYNE

I felt sorry about pelting that rabbit near the railroad tracks on Campus View Road. But by the time I returned to Tulip Tree, I wished I'd killed it outright. That damn rabbit had been Wayne incarnate after all. Look at how it had approached me, and the expression in its eyes. I felt nothing but regret.

Wayne was on the Tulip Tree terrace, showing someone the same letters he'd shown me. Proudly, he told the person I'd already seen all three. He seemed to speak louder for my benefit.

Then, as I perused the ads on the bulletin board near the management office, I overheard another person say, "Hey, Danton. I heard some of your stories are getting published. Congrats!"

I got into the elevator, and so did Wayne. Luckily, somebody else came in too. If he hadn't, and there had been no one else around, there was no doubt about it. I would have punched him there and then.

One afternoon, I was taking a walk near the tulip garden when I saw Wayne scurry by. He had Steven with him. In his usual manner—timid, bewildered, stealing furtive glances—he was walking along the footpath, not far from me. I sensed that he was seeking me out on purpose. His expression was one of terror, but he also seemed itching to insult me.

He came over when I called out to him.

"I can't wait to see my stories in print," he said with a grin.

"I can't wait to punch you in the mouth," I replied.

And then I punched him in the mouth. He went sprawling. And Steven copied him and fell down too. After wiping the blood from his mouth, he got to his feet and walked toward me. He showed no sign of wanting to punch me back, but rather, of wanting to insult me more. Steven got to his feet, too, but moved away.

This time I punched Wayne in the nose. He went sprawling once more. After wiping the blood from his nose, he stood up. He looked like he wanted me to punch him again. So I socked him in the chin. Again he went sprawling. More blood dripped from his lips. He spent a few seconds wiping it away, then rose once more. "Hit me again if you dare," his eyes seemed to say. So I hit him in the nose and he went sprawling again. He wiped the blood from his nose. Again he stood up. This time, I punched him in the mouth.[17]

Steven kept his distance, but he showed no fear or puzzlement or anger at the sight.

A few people must have seen what was going on from their apartment windows. And they must have called the police. Before long, not only the campus police came, but the Bloomington cops as well. And an ambulance from the university health service and one from Bloomington Hospital followed in close succession. A few reporters even showed up, with cameras too.

Wayne admitted he was to blame. He told everyone he'd cursed me out and had deserved his beating. According to him, he'd said such things as, "Fanton Drummond, you suffer from a leprosy of the soul," and "You're a coward when it comes to everything except whores," and "You have a sledgehammer for brains," and "You're worthless and have no sense of decency," and "You don't deserve to be called a human being, you hellspawn, you son of a bitch," and so on.

He continued. "Of course this man punched me! I treated him like an animal, not a human being. He was right to be mad. My insults hit home and he knew it. I'm no match for him in the strength department. What chance does a civilized person have against a wild animal? And I'm no animal, so I wasn't going to resort to brute force."

He raised his voice for his audience—the police, the reporters, the paramedics, and everyone else. It was as if he'd spent several days memorizing his lines.

He was deliberately insulting me. I knew it. He'd never said anything of the sort, but by claiming to have said these things, he intended to make me ashamed of myself. Also, he was using the opportunity to call his wife a whore. He'd waited for the right moment all this time to force me to admit his superiority.

PART II

CHAPTER 1

OLENKA'S REPLACEMENT, JANE

She was tall and skinny and worked at the nightclub because she preferred to sleep during the day. And she was constantly flapping her gums, as if only death were capable of shutting her up. That was my impression of Olenka's replacement, at least from what I could see of her head through the window.

Only when I actually entered the club did I find out she was an avid admirer of Olenka. I sat near the counter where she worked, and in the span of a few minutes, the phone rang a number of times. All the calls were for Olenka. From what Jane told them (Jane was the name of Olenka's replacement) I could tell they were customers who'd been away and had recently come back to town.

"Oh ho! Well, she moved a while ago." "No, she didn't leave an address." "Oh ho! No, I don't know where she is now." Her replies were seasoned with all sorts of praise for Olenka—a sign of her esteem.

"Who's Olenka?" I asked.

"Oh ho! You're new here, aren't you?"

She said if it weren't for Olenka, she wouldn't be working out front like now. "It's boring back there," she told me. "No one to see. No one to talk to. But talking's important, don't you think?" She laughed. "Oh ho! You agree, don't you?"

She said business had improved after Olenka started working there. Everyone liked Olenka. "She could work the cash register and chat on the phone, all at the same time. Not only that. She'd be making eyes at customers too. Then she'd jump up and pour beers. Then she'd be back on the phone again, butt in her chair, but swaying to the music nonetheless. While making jokes too."

"How about art? Did she like to draw?"

"Never saw her draw, but I bet she could if she wanted to. She had graceful hands—like a magician's. And she could dance from eight at night to four in the morning, nonstop. And she'd still have lots of energy and wouldn't look tired at all. One time, she danced till all her buttons popped off and her zipper busted and her seams ripped. Even the seat of her pants split open. But she still kept at it. She jumped so high her head touched the ceiling. Then she got down low and began twisting and turning on the floor. All of a sudden, there she was in someone's lap. The guy was bald, so Olenka began drumming away on his head with her fingers and he cracked up. He must have wanted to see Olenka's face, but he was cross-eyed, so he ended up looking somewhere else. So when he tried to kiss Olenka, all he wound up kissing was air. In the meantime, Olenka had slipped away. The whole room was filled with applause. When that girl danced! You didn't know if she was moving to the music or if it was moving to her. That's why people started writing music in the first place—to see movements like hers. Know how I know all this? I was spying. From back there. See that peephole? Oh ho! In other words, everyone who knew Olenka fell in love with her. She's gone now, but the club's still doing great. That's why I got promoted to her old job."

Then she told me that Olenka had mentioned moving to Chicago.

"Chicago?" I repeated.

"Yeah, Chicago. Oh ho! I bet that's where you're headed now."

CHAPTER 2

I TRAVEL TO CHICAGO

I stopped in Indianapolis on the way to Chicago. It was foggy and damp. The bus station was pretty crowded, but still, loneliness pecked away at my heart. I hoped the drizzle would hasten the nightfall[18] so I could sink into the dark.

It baffled me—why, since hitching a ride to Kentucky on that eighteen-wheeler, I'd felt like a billiard ball. I'd rolled from Indiana to Kentucky for no apparent reason. I'd rolled back to Indiana after seeing Olenka leap out the window. And now, I was about to roll off to Chicago, the biggest city in Illinois, even if it wasn't the state capital. Even if Jane hadn't told me about Olenka that night at the club, I'd have taken off for Chicago all the same. Some greater force was driving me there—though I didn't know what, or who, wielded the cue. Jane's story had merely hastened my rolling in that direction.

While waiting for the bus to Chicago, I saw a man sitting on his own. He was like a bronze statue. Then he turned in my direction, robot-like, and gestured. He stood up, walked over, and introduced himself by way of a card.

Apologies, I'm deaf and mute, it read. *My name is John. Would you like to buy a bracelet, ring, necklace, or anything else? The money goes to charity. Thank you.*

He proceeded to open a small suitcase of trinkets, each one labeled with a price. They cost two or three times more than they would in a regular store. To help him out, I bought a pendant. The shape of it was very pretty indeed.

He took out another card, on which was written, *Thank you*. Then he walked off toward someone else. I called after him. For some reason, I felt the sudden urge to buy a ring. But he kept going, and I remembered he was deaf.

Wayne sprang to mind. Pitiful, really. He'd been dubbed the Mute, though all his coworkers had known he wasn't mute at all. I'd even found out later that some of the regular patrons had known he'd been pretending too.

I don't know how exactly, but I suddenly found myself in conversation with a young woman. There was another young woman with her too. I learned they were in need of a traveling companion. Though we'd only just met, we got along well.

We made the decision to band together, to help and protect one another. As it happened, none of us had ever been to Chicago before.

The two women were built very differently. The first, Mary Bentley, was flabby, and a bit older than the other. She dominated practically the whole conversation, turning everything into fodder for discussion: the color of the walls, the station clock, the vending machines, the convenience store in the corner, the bus that had just come in from Cleveland, Ohio, and whatever else. The communication between her eyes, brain, and mouth seemed instantaneous. The mere sight of anything prompted her eyes to relay it to her brain, which commanded her mouth to speak.

The other woman, Mary Carson, was slender. Everything about her suggested she was fearful of doing something wrong. She preferred to listen and smile, nod and shake her head, and once in a while say, "Yes, probably. I'm not entirely sure."

Since they were both called Mary, I proposed calling them MB and MC. They laughed in agreement.

They had started out as pen pals. It had begun like this: MC had won first prize in a magazine crossword puzzle contest, and MB had won second place. A few months later, MB saw that MC had won third place in a sewing machine slogan-writing contest. She kept seeing MC's name in various newspapers and magazines. Later, she saw MC's name appear yet again, in another magazine as the second-place crossword puzzle winner. MB was impressed with MC. And to express her admiration, she sent MC a letter. That's how they became friends.

They had even visited each other before. MB had gone to see MC in Aliquippa, and MC had stayed with MB in New Kensington—both lived in Pennsylvania. Now, at MB's suggestion, they were off to see Chicago.

"Too many people travel in summer," said MB. "Better to visit Chicago when everyone else is at home."

She added that MC thought the same way. They liked to watch movies and go swimming and sightseeing at times when there were fewer people around.

After a while, I had the feeling that MB was treating MC like a ball. That is, she was dribbling her in my direction. She kept praising MC to the skies. Everything about her was worthy of admiration. For example: "Still waters run deep. That's MC. Loud gongs ring hollow. That's me. If I make a decision, don't be too quick to agree. You should always ask MC first."

I enjoyed hearing all the good things she had to say about MC. And gradually, I was won over. I would buy a pair of handcuffs and chain MC's wrist to mine. Then off we'd run, diving into Lake Michigan from the shores of Chicago. We'd swim, climb on a boat, cross the lake, and head for Canada, without so much as a farewell to MB. There, MC and I would get married and have five kids.

I liked MB, I really did, but I was starting to get sick of her. I found myself wanting to solder her mouth shut, or punch her in the throat to render her mute. Part of her seemed to know how I felt, but another part couldn't suppress the urge to keep talking. So she kept at it, seemingly aware of how much I disliked hearing her talk.

In addition to all this, a desire to forget about Olenka would well up inside me every now and then. I would become a recluse, along with MC. She and I would live like cavemen, wearing loincloths in summer, sheltering underground in winter, and my fare of choice would be raw fish.

According to a saga written by James Fenimore Cooper—a series of books known as *The Leatherstocking Tales*—back when people were settling the area near the Canadian-American border, there was a white man named Hawkeye who became fed up with so-called civilization. Consequently, he was always retreating into the wilderness to be with his Indian friends.[19]

I wished to retreat even further into the past than Hawkeye. He persisted in carrying a rifle, which I hadn't the least desire to do. My children would be the ones to discover and use tools—for starting fires, for chopping wood, for catching fish. I myself wanted to regress even further, back to the animist stage.

Now I began to doubt the place Olenka held in my heart. Had I wanted to marry her specifically, or had I merely wanted to get married—not necessarily to her—and have kids? The mere mention of children had been enough to make her tremble, but why—despite having roundly condemned the mother of those three scruffy children in Tulip Tree?

There was another incident I remembered even now: one day, Olenka had been flipping through a book by Thackeray called *Vanity Fair.* She'd already known its subject—human folly. Thackeray likened the world to a play, with the players manipulating each other, preying on each other, causing each other harm. Everything and everyone was false, true love and loyalty the object of ridicule, all this Olenka had known. But she hadn't anticipated that she would find a sentence inside that would cut her to the heart: "Mother is the name for God in the lips and hearts of little children."[20] From what I had observed, Olenka behaved as if Steven didn't even exist.

Then I realized—I had bought the necklace *after* first laying eyes on MC, not before. I'd seen her standing near a mailbox, keeping watch over two small suitcases. I'd seen her and *felt nothing.* Then I'd bought the necklace. And only then had I seen MB walking over to her, jabbering away.

And then I realized—I hadn't actually felt nothing when seeing MC for the first time. And I'd called after the mute to buy a ring from him before laying eyes on MB. Now I knew why I'd had the sudden urge to buy a ring after the mute had already started walking away. I must have said to myself, unconsciously, "Why only a necklace? Why not buy her a ring as well? Also, don't forget to buy her the real deal someday."

And now I recalled it—that after trying to call the mute back, I'd said to myself, "Ah! If only I could buy a real necklace and ring right now."

Yes, I recalled it now. And how, at the time, Olenka hadn't been on my mind.

CHAPTER 3

A PROPOSAL OF MARRIAGE

The more time I spent with MC, the more I forgot about Olenka. It was as if my sole reason for heading to Chicago had always been to get to know MC. No longer did I wonder why I was rolling, billiard-ball-like, from Kentucky to Indiana to Illinois. I surrendered myself to what I perceived to be "chance." I had stopped over in Indianapolis and taken my sweet time in boarding the bus to Chicago because chance had made me its object. I'd wound up meeting MB by chance—and the fact that MB encouraged MC to spend more time with me was pure chance too. And the fact that MC and I seemed to be a good match—that was also by chance.

But still, at some point I'd have to take action. Circumstances wouldn't allow me to remain an object of chance for good. At some point, circumstances were sure to give me the opportunity to become a subject.

And so, when the time was right, to be precise, when MB suddenly left us alone for a long period of time for no apparent reason, I professed my love openly to MC. I declared that, verily, I adored her hair, her eyes, her nose, her hands, her skin. I adored the way she walked and talked and ate and everything else. I declared my intention to make her my wife and the mother of my children. Nor did I omit to state the exact number of children I desired. Nor did I omit to assert that though I hadn't loved her for very long, I would love her till my dying breath. Every second of my life thenceforth—such did I profess—would serve only to ever increase the love I felt for her. Hence—thus I pleaded—it was my hope that she accept my marriage proposal with no doubt as to the quality of my love.

"And?" she asked once I was done, as if she were challenging me to continue.

"That's all," I replied, crestfallen.

She asked whether I had the wrong woman—that my gaze was on her, but she sensed my heart was set on someone else. She could tell from the look in my eyes that I regarded her merely as a stand-in.

I denied her accusation and urged her to say yes.

"I want you to know," she said, "I have no intention of marrying yet. But if I did, you should know what kind of man I would deem fit to be my husband. I need someone brave and strong, in spirit and in flesh. Like a general from days of yore, he must be capable of rallying his troops without the aid of a megaphone. Someone physically powerful, with a brilliant mind. When he sallies forth into battle, I'll be duty bound to follow behind. I'll follow his commands, watch him slay his enemies, and wipe the sweat from his brow whenever he requires.[21]

"I'm a woman, but as fate would have it, I have the same advantages as any man. The same level of education, the same job opportunities, more or less, and whatnot make me fully aware of my ability, freedom, and right to determine my life's path. I could be a doctor if I wanted to. Or a grassroots lawyer. Or a professor, company secretary, or post-office manager. Or a bus driver or sidewalk paver. A barber, an electrician, or anything else. I no longer regard men as my superiors but as equals. Because I have the same abilities, I don't feel any particular respect for men. Whatever they can achieve isn't too difficult for me either. Men no longer have a monopoly in any arena. Circumstances have put women in a position to take on other roles apart from becoming wives, running the household, and raising kids.

"The only thing is, I'm afraid of slipping up like a lot of women do these days. What if I get married and have kids only to end up miserable as a result?"

"Are there any men out there who meet your ideal?"

"Why not ask whether there are any strong women out there? Take Semiramis, queen of Assyria, or Dido, queen of

Carthage. They treated men like men treat wives. They had harems filled with men. They were leaders in battle and brilliant politicians. A man could only be satisfied with his wifely status if he were married to a woman like that. Such a man would have no choice but to tend to the house and care for the children."[22]

"You must be dreaming."

"I *am* dreaming. But I won't dream *forever*. As long as I am dreaming, though, I wish we could go back to primitive times. When strong men who worked hard accumulated wives, while weak men had no choice but to marry inferior women no one else wanted. The strong would beget the strong and the weak beget the weak. And the strong would prevail."

"And dreams aside?"

"I've come up with a plan for turning my back on reality in order to live out my dream: I'll marry a college professor—someone fully aware of his smallness, his stuntedness. The kind of academic who writes scholarly papers without any regard for quality, as long as he does the bare minimum to get a promotion. The kind that students sidle up to for the sole purpose of getting a good grade. In short, nothing less than an idiot. Yet at the same time the perks of his position will shelter him. Because he's published X number of articles and X number of books, he'll still command respect. Students will still flock to him and he'll never need to descend to the level of the common people. He'll never have to endure being tested by real life, surrounded by the thick protective walls of the university, known as 'knowledge.' Meanwhile, let his soul be dashed to pieces in the clash between his true smallness and false importance. Whenever his opinion of himself is on the wane, I'll point to how great he is. And by the same token, if he gets too full of himself, I'll lay bare how little he is. That's the kind of man I'll take as my husband. If people are still going to put stock in the members of the elite and consider them bulletproof, then I'll align myself with the elite."

I asked if she was sure she didn't want to accept my proposal.

Her reply was frank. "You don't seem very strong in spirit

to me. You might turn out to be the kind of man who can't stand on his own two feet, who needs coddling and relies on someone else to take the lead.

"From what I've seen, you seem the changeable type. And sometimes you're unsure of yourself. Any woman who marries you will have to be perpetually on standby, just in case she has to help you out. She'll have to be patient and be prepared to be miserable. She'll have to be willing to make sacrifices."[23]

And so goes the story of when I asked MC to marry me in downtown Chicago, at the La Salle Hotel, where I was staying with her and MB.

That same night, I went down to the lobby and made a beeline for the pay phone. I opened the phone book to a random page. I found a name that interested me—a Vera Ford. I'd seen the same name in the Bloomington phone book as well, if I wasn't mistaken. So I picked up the receiver and put in a quarter.

"Hello? Is this Vera Ford?"

"Yes?"

"My name is Fanton. Fanton Drummond from Bloomington, Indiana. I happen to be in Chicago right now, at the La Salle Hotel on La Salle Street, downtown. I'm lonely. Want to go to a nightclub with me? I'll call a taxi in a little while. I'll buy some handcuffs. I'll cuff your hand to mine. We'll dance till morning. Whaddaya say?"

"Are you nuts?"

Vera hung up.

I sat alone in the lobby for a long time.

CHAPTER 4

MC LEAVES FOR HOME BY HERSELF

The next day, after getting some coffee from a vending machine near the same pay phone, I resumed my sitting.

Around ten minutes later, I was joined by MB and MC. As usual, MB was beaming away. Perhaps she had no brain, so pleased was she with everything and everyone. MC's expression was as usual too—not beaming, but not gloomy either. She must have had thick skin—thick as concrete. Last night's conversation seemed to have had no effect at all. She behaved as if I were someone with whom she met regularly, with whom she'd always gotten along, with whom she'd never argued or even differed in opinion.

I wondered whether she mightn't accept me after all. I just had to be a little patient. There were several indications that she tended to see everything as one of either two things: a matter of principle or not involving principle at all. Regarding anything that wasn't a matter of principle, she was extremely easygoing. She was happy to go along with not only MB's wishes but my own. When we were deciding where to go that day, for example. The John Hancock Center first, followed by the Playboy Building, then the Mosque Maryam—it didn't matter to her.

Her only wish was to see the Picasso. This was an absolute must. We spent a lot of time just trying to find the sculpture. We searched all over, but it was nowhere to be found. Finally, someone explained that the sculpture had been taken down.[i]

"Where did it used to be?" asked MC.

The person told us. MC was still dead set on going—which would take even more time. If the sculpture really had been taken down, there would be no signs, either, and it would be difficult to find. Once we located the site where the sculpture used to be, MB suggested we head to Lake Michigan.

But MC refused. "We have to go to the Metropolitan Art Archive of Chicago. I want to find out more about the sculpture."

Then we wasted an inordinate amount of time hunting for the archive.

We had coffee and doughnuts. Then MB suggested we head to the Sears Tower.

"Hold on," said MC. She wanted to call her mother.

She explained that her younger sister was away, chaperoning some elementary school children on a camping excursion near Beaver Falls. Her sister was supposed to have returned yesterday afternoon.

"I forgot to call last night," she told us.

Sure, said MB. She wanted to call home too. I tagged along. Not far from where I'd been sitting, and where they'd been sitting, was a wall with five pay phones all in a row. I intended to call my own apartment. The phone would keep ringing because no one was home. I just wanted to stay close to MC—to eavesdrop on what she said to her mother and sister.

A partition separated each phone from the other, so I didn't see the change in MC's expression. I could only hear the tremble in her voice. Unusually for her, she sounded emotional: "Oh! . . . Our poor family . . . How can we be so unlucky . . . When something bad happens, more bad things are bound to follow . . . Oh! . . . Oh! . . . Yes, I know . . . Once anything goes wrong, it can never be put right again . . . Our poor, wretched family . . . Oh! . . ."[24]

When she was done, she tottered unsteadily to a nearby seat. I hurried over. Her face was a fiery red. For the first time, I could see she had feelings. Ordinarily, she was a concrete wall.

For a long time she said nothing. When she spoke, her voice faltered. This was the gist: yesterday morning, her mother had slipped and fallen in the bathroom. The pain was unbearable. She called the hospital and an ambulance came to pick her up. Her hand was declared broken and she had sprained several muscles. She'd been discharged from the hospital that same day, though the pain was still excruciating. A few hours later, she received a phone call. The bus carrying the schoolchildren and MC's sister had crashed into a semitruck. A lot of the children were wounded or unconscious. Her sister was also hurt. Everyone was being treated at a hospital in Marion Hill.

"I have to go home right away," said MC. "I'll catch a flight."

MB and I tried to calm her down. MB suggested calling the hospital in Marion Hill to find out how her sister was.

"Maybe she's not too badly injured," said MB, hopefully. And if that were indeed the case, MC might not need to rush home. If MC really did need to go back right away, though, taking a plane was hardly necessary.

MC rejected her friend's suggestions, and MB's offer to accompany her on the flight home met with refusal too.

"It'll be too expensive. And according to the schedule, you're supposed to go home tomorrow. Don't let me change your plans. Especially since you've already bought a return bus ticket home."

She refused my offer to accompany her as well.

"Sorry about last night," she said, her voice trembling, her eyes filling with tears.

Yes, it seems she did have feelings after all.

At O'Hare International Airport, MC and MB hugged each other goodbye. From MB, I learned that MC's father had died a while ago, and MC had no siblings apart from the one who had been in the accident. So once more, I offered to accompany MC. She still refused. Then she regarded me for a long time, her eyes still glistening with tears.

"Sorry about last night," she said again.

She shook my hand—and didn't protest when I kissed hers, then her forehead, then finally, each cheek.

She said it again. "Sorry about last night." Then she gave my hand a squeeze.

MB and I waited until MC had boarded the bus that would

cross the tarmac to the plane. I wondered which was a better analogy for MC—a punter or a pendulum? True, for the time being she had booted Olenka aside. Gone was Olenka, uprooted from my heart, my mind, my every breath. MC had replaced her, seeping into my skin, sliding into my life.

But if MC were a pendulum, before long I'd be shooed away and returned to Olenka. Which was she? I had no idea. And I couldn't tell which one was better for me.

MB and I decided to leave Chicago immediately instead of waiting until the next day.

So we started homeward, MB and I, on a bus back to Indianapolis. The plan was for her to call MC from there. But when we arrived, it turned out the bus to Pittsburgh via Columbus was ready to depart. She jumped on in the nick of time. It was this very situation that MC had feared might happen. "What if I take a bus and something happens on the way?" she'd said. "I might have to spend the night in Indianapolis. I want to avoid any delay." That was why she'd decided to take a plane.

After a hasty handshake, MB left. She was her usual happy self, her voice still strident as a gong. It turned out the bus to Bloomington had already left about ten minutes prior. It had been the last bus. The next one would be at a quarter past five in the morning. I would have to spend the night at the bus station, thanks to the roadwork between Remington and Lafayette, which had delayed our arrival from Chicago. It was a good thing MB hadn't ended up here too. She'd still had a few minutes to hoof it to the bus to Columbus. If she'd had to stay overnight at the station like me, it would have been my bad luck. Imagine spending the whole night with a gong ringing in my ears.

CHAPTER 5

OVERNIGHT IN INDIANAPOLIS

A deaf and mute man came up to me. Only then did I recall the necklace I'd bought before. It was still in my suitcase and now I regretted not giving it to MC before she boarded her flight. I don't think she would have refused the gift.

Like the other man before, this man introduced himself with a card. He opened his suitcase and invited me, through hand gestures, to buy his wares. I declined. Politely, he took his leave. Perhaps the same school for deaf and mute people had trained them both. Just look: they all did the same thing. I had seen people like them in bus stations in various states—Michigan, Ohio, Virginia, and more. But I was only taking notice of them now.

Wayne sprang to mind. There were similarities between their mannerisms and his. What those similarities were exactly, it was difficult to say. I felt they were the same without being able to explain why. If only I could see them and Wayne all walking hand in hand—perhaps then I'd be able to pinpoint it. How sorry I felt for them, and how sorry I felt for Wayne. If anyone familiar with these men ever came across Wayne, he would probably assume that Wayne was one of them.

After wandering around the bus station for a while, I stopped in at the arcade. I played some pinball. I wondered at how some people could keep losing at it, while I kept winning game after game.

I found the other games easy too. Shooting down planes,

driving cars, playing two cowboys in a duel, wrecking a submarine, gunning down rabbits—none of it was hard. I attracted a small following, probably due to the fact that I was on a winning streak. Eventually, I returned to the pinball machine. My followers came along. And the same thing when I went back to the game where I had to shoot down planes. And when I returned to the car-racing game, a deaf and mute man joined the onlookers. I could see him clearly, his face reflected in the glass of the screen. But over time, the person I was seeing in the glass seemed not to be him but Wayne. When my opponent crashed and went flying, which the onlookers greeted with a roar, the mute gave me a thumbs-up, as if to say, "Great!" I gave him a nod. Perhaps he would interpret my nod as an expression of thanks.

In the end, I left the arcade. It was too noisy. And my time there left me with two thoughts: all the games were too easy for me, and a Wayne had deemed me worthy of a thumbs-up.

Sipping a cup of chicken soup from a vending machine, I asked myself: *Now what?* The bus station was a lot like my everyday life, wandering here and there, looking for ways to pass the time, with no real purpose. It was the same out there, every day. I would flow from one place to the next, who knew where and to what end? Sure, after this station, Bloomington would be my final stop. But once I got there, what would I do? Take walks every day, work when I felt like it, and if I was bored or unhappy, go out?

Eventually, I went over to a coin-operated TV. I sat down and put in a quarter. *The Lawrence Welk Show* was on channel 15—popular songs from the fifties. I got bored.

Channel 13 was playing *Sha Na Na*, a variety show with songs and comedy skits. I turned the dial to change the channel. A soap commercial. I changed the channel again. And on it went.

The TV set went dead. I put in another quarter. The set turned on again. After flipping from one channel to another, I finally found something interesting: a wrestling match between Orez, a wrestling champion from Detroit, and Yorrick, from St. Louis.[i] Only then did I remember that I knew someone in Indianapolis. His name was David Chiang. He was Chinese, born in Hong Kong. When he'd lived in Bloomington, I'd hired him to teach me jujitsu.

I went to the pay phone and searched for Chiang's name. When I found it, I put in twenty cents. The phone rang. Someone with a Chinese accent told me Chiang was on vacation in Cincinnati.

"Can I take a message?" asked the voice.

I hung up. It had been a while since my last jujitsu session, but if I had to, I was sure I still had the skills to fight.

It was then that the convenience store on the corner caught my attention. I sauntered over. My gaze landed on a magazine—*The New Yorker.* The latest issue too! I picked it up and flipped through. Sure enough, there was Wayne Danton's story, "The Mute and the Books."

Naturally, if I hadn't known Wayne, I wouldn't have wasted my time reading it. But since I did know him, I thought, *Well, why not.* But as I read, my pulse began to quicken. Who was the Mute based on? From his way of walking and arranging his bed, from his habit of accumulating books without reading them, from his poor moral fiber and aimless wandering, fickleness and irresponsibility, I had more than an inkling. Wayne was writing about me. It was I who had furnished the template and content for his story. I may have been insensitive and stupid, but I could still tell how he'd mined my life for the purposes of his tale. Wayne may have come up with a lot of the finer details, but he had perceived who I was in essence, and had captured the energy of that essence in his writing.

And where did he find out so much about me, if not from his wife? One of the sentences went as follows: *The Mute always slept with three pillows, two beneath his head and one on top. He'd sometimes prop his feet up with pillows. And if so, a double stack. So the Mute would end up using five pillows all at once.* Olenka was the only one who knew this habit of mine.

Throughout Wayne's story, I felt as if Wayne were paying me a visit, inspecting my whole apartment, ordering me to strip, bathe, brush my teeth, cook, eat, sleep, watch TV. The story's tone was angry, mocking, demeaning. The whole thing was seasoned with the bias of an aching heart. Its language was alive and fluid. When writing the story, Wayne must have actually been berating me, taunting me, manipulating me in his head.

Had Olenka conspired with him to play me for a fool, or had she merely given him information? Or, without meaning to, spoken to him about me? Perhaps she had brought me up for the purpose of commending me and putting him down. Yes, it was possible. All of these were possibilities. But whatever the case, I now knew that Olenka hadn't kept me a secret from him. Perhaps Wayne knew just as much about me as I knew about him—both of us knowing the other through Olenka.

I was angry. Sure, some of what Wayne had written was true, but he was exaggerating. To call the Mute someone "who suffered from a leprosy of the soul" was going too far. And in such an offensive tone! Objectively speaking, I enjoyed the story. The writer's skill was such that I found myself despising the Mute. He had to be banished from society, not because he was mute, but because he harbored an extremely dangerous psychological illness that might easily spread. No wonder the editorial staff of *The New Yorker* was going to include it in their yearly anthology of best short stories. Still, as the person who had been made the butt of this joke, I felt no disgust at the Mute, just the author. If Wayne were here, I would have socked him in the jaw.

In this state of rage and frustration, I set out on foot from the bus station. Strong winds gusted through the city. The streetlamps glowed weakly, struggling against the fog. How cold it was. A few taxi drivers crowded around me, offering their services. If I really wanted, I could take a cab home this very moment, wake Wayne up, and punch him in the jaw. But I thought it would be better to wait until morning.

I walked on, down wide roads and side streets and narrow alleyways. In one alley, a dog bolted past. I kicked it in the rear, its body soaring into the air, its howl piercing the night. Farther down was another dog, sniffing at a wall. I broke into a run and kicked it in the rear as well. The dog went flying, letting out a long howl.

On I walked, through blocks of warehouses and abandoned buildings. A few of the windows had been boarded up. I struck one of them and heard the sound of breaking glass. I fled to the main road.

I wondered then: perhaps Wayne had been angry at himself for being such a jerk. And perhaps his anger at himself had melded into his anger toward me. Then again, it was the Mute who was the real victim in all this, not the author who wrote him.

Eventually, I decided to go into a nightclub. I felt pretty tired and in need of a drink. I wasn't thinking too clearly, and my energy was flagging. I'd once heard that a Bloody Mary was good for calming the mind and boosting vitality, so I ordered one.

In a corner near the exit was a man with thick sideburns trying to chat up the cashier. She was giving him the cold shoulder. He was getting pretty mad, his face turning red. I wondered what Olenka had looked like when dealing with men like this. True, I used to be jealous. But whether I'd feel jealous now, I wasn't sure.

Also, I was still unsure about MC's role, pendulum or punter. Would I be swung back to Olenka, or had Olenka been booted out? Reading Wayne's story hadn't much changed my feelings for Olenka. She had furnished him with information, yes, but I didn't know the full story behind it. If she'd been making fun of me like she made fun of him in my company, then perhaps I was to blame as well. I'd never stopped her when she talked badly about Wayne. I'd even enjoyed it. Not infrequently, to mock him more, I'd even throw in a comment to spice things up. Not only had I stolen her from him, I'd subjected him to close scrutiny, for the purpose of turning him into an object of ridicule. Both acts of malice had given me great satisfaction, and it wasn't impossible that Olenka had treated me the same way she'd treated him. It only made sense that Wayne, in turn, be allowed to scrutinize me and turn me into a laughingstock.

I left the nightclub and flung myself into another one, but this time, not out of aimlessness or boredom. I knew exactly what I wanted. I wanted to wear myself out in order to regain my strength—to sleep soundly on the bus ride home, and upon reaching Tulip Tree, to sock Wayne in the jaw. And also break his nose.

The atmosphere was rather different in this nightclub. The front room was as per usual, but there were sounds coming from the back room—a big ruckus, with laughter and cheering.

I downed my Bloody Mary, stood up, and headed to the back. Someone stopped me at the entrance.

"It's an arm-wrestling match," he told me. "A dollar to enter."

So I paid.

The room was arranged like a miniature Roman amphitheater, with the chairs in circular rows and the floor sloping down toward the middle of the room. The center was spacious. They probably held shows here, dancing, singing, and the like. Tonight's event just happened to be arm wrestling.

The defending champion was a bald black man. He sat at a round table, above which hung a lamp that shone very bright. The man's head gleamed. I wondered if he'd oiled it with ghee.

Another man sat across from him. They were both of a large, sturdy, rugged build. Each had his right elbow on the table. They gripped hands in a battle of strength. From the shouts of the people around me, I learned that the black man was known as the Mute. His opponent was known merely as Joe.

It was an uneven match. Several times, the Mute got the upper hand, but even so, Joe still held his ground. Whenever his arm was about to be pinned down by the Mute, he resisted with all his might and managed to right it again.

I learned from some of the other people that the Mute was, in fact, mute. Like the other mute people I had seen around the bus stations, he also had something of the Wayne about him. And now I had an idea of what made them all so similar. In everything they did, there seemed to be an underlying awareness on their part of their muteness. This was the fine thread that seemed to connect them all—something about the way they acted, which I couldn't articulate. I knew it only because I could sense it. Wayne had the same feel about him. He wasn't mute, but I was certain he felt as if he were. In one respect, writing the story allowed him to vent his rage at feeling this way. But at the same time, writing it enabled him to cast me as mute.

The pimply guy next to me was backing the Mute. He invited me to wager five bucks. I was sure the Mute would win, but I accepted his challenge and backed Joe. Before long, the Mute won. I lost my five dollars.

After downing a few drinks, the Mute took on other challengers, felling numerous opponents with ease. The longer I watched, the more I despised his arrogance. He behaved as if all his opponents were lightweights, easily vanquished, worthy only of scorn. I caught glimpses of Wayne in him every now and then, as if he were Wayne incarnate, Wayne Number Two.

My hatred came to a boil. I stepped forward. Everyone cheered. The Mute's expression suggested he'd say "Hah!" if he could. I shivered. Wayne's story made me realize: I, too, was mute. It dawned on me then, my deficiency, whatever it was. And to hide this nameless deficiency, I did as I pleased. My little world, just as I had realized earlier, was no more than a bus station at night. Now here I was, challenging the Mute—in another attempt to forget the deficiency I had no name for. *You're right, Wayne. I'm mute*, I thought. But I still felt mad, for the way he had treated me in his short story had gone too far.

I wasn't ready, and would probably never be. But I said I was anyway. The match commenced. I fell into a dream state. The person in front of me was Wayne. His sunken eyes. His cunning gaze. His cowardly attitude. But beneath it all was a malicious desire to crush me. He hung back, but I could tell from his movements that he was waiting for an invitation. It was exactly like the time I had punched him before. So I motioned for him to come closer. I invited him closer, for a pleasant chat. He was silent. Again, I tried to get him to talk. He spit on the ground. It was my turn to be silent. Then he spit in my face. I got angry. I punched him in the mouth. He went sprawling. His lip was bleeding. Then he rose and advanced again. I hit his nose. He went sprawling once more. Now his nose bled. He paused for a moment to wipe the blood away before getting to his feet. I socked him in the chin. He fell down yet again.

When I came to my senses, the Mute's arm was nearly down for the count. The crowd roared. Most of them were betting on the Mute. Meanwhile my throat was dry and I was pouring with sweat. I still had the upper hand. The Mute grinned. There was a vengeful glint in his eyes. Wayne's eyes.

The Mute's arm descended, overpowering mine. My throat felt even drier, my sweat more copious, and colder. I felt tired. For the past few days I'd slept little, rested little, and had eaten at odd times. Slowly but surely, the Mute's arm went back up, bit by bit. The crowd roared. I fell back into a dream state. My dream went like this: dressed only in a loincloth and armed only with a stone club, I bellowed as I led the charge against a band of primitives. I myself was a primitive. And from her sedan chair, MC sat watching, gnawing on a haunch of raw meat. She was dressed in a loincloth, like me.

By the time I came to my senses again, the Mute had gained the advantage. People were yelling themselves hoarse. I was beginning to see stars. If only I could dream about socking Wayne. Then I'd probably win. But I wasn't dreaming anything now. I had the growing sense that despite my ability to speak, deep down, in my soul, I was mute.

Why was I doing this? I wondered. Back when I'd trained with David Chiang, I'd been a star pupil. He'd said with my natural talent and abilities, it would be difficult to find my match. If I trained diligently—he had told me—I could even defeat him someday. But I hadn't been taking lessons very long before I grew bored. I'd told him I no longer needed his services. He'd expressed his disappointment.

Once again, I succeeded in righting my arm. I had regained the upper hand. And for the remainder of the match, I didn't lapse into any dreams. I was merely conscious of the fact that I was mute. Wayne and I were the same.

A few moments later, my arm dropped to the table. People cheered in satisfaction. The emcee clapped me on the back. "This was one of the longest matches of the night. You're the real deal, if you ask me."[25]

This made me happy. I promised myself I'd tell MC all about this when the time was right. And I now knew she was a punter, not a pendulum. Olenka had been ousted from my heart. Never once had I seen my relationship with Wayne as part of a greater triangle. Sure, Olenka was our point of connection, but I'd never thought of Wayne as linked to her. To me, Olenka was a living entity in her own right, separate from the living entity known as Wayne Danton. It was true before and even more so now. I would face Wayne head-on, as an enemy, wholly separate from Olenka.

CHAPTER 6

WAYNE, GALPIN, AND ME

When I got back to Tulip Tree, I discovered that Wayne had left the building for good. He'd moved without even leaving the building manager his new address. According to the neighbor across the hall, Wayne planned to "devote all his time, energy, and attention, his entire body and soul, to developing his craft." How pretentious could you get.

Unable to carry out my intention to punch Wayne, I resorted to loafing about. I thought I might as well check my mailbox. I found a bank statement saying that I still had a balance of $5,375.42. If I tightened my belt, I could keep taking it easy and not work for another ten or so months.

I'd made around the same amount in a mere two weeks once, on a gig for 20th Century Fox. They'd been filming *Breaking Away*—a movie set in Bloomington about a bike race and the aspirations of some college-age kids.[26] I'd helped arrange the shooting locations. Now they were turning the film into a TV series. The director, Peter Yates, had contacted me about it, inviting me to relocate to Hollywood for the project, and offering me a big salary too. I'd turned him down. Something inside me had said no and I couldn't explain what it was.

I glanced at my bank balance again. It was the equivalent of about four weeks' worth of pay at my old job directing TV commercials at the ad agency. Galpin Danzig, on the other hand, had earned $25.00 an hour as a low-level employee, and only whenever there happened to be work for him to do. And even though the work kept coming, he chose to quit and take a job at the library for $3.20 an hour instead.

He was happier being a prole, though for different reasons than mine. Maybe Wayne was right. Maybe I did suffer from a leprosy of the soul.

A black-and-white film advertisement for the film *Breaking Away,* directed by Peter Yates and starring Dennis Quaid, Barbara Barrie, and Dennis Christopher—clipped from the Thursday, July 29, 1982, edition of the Indonesian-language newspaper the *Surabaya Post.*

The ad is a collage of different scenes from the film and text in different sizes and fonts. On the left, a young white woman with long dark hair has her hand on the shoulder of a young white man with wavy blond hair. The woman gazes earnestly at him and the young man looks down, avoiding her gaze. To the bottom left of that image is a smaller image of a young man brandishing a trophy, his arms held high in triumph. To the right is an image of a group of four young men dressed in T-shirts and jeans, advancing, three on foot and one on a bicycle. Farther to the right are an older man hugging a young man as an older woman looks lovingly on; a few young men engaged in a scuffle, arms locked around each other; and a young brunette woman looking off into the distance with a smile on her face. There is also an image of six Oscar statues in a row, in a circular frame, with the English-language text *Winner of 6 Academy Awards.*

The text at the very top gives the date the film starts showing (July 29, 1982), the times, and the locations (the Surabaya Theater, the Ria, the Indra). Other text includes a three-star rating from the newspaper *Kompas* (the highest rating), the ticket price, and praise for the film.

When the director Peter Yates was shooting the film *Breaking Away* in Bloomington, Fanton Drummond was employed as a location manager, arranging the locations for the bicycle race scenes. The film won six Oscars. After seeing the movie on TV, Mary Carson revised her assessment of Fanton Drummond. Fanton himself didn't think much at all of his involvement in the film. *Breaking Away* only came to Indonesia in 1982.

PART III

CHAPTER 1

FIVE MASTURBATORY LETTERS

I decided to masturbate via letter writing. That is, I would write a letter addressed to MC, then put it away for about as long as it would take for the letter to reach her by mail. Then I would read the letter, as if I were MC, and write a reply addressed to me as myself, Fanton Drummond. I would keep this letter for a few days too, for as long as it would take for the letter to reach me. Then I would read the letter and proceed to write a reply. In short, masturbation. But I hoped that by this method, I would be able to scratch beneath the surface, to discover who I really was.

I had already learned much about myself from Olenka. Her presence in my life had also encouraged me to figure out who I was. Then there was Wayne's story—also an attempt to expose who I was, though it wasn't very accurate and, in fact, went too far.

I knew if I actually wrote to MC, she'd never respond. And as for MB, I wanted nothing to do with her. Being, in essence, a gong, she would be of no use. If I wanted to know whether I should go sailing on Lake Michigan, then maybe I'd contact her, but not for anything more important than that.

But masturbation would enable me to formulate my own questions and search for answers. "Engaging in dialogue with myself" was the proper term. In other words, I would perform a dramatic monologue wherein I would talk to myself before an imaginary audience. The type of audience, and my relationship to that audience, was important as well. If my audience were Wayne, the questions I'd pose were sure to be angry, and my answers would end up sounding defensive, and oppositional too. I'd end up railing against my audience for their rudeness, and insisting I didn't deserve to be ridiculed or put down or dismissed as "someone suffering from a leprosy of the soul." But if MC were my imagined audience, I'd come up with questions whose answers would increase the chances of her accepting me. Looking inside myself, looking into my past, assessing myself—I would only be able to do these things if my audience were MC.

The opening line of my masturbatory letter would go something like this: *MC, we must make a distinction between cause and effect.*

I would go on to say that she'd been right, that my spirit lacked strength, that I couldn't stand on my own and required care, assistance, and direction—but I needed these very things *so* I could grow strong in spirit and stand on my own, without care, assistance, or direction from anyone else.

I often found myself treating myself as an enemy, and attempting to flee my own self. Under such circumstances, what I wanted to do instead was treat myself as an object of study.

Then I would tell her about the time when I'd worked as a railroad hand. *How come I'm not a train engineer?* I wondered at the time. The answer that first sprang to mind: *Well, I'm still young.* The next question, then, as someone who hadn't reached full adulthood: *How come I'm not old?* The answer was simple: *I need more time.* However, there was yet another question, more difficult to answer: *Let's say I were old enough. Would I have the ability to be a train engineer?* It was certainly a cushy job, sitting in front, obeying orders, pulling out of the station, the path ahead all set. Every now and then you'd come across a signal. All you had to do was follow what it told you, not much thought required. The pay was good too.

I would then go on to tell her about another question that would often spring to mind: *Let's say I did become an engineer one day. Would I really be happy?*

I once overheard an engineer complain, "I regret getting a

good education and I regret being so ambitious. If only I'd been more of a dimwit, more content with my lot in life. Then I'd be happy doing anything. I wouldn't have become an engineer."

He'd muttered this right after he'd gotten told off for violating the rules.

I'd asked, "Are you saying that if you were stupid, weren't educated, and had no ambition, you'd be content with being a railroad hand?"

His reply had been confident. "Yep. It would be more or less the same as now, anyway. For example, I have no desire to be a stationmaster—because I know I don't have what it takes."

I would then go on to write in my letter about how I often thought about the two philosophers Chuang Tzu and Hui Tzu. They had been taking a stroll one day, enjoying the fresh air, on the bridge over the River Hao. Though they were merely passing the time, looking at mundane things and chatting about nothing of great import, a lot was made of their conversation. They were philosophers, after all.

The full story went like this: Chuang Tzu said, "Look at those minnows darting hither and thither. Such is the pleasure that fish enjoy!"

Hui Tzu replied, "You are not a fish, are you? How do you know what gives pleasure to fish?"

Chuang Tzu said, "You are not I. How do you know that I do not know what gives pleasure to fish?"

Hui Tzu said, "If because I am not you, I cannot know whether you know, then equally because you yourself are not a fish, you cannot know what gives pleasure to fish. My argument still stands, my fellow philosopher."

Chuang Tzu said, "Let us go back to where we started. You asked me how I knew what gives pleasure to fish. But you already knew how I knew it when you asked me. You knew that I knew it by standing here on the bridge at Hao. Not all knowledge can be gained through argumentation."[27]

And so their conversation reached a stalemate. The same went for me. I often found myself hitting a wall if I relied too heavily on assumptions. Just like Chuang Tzu. For example, I'd never made any serious attempt to achieve anything because I'd seen how many people who did achieve something were nothing but idiots. Like the college professor MC planned to marry someday.

I also found myself running into walls whenever I placed too much faith in the importance of experience. Nobody could properly assess something without getting involved and experiencing it for oneself—and such was the argument, more or less, of the philosopher Hui Tzu. In the past, I had leaped from one job to the next, wanting to experience something new before drawing my own conclusions. The result was always the same. Each new experience only increased my appetite for still newer ones.

These, more or less, were the main thoughts I would express in my first masturbatory letter.

The second masturbatory letter would contain thoughts such as these:

I don't know who brought the matter up that day, back when I was little. But we all had a discussion about where babies came from. Nearly everyone agreed that babies fell out of their mothers like excrement (alias, poop).

A few kids begged to differ. They said babies came from the sky, carried by birds.

"How can birds be strong enough to carry babies?" others objected.

"They are! We just never see them because we don't know when they're going to show up. They carry the babies in their beaks."

The debate ended with no clear consensus.

Actually, my opinion at the time was that babies came from bodies like excrement (alias, poop). But if this was the case, I thought to myself, how filthy I must be! Then I tried my hardest not to believe it. I forced myself to hold devoutly to the theory that babies were brought to earth by giant birds, like storks. I began sneaking off to the fields. Who knew, maybe I'd see a bird descending with a baby in its beak.

One day I asked one of the gardeners—Mr. Manning, if I'm not mistaken—if he knew where my father and mother might be living now.

Mr. Manning said they lived in heaven.

When I asked where heaven was, he replied, "Way up there, in the sky. If you're wise, clever, and hardworking like your parents, then you'll go to heaven, kid. In the sky, see? Up there?"

During that time, there was a teacher—Mr. Allyn, if I remember correctly—who would send me to the post office to mail his letters. Most of them were from *John Allyn, 146 Lawrence Street, Rockdale, Kentucky, 49562*, addressed to *Ernest Allyn, 257 Martin Avenue, Donson City, Ohio 35269.* (I can't remember the real names and addresses, but they went something along those lines.)

One day I asked Mr. Allyn, "Is Ernest Allyn your father, Mr. Allyn?"

Mr. Allyn nodded.

"Why do you have to stick a stamp on the envelope?"

"Stamps are like money. When there's a stamp stuck to it, it means you've paid for the letter to be sent."

"What happens if there's no stamp on it?"

"Then the post office won't send your letter because you haven't paid."

I didn't quite believe him. How could stamps be like money?

One day I wrote a letter to my mother and father. On the back of the envelope, I wrote:

Fanton Drummond

535 Organ Avenue

Rockdale, The State of Kentucky, zip code 49562

The Midwest

The United States

The American Continent

Planet Earth

THE UNIVERSE

Then I wrote my mother and father's address:

My Dear Mother and Father

Mr. and Mrs. Drummond

Heaven

THE SKY

The letter went like this:

> Mother and Father. This is Fanton. I am well. People say if I am good I can go to heaven. Robert drew an elephant. The nose was too long. Jason drew a stork. A big one. It was on its way to deliver a baby. I am well. I am sleepy. Tomorrow a magician from Tennessee is coming here. F. Drummond.

No stamp.

About five days later, the headmaster called me in. I was told there was a letter for me. The headmaster advised me not to write any more letters. The return address read only: *Drummond.*

It went: *We're glad you're well, Fanton. We're too old and won't be writing again. Sorry if we don't reply to any more letters. Your beloved parents, Mr. and Mrs. Drummond.*

After receiving this reply, I wrote my parents two more letters, neither one with stamps. And neither of them got a reply.

That would be the gist of the second masturbation letter.

In my third masturbation letter, I would provoke MC to jealousy. It would go something like this:

> I followed Patricia one day. At the edge of the cornfield I said, "Patricia, can I kiss you?" "No." "Why not?" "Then I'll have a baby." I did kiss her in the end, but she never had a baby.

In the fourth masturbation letter, I'd wax philosophical.

> MC, what's the point in working hard when I can take it easy and live a good life anyway? Some other guy—Jerry, say, or

Mike, or Abrolin—might work himself to death and get nothing but three dollars and twenty cents an hour in return.

I used to have a job where I got paid twenty-five hundred dollars a week. But the professor you marry? He'll be nothing but a Jerry, Mike, or Abrolin. That's right. The man you're so besotted with will spend all his days in the library. What a waste of time. Why pick someone stupid like him? Pick me instead. I'm sure if I wanted to, with a little effort, I could write a bunch of articles and a few books—just like the professor you plan to take as your husband. Except I think this kind of work is pointless. Hard work is for idiots. And you're not an idiot. You know, MB the Gong admires you for good reason. You're no Jerry, Mike, or Abrolin.

In the fifth letter, I would write, *I've taken up jujitsu again. Before long, I'll be appointed commander of the Mongol Army. Come hither and wipe the sweat from my brow.*

My brain was exhausted. Not from lack of sleep but from the effort I'd expended outlining those five letters. And animating those five letters was a desire to defend myself. Let's say she was right about me being changeable. By right she should admire me for it. I was changeable because I had principles. Never mind whether these principles were right or not, they were principles all the same. This was something worthy of respect, actually—my refusal to stagnate. My life was composed of continual thought. Sure, I wouldn't be changeable if I were like her, hell-bent on marrying some stupid professor. If a principle caused someone to stagnate, then it was wrong. I wanted her to see that. Better to try out different things than climb straight into the grave merely because you knew you were headed there anyway. That was essentially what she wanted to do.

CHAPTER 2

DISASTER

I was tired. But I knew I wouldn't be able to fall asleep if I went to bed. So I turned on the TV. There was nothing good on. I hopped from one channel to another before finally landing on the news: "This is channel seventeen, Bloomington, Indiana—where viewers come first. I'm Brian Troring and here's a roundup of today's news."

After a message from their sponsor, Troring returned to deliver the following report:

"Of the forty-six people critically injured in the recent crash of a DC-10 airliner in Pittsburgh, fourteen more people have died. This brings the total number of deaths to ninety-six, including the pilot and flight crew. The cause of the crash is still under investigation. According to Albatross Airlines' spokesman in Pittsburgh, engine failure is the suspected cause. The crash that befell Flight F52 occurred when the DC-10 was stopping over in Pittsburgh, en route from Chicago to New York."[i]

Worried that I might have heard wrong, I went down and bought a paper from a newspaper vending machine. I hadn't misheard at all. MC's plane had crashed just as it was about to land at Pittsburgh International Airport. Accompanying the article were several photos of the wreckage and a few victims.

Maddock, the Tulip Tree building manager, happened to be passing by. As usual, he wore sunglasses, which he sported day and night, whether it was sunny or cloudy outside. On his belt hung dozens of keys, who knew what they all were for.

"Big news!" exclaimed Maddock.

"What?"

"Baseball! Pittsburgh beat UIC. And I know that UIC will beat Louisville next week. Texas doesn't stand a chance, much less Georgia."

"Yeah, but not if Benson doesn't play," I said.

"Well, then there's always Dimsdale, Stevick, and Tave. Point is, Pittsburgh can't lose. Don't believe me?"

"Yeah, maybe you're right. Anyway, I was just reading about this plane crash."

"It's not like the one last year, is it? Remember, when Florida's top player, Mercer, was on that flight that crashed in Tallahassee?"

I told him about the recent incident.

"That's a shame," said Maddock. "Shouldn't've flown if there was engine trouble. That's not like what happened to Mercer. The engine was fine, the weather was fine, and out of the blue it crashed into another plane whose pilot was just learning to fly. That's what you call bad luck. Poor Mercer. If he were still around, Pittsburgh would be shaking in their boots."

Then Maddock left.

I tried to reach the Albatross Airlines Pittsburgh office but failed. All I got was the following message: "Thank you for calling. We're sorry we can't answer the phone right now. Apologies again and thank you. This is a recorded message from Albatross, King of the Skies." Then the phone automatically hung up.

I received the same message when I called their Chicago office. I resorted to phoning the Bloomington branch. They told me they didn't have a list of the victims in the Pittsburgh crash.

"My fiancée was on that flight. Can you please check for her name? Carson. Mary Carson. We're supposed to get married next month."

"I'm sorry, sir," said the woman on the line. "Like I said, we don't have a list."

"Fuck you!"

"Excuse me, sir?"

"Fuck you!"

"Hey, don't swear at me!"

"Shithead!"

"Stop it. If you're going to be rude—"

"What are you, some kind of whore?"

"I am not, sir! I'll have you know I'm a respectable woman. Why, I—I . . ."

CHAPTER 3

MADAME SOSOSTRIS

Eventually, I fell asleep and had a dream. I was glad I was still capable of dreaming. If I weren't, it would mean my life really had run dry. I was sure people who led dry lives weren't subject to reveries or fantasies, and I was positive they never had dreams. They were probably incapable of deception too, whereas I knew how to deceive people—or at least, myself. Case in point, the effort I had expended in composing those masturbatory letters.

Obviously, Wayne's gibe—that I suffered from a leprosy of the soul—was going too far. Still, he wasn't mistaken about something inside me being not right. And sure, at first glance, MC may have appeared more upright, but her determination to marry a man who felt himself entitled to adoration, whom she would then jeer as she pleased, made her no different from Olenka. I'd even go so far as to wager that she would treat her husband, that professor of hers, the same way Olenka treated Wayne. I bet she would be even crueler than Olenka. As far as I knew, when Olenka had settled on Wayne, she had pinned her hopes on Wayne becoming a true writer. MC, on the other hand, was planning to marry someone she didn't respect at all—a man whom she could praise or ridicule as she saw fit. However you looked at it, at least Olenka was an idealist at heart. Since MC thought her ideal unrealistic, she was deliberately resigning herself to what she did see as real—an unideal situation, which would only cause everyone to suffer. Inevitably, she would get sick of her husband and feel the urge to ridicule, degrade, and laugh at him. Like I said, upon sighting the grave, she was choosing to climb straight in.

As opposed to Madame Sosostris, famous clairvoyante, known to be the wisest woman in Europe. Cards in hand, Madame Sosostris could see both future and past. She perceived the entire universe sinking into decay, a fact unseen and unfelt by anyone else. With her strength of sight she could penetrate great mysteries. Like how the ancient civilization of Phoenicia fell into ruin. She knew the exact moment the sailors of said nation perished, drowned in the raging sea. She saw Belladonna too, the most beautiful woman in the history of the world, transformed into a poisonous plant. How many men died, slain by her beauty, the very venom of death itself! Before Madame Sosostris's eyes, the Virgin of the Rocks, the Madonna in Leonardo da Vinci's painting, morphed into a cold-blooded killer. Naturally, her view of reality was far more sublime than MC's. So, unlike MC, Madame Sosostris was able to say:

What shall I do now? What shall I do?
I shall rush out as I am, and walk the street
With my hair down, so. What shall we do tomorrow?
What shall we ever do?

Whereas someone like MC wouldn't worry or fret at all. She could only see the world as it was, lacking any power whatsoever to see past literal fact.

My chest swelled with pride, for what Madame Sosostris uttered was my very life in practice. All right, so I'd never read cards or gazed back into the past or far into the future, but at least I could recognize that I was falling into decay. Which was why, like Madame Sosostris, I was always rushing here and there.

Naturally, my powers of sight couldn't compare to those of Madame Sosostris. Even so, I had good reason to believe that I was superior to Olenka, and of course, to MC. Come to think of it, maybe I was even greater than Madame Sosostris herself. There was nothing special about MC apart from her eagerness to hop preemptively into the grave. And Olenka, forced to give up her hopes and dreams, had turned to a life of self-destruction.

Madame Sosostris, in contrast, never had hope at all. To her, everything was in ruin. Nothing was good, or pure, or noble. She roamed the world. How sweltering every inch of the universe seemed, and yet she knew she would find no shelter, no safety, no peace. Land, air, sea, and everywhere else—all belonged to the enemy, who bore the name Death.

But me, I was different. If I saw a well before me, I'd never think about diving in. And when dealing with Olenka, I had been confident about taming her wildness. And in my dealings with MC, I had showed myself capable of surrendering to the realm of romance.

My roamings were my way of defying my circumstances. I refused to give in; circumstance would not be the master of me. I was a man of strength and had evidence to prove it, like I'd said in one of my masturbatory letters: my time was mine to do with what I pleased. I didn't have to let some schedule rule my life. I'd already shown that I wasn't your average Jerry, Mike, or Abrolin, scrounging around for scraps like a dog. And of course, I was no Madame Sosostris either. Remember how she felt about the great cities of the world? Jerusalem, Athens, Alexandria, Vienna, London—to her they were merely "unreal." Remember, too, her sentiments toward London Bridge in all its sturdiness and grace. In her eyes, it was already crumbling, falling, falling. "London Bridge is falling down, falling down, falling down"—that was how she felt.

For all my stupidity and erratic behavior, I was still able to take pleasure in all life had to offer. To me, London *was* real, and grand, and delightful. All right, so I'd never been to London, but from what I'd seen of it in pictures, movies, and books, not to mention the stories I'd heard, I knew enough. I was sure of my ability to stroll around Piccadilly Circus, visit Nelson's Column, ride the Underground, and whatnot with a joyful, happy heart. And in my eyes, London Bridge was still graceful and resilient, unlikely to collapse unless deliberately destroyed. But even Hitler hadn't succeeded in bringing it down.

Remember, too, here I was, having a dream. So my life was far from dry. In fact, it was wet. For however empty my life was and how easily bored I could get, I could still see the pleasure in things. For example, in the bus station in Indianapolis—I could still play pinball, sip chicken soup, rejoice at parting ways with the Gong, et cetera.

For all my degenerate ways, I still had shining qualities. I always kept my hopes up, I always had tomorrow, even though tomorrow I'd do nothing but wander around aimlessly some more. With these qualities of mine, I deserved to have a girl waiting for me, who would always yearn to be at my side. I deserved to be like an Irish sailor, missing his hometown yet knowing, somewhere out there, his beloved was waiting for him. And so, as would befit an Irish sailor, I mumbled a tune:

Frisch weht der Wind
Der Heimat zu,
Mien Irisch Kind,
Wo weilest du?[28]

Upon realizing that what I was singing was a snippet from the opera *Tristan und Isolde*, I wondered if my relationship with Olenka could be mended after all. I knew, of course, I had no right to compare myself to Tristan, but it wasn't wrong to say he and I were alike in certain ways. For the very tips of Tristan's fingers were widely held to be possessed of the gift of *venerie*. He had extraordinary abilities, and whatever he did would meet with success. I may not have been as talented as he was, but I was certainly no Jerry, Mike, or Abrolin. At the ad agency, every client who'd hired me was guaranteed to be satisfied with my work. Galpin had said it himself, that I possessed a knack for things that your average person wasn't lucky enough to have. And Peter Yates had invited me to come live in Hollywood precisely because of his faith in my abilities.

Like Tristan, I never knew my parents. He and I were both orphans. True, I was probably the son of someone ordinary—not a senator or congressman or the owner of a big bank—where Tristan was actually the son of a king. Maybe it was because I wasn't born to anyone famous that I had no ambition at all. Never, for example, had I desired to become an ambassador, or to monopolize the pharmaceutical market, or to buy an airline on the verge of bankruptcy for the sake of turning it around. Nothing like that. In contrast, Tristan always set his ambitions sky-high. He wanted to do battle, to vanquish his enemies, to make his name revered throughout the land.

That Tristan had engaged in deception was common knowledge. He served under King Mark. And by King Mark, he was ordered to Ireland to fetch Isolde, the King's bride-to-be. The king found out about Tristan and Isolde falling in love and flirting, and you can guess what happened next. The king was furious, and Tristan was forced to take flight.

Sure, everyone knows they didn't mean to fall in love. As Tristan was bringing Isolde over to hand her to the king, the two of them unwittingly consumed a love potion. It was at this point that their adulterous passions began.

As everyone also knows, Richard Wagner didn't pull the opera *Tristan und Isolde* out of thin air or his own head. It was based on a legend that had been passed down by word of mouth over the centuries. When he had depicted them swallowing love's poison unawares, he wasn't just making things up. He'd composed his music based on a preexisting story, and a preexisting story had to have its roots somewhere.

For hundreds of years, people must have wanted to believe in the reality of Tristan and Isolde's love story. Whenever I'd watched this opera—in Indiana and Michigan, and once in Ohio—the audience would always cheer when we got to the scene where Tristan and Isolde drink the love potion. The same thing had happened when I'd attended readings of Tristan and Isolde's tale—not just of Gottfried von Strassburg's and Béroul's versions but also of Eilhart von Oberge's. The audience positively pined for it, for love to blossom between the two young lovers, despite how close their love came to betrayal. The audience was always happy, itching even, to see Tristan and Isolde deceive the king.

And everyone knows why. Mark's right to Isolde comes only from his status as king. If Mark weren't royalty, born to beggars, say, then he wouldn't have any power. Even as a king, he can't do very much. When he has enemies, Tristan is the one he sends to get rid of them. Even when it comes to fetching his wife, Tristan is the one in charge. It's not surprising, then, that whatever Tristan does, good or bad, people admire him. And the more the king suffers, the happier the audience is.

Supposing Olenka, Wayne, and I were brought before a panel of judges. I was certain Olenka's every action would elicit approval and praise. My behavior would also garner their sympathy. Wayne, who should by right be pitied, would be censured instead. All the panel members would be sure to hope that Olenka and I would stab Wayne in the back. Just like Tristan and Isolde's audience and readers, the panel members were sure to side with Olenka and me.

Even so, I was sure that all stories had to have a moral, by however slim a margin. No story would ask its reader or viewer to admire or side with wrongdoing and curse what is right, much less cheer when good is defeated. The same applies to Tristan and Isolde. Their wrongdoing inspires admiration; the king, deserving of pity, is hated—for everyone wishes to side with Tristan and Isolde. But where would the moral of the story be, if the king were allowed to continue to suffer while Tristan and Isolde carried on as they pleased, committing deeds that should be criticized, if not outright cursed?

And in the end, they do receive their curse. Tristan is mortally wounded in combat. The only one in the world who can save his life is Isolde. As he waits for Isolde to come, he receives false word that she refuses to come to his aid. Thus gone is Tristan forever. Isolde arrives too late. Upon discovering Tristan's body, already cold, Isolde decides to join him by stabbing herself in the heart.

I was certain that, when it came down to it, my relationship with Olenka was irredeemable. Like Tristan and Isolde, Olenka and I would be punished, whatever form it might take. That which was wrong would, in the end, receive what was deserved. And the same would apply for that which was good.

CHAPTER 4

A DREAM

Again, I fell asleep and dreamed. In my dream, I was sitting in the Bloomington meteorological radar room. The DaVinci TransAmerica balloon was approaching Bloomington at forty miles an hour. I had made contact with them half an hour ago. I was urging them to land. The radar showed that freezing fifty-five-mile-an-hour winds, along with heavy rain and lightning, were headed for the Richmond area, near the border between Indiana and Ohio.

"We've come so far—eighteen hundred miles, all the way from Oregon. Do we really have to land?"

"There's no choice," I said.

They asked if they could detour to Ellettsville, before heading on to Ohio.

"Didn't you hear the Terre Haute control tower? A big storm's due to hit all of southern Indiana, northern Kentucky, and greater Ohio!"

"Yeah, we heard."

"Sorry, guys. There's no other way. You've got to land in Bloomington. Or Columbus, Indiana's the furthest you can go."

But they wouldn't land. Then I woke up.

My first thought was, *If I were them, I would've landed for sure. What's the point of trying to go against a storm?*

It was almost half past two in the morning. I was hungry and there was nothing good on TV. All that was showing were old films with actors I didn't recognize.

Eventually, I phoned Pagliani's and ordered a seventeen-inch pizza and a bottle of California Chablis.

"Don't skimp on the pepperoni," I told them. "Or the hamburger. Or the olives. But no sausage. I don't eat pork."

I could still recall what a friend of mine had once said—that the Quran forbade Muslims from eating pork. I wasn't Muslim, but I thought I might as well comply. Human history was littered with hundreds of prophets, thousands even, but there were only three holy books. It was only fitting to follow what a holy book said—of this I was sure. And I could still remember what I'd read in the Quran when I happened to be flipping through a copy in the library:

Those who believe (in the Quran)
And those who follow the Jewish (scriptures)
And the Christians and the Sabians,—
Any who believe in God
and the Last Day,
And work righteousness,
Shall have their reward
With their Lord; on them
Shall be no fear, nor shall they grieve.[29]

So it seemed only fitting that I not eat pork. All right, so maybe I had accidentally eaten pork in the past. But whenever it had happened, I regretted it deeply—that I'd failed, as a believer in God, to obey His word, as given in one of His holy books.

About twenty minutes later, there came a knock on my door. Two young women had brought me my order. They looked slender, pretty, and bright. Each carried a walkie-talkie and a revolver. It seemed they even knew martial arts. I was impressed.

According to their name tags, they were called Mary and Janet. In the brief conversation that followed, I learned that Janet worked full time and Mary was in college, majoring in communications. Mary had spent two whole weeks last summer making a video about Bloomington's nightlife for a practicum. That was how she'd found out about delivering pizzas at night.

I asked whether I would get hired, if I applied for a job like theirs.

"Probably," replied Janet. She explained that a lot of college students studied late at night in the fall and winter. They would get hungry but couldn't be bothered to go out.

Their uniforms, walkie-talkies, and revolvers intrigued me. How handsome and manly I'd look if I worked there. It wasn't a bad thing, to act macho every now and then.

"What's the pay?" I asked.

"Seven fifty an hour after midnight," said Janet.

Or maybe "macho" is overrated, I thought. *It's not like I'm Jerry, Mike, or Abrolin. For that kind of pay, I may as well take Peter Yates up on his offer.*

I asked Mary her last name.

"Carson," she replied.

I chuckled. "By happy coincidence, my girlfriend's name is Mary Carson too. We were going to get married next month."

"For real?"

"For real. But she died."

Then I told her about the DC-10 crash in Pittsburgh. They expressed their condolences and said it was the first time they'd heard about it.

"Any interesting news lately?" I asked.

Mary and Janet gave me a brief rundown of what was happening in the World Series.[30] They reminded me of Maddock.

I tipped them a dollar each. They were already almost at the elevator when I called them back. I gave them each another dollar. I felt sorry for them, but I admired them too. At first they refused, but they eventually took the money.

I uttered a prayer once they had left. "Oh Lord, bless each of them abundantly. Grant them good husbands—fine, honest, godly men. Grant them healthy children who will respect their parents and have a sense of duty toward their fellow man. Amen."

PART IV

CHAPTER 1

A LONG LETTER FROM OLENKA

A week before the DaVinci TransAmerica balloon had crossed over Bloomington, I remember Olenka saying, "I'm not going to write to you after we part ways."

If she needed to call, she said she would use a pay phone. That way, if she didn't put more money in, after three minutes the line would go dead.

"That way I'll say only what I need to," she'd explained before adding, "but it would be best not to keep in touch at all."

But she'd written to me after all—a letter of great length. As if it contained her whole life. This was the letter in full:

I promised I wouldn't write. Still, I'm sure this letter won't surprise you. You must be so different now—strong as a giant, disciplined as a monk.

I won't mention my location. It's no longer of any importance. [My note: unfortunately, the postmark on the envelope was blurry.] For a while after leaving, I'd keep seeing glimpses of you. Then you vanished entirely. I tried hard to forget you and succeeded for a while. Of course, by now, you haven't caught any glimpses of me for a long time yourself. Does this mean our spiritual affinity is gone?

Anyway, I'm writing to you about a more important matter. You probably won't consider this a real letter. I don't either. This is my attempt to fulfill a promise I made to myself—that one day I would tell you the story of my life. I probably won't ever contact you again after this. But until that point is reached, permit me to keep my word.

My father's family was originally from Pennsylvania. Their situation wasn't very good, so they moved to Kentucky. There, he met the girl who would later become my mother. My father's life story is similar to that of Abraham Lincoln's father. Lincoln's father moved from Pennsylvania to Kentucky before meeting a girl and getting married. Coincidentally, my father's family came from a village just ten miles from Lincoln's birthplace. That's where I was born.

My life was different from that of other children. Everyone else had siblings, whereas I was an only child. Dad liked to hunt, but the hunting grounds got smaller and the government shortened the hunting season, so he took to tinkering around more with his old pickup truck. He still kept his double-barreled rifle, though. He maintained it well, even whispering to it like a lover. Mom let him be. A man needs his hobbies, she'd always say.

Mom was always the stronger one in the relationship. She had the more dominant personality. They both seemed aware of the situation, but it wasn't an issue, and Mom made most of the decisions. Dad went along and Mom never bossed him about. And I never doubted that Dad loved me half to death.

Dad always told me to be like my mother when I grew up, capable and fearless. Though Mom never overtly acknowledged what Dad said about her, she raised me to be like her.

At first I had no idea that my parents had actually wanted a boy. My birth must have disappointed them. They never said so, but I felt it as time went on. They were also dismayed at my fondness for drawing. They gently pointed out that I daydreamed too much and didn't take enough interest in useful things. When they reprimanded me and I still couldn't curb my inclinations, I was forced to draw on the sly. Mom always found out. She seemed more disappointed with me by the day.

One day they took me deer hunting. As usual, we rode in Dad's pickup truck. I still remember how broken down it was. Mom had actually suggested multiple times that he buy something newer, but Dad always refused. If it was still usable, then why replace it, he argued. Besides, he liked old machines. Also, fixing old engines was his hobby. And Mom never tried to meddle when it came to Dad tinkering with his truck. Though if she ever were to help out, she was sure to do a better job. That's what happened on this trip, in fact. The truck stalled and Dad tried to fix it. He worked on it for a long time but still couldn't get it to work. Mom had to pitch in. The truck was up and running in no time. Dad urged me to follow her example. "A girl's got to be smart," he said. "Or she'll get taken advantage of when she grows up." At the time, I didn't know what he meant.

Dad parked the truck in a remote village and we walked on foot to the hunting grounds. I got the impression that they both wanted me to be good at shooting. Dad gave me some tips. I took a few shots, most of them misses, of course. Dad repeated himself, that he hoped I'd grow up smart. So I'd be happy and have a good life.

When he fired his rifle, the sight of him filled me with awe. Then, for some reason, Mom took a turn, and I realized she was a much better shot. Though, as far as I knew, this was the first time she'd ever held a gun.

I won't go on about the hunting; suffice to say, we camped for several days before it began to pour. Quickly and unexpectedly, the weather turned awful. And Mom fell ill.

This was the point at which her health began to deteriorate, and our living conditions too. Of course, such circumstances had befallen other families, but in those cases, the father had gotten sick, not the mother.

Dad began to suffer from bouts of gloom. Even Mom seemed to feel sorry for him. My suspicions grew with each passing day that they wished I were a boy. Perhaps, I thought to myself, because I was neither a boy nor as bright as my mother, they worried I wouldn't do well in life. I grew more conscious of their subtle reproofs—that I spent too much time dreaming, not engaging in useful tasks. And they outright scolded me whenever they caught me drawing secretly. My mother even accused me of being sneaky by nature. If I was already secretive at this age, she said, then I might start stealing things when I grew up. If I didn't get what I wanted or were thwarted, she said, then maybe I'd wind up doing bad things. At the time, I didn't know what she meant.

As usual, Dad would still travel to the other towns in the area, still in the same old truck. The pickup got older and more beat up, and broke down more than before. Mom's attempts to coax him into buying a newer vehicle failed, as usual. Dad said the truck had served us well. If it had served us so well, why throw it away, he argued. If Mom's health had been better, I'm sure Dad would have eventually given in. But she was hardly able to get out of bed, so she couldn't enforce her wishes in the same way.

One morning, Mom suggested he postpone that day's trip. He refused. He'd already promised some customers that he would be delivering pumpkins and squash. She tried again, telling him that she'd had a bad dream the night before.[31] She worried it would come true. What she dreamed exactly, I didn't know.

Dad argued back. It was Halloween season. He said nightmares were normal, what with people putting out jack-o'-lanterns, and kids roaming the neighborhood on the night itself, trick-or-treating in all sorts of devilish garb, and restaurants giving their dishes ghoulish names, the waitstaff dressing up as fairies and vampires.[32] Given all this, bad dreams were to be expected, he said. He proceeded to leave, and she began to cry. She hugged me tight. "I hope nothing happens to your father," she sobbed.

It was the last time we saw him. His truck stalled crossing the railroad tracks. A train ran into him and smashed both him and the truck into a pulp.[33]

After that, Mom would disappear in the mornings. I never knew where she went. After the accident, she also began saying she hoped I would be careful when I grew up. I should do useful things, and stop daydreaming so much. If I tried my hand at something and it didn't turn out, I should give it up for something more practical. Don't sneak around. Don't be so secretive, she'd say.

She would often sit in Dad's old room and cry. I really didn't want to bother her, but over time I began to suspect she was up to something. As time went on, I tried spying on her but with no success.

One morning, she woke me up very early. After giving me the usual advice, she said, "Sneaking around is all right if it's for a noble cause. But if you fail at something and spend your time doing frivolous things for no good reason, that's what you call shameful." I didn't know what she meant.

When she went out, she took me with her. She was carrying a small rolled-up carpet. I was suspicious of what might be inside, but I didn't ask questions. We hurried along, over footpaths and fields that had long fallen into disuse. I knew how tired she was, and sometimes she'd stumble. But her energy still burned bright. Like a bonfire, it would only go out when the last log had turned to ash. She was more man than my father ever was.

We reached a small hill sheltered by some trees and my mother came to a stop. Here, she unfurled her secret: she had been studying the schedule for the train that had killed my dad. She'd found out who the train engineer was. She knew what days he worked. She even knew his name—first, middle, and last. "Oh Olenka, if only you were a boy. Then no one would look down on you, no matter what happens next. But you're a girl, so you have to be careful, and determined and strong. You must be brave. A warrior . . ." She wasn't sobbing now. She was ready to take her revenge, come what may.

The carpet bundle's contents turned out to be nothing other than Dad's rifle. She had disassembled it, so it would be more compact. Now she began reassembling it. Her movements were sure—far surer than Dad's had ever been.

Right on schedule, the train chugged into view. But now my mother faltered. She seemed to hesitate, as if distracted by something on the tracks. Nevertheless, she took aim and held it as the train drew near. I wondered why her hold on the rifle was so unsteady this time. She saw the target: the engineer's head. If she were to shoot my father's killer, she could do so easily. It wasn't too far away, she had a good shot, and the train wasn't going too fast. Shooting a deer in flight would have been harder, and I'd seen my mother take such shots without any difficulty at all. She wouldn't even need to take proper aim in order to pull it off. But this time was different. It was as if something were standing, shielding the engineer. I tell you, Fanton Drummond, I couldn't for the life of me explain it at the time.

But after meeting you, Fanton, I could finally guess what was holding my mother back—my father. I'm sure it was Dad that she saw, leaping about on the railroad tracks, then around the engineer, blocking him from view. I knew this, Drummond, because when you were still trying to find me, I would see flashes of you. When I saw you the first time, I knew that you loved me, oh, Fanton. And, Drummond, the moment I glimpsed you, I knew then that it had been Dad standing in my mother's way.

Wayne does know this story in part. Again, only in part. I've never told anyone the whole of it, except you, Drummond. Fanton, do you know why? Because I've never loved anyone else as much as I do you. Oh, Drummond. I only told Wayne because I pitied him. He used to complain all the time, saying he didn't have any material for his stories. He needed material, he told me, that would inspire him to write. Then he kept saying he thought I must have the material he needed. I ended up telling him part of what I've just told you. Again, only in part. It's true I was drawn to Wayne at the time. And it's true that I admired his primitive qualities. But mainly, I felt sorry for him when he complained that he didn't have material to write about.

All I told him was how sad my mother was. That in her sad state, she would dream about shooting the train engineer in the head. Then Wayne gave my story a rehaul, turned it into "Olenka," appropriating my name, my voice, my very breath. Dad became Albright. The engineer became Albirkin the sheriff. In the story, Albright hides when the sheriff comes, telling his wife to pretend not to know where he is. This was taken from my father's relationship with my mother—when anything cropped up outside of the usual chores, Dad would step aside and let Mom take the lead.

Wayne gave my mother an overhaul too, turning her from a woman able to handle any and every situation into Mrs. Albright, tactically shrewd, playing dumb about her husband's whereabouts. If my actual mother had been faced with such a situation, she would have stood up to the sheriff and argued with him while my father ran away and hid. The rifle Olenka uses in the story is Dad's rifle. And in place of Dad's death—the destruction of the Albrights' source of livelihood, the annihilation of the dam.

Wayne was truly a magician, the way he could take a true story and fictionalize it into something so divergent from real life. Even the character Olenka was well written—cold-blooded, cruel, collected, eloquent. Once we were married, I would find myself wishing I could act as she would. She would torture him slowly, watch on as he died in agony, then rejoice in his end.

I only felt this way <u>because</u> Wayne was so overbearing. I considered submitting to my husband to be part of marriage, but every time I'd submit, he'd merely take advantage of me. I wanted for him to become a good writer, but he began demanding the privileges of being one without feeling any obligation to write well. As such, he felt entitled to treat me a certain way.

To go back to my mother for a bit—her health continued to deteriorate. She died shortly after failing to kill the engineer.

Since there was no one else left, my uncle took me in. He had left Kentucky a long time ago and settled in Silverstone, Illinois. All the proceeds from the sale of my parents' estate went to me, though it wasn't quite accurate to say it had belonged to them both; Mom had been responsible for everything they'd owned. She'd been the one to develop the land and hire people to work it, whereas Dad's job—making the deliveries—had merely been an outlet for what he liked to do. Without Dad, Mom could have hired someone else, who would have been much better at the job. Dad liked getting out of the house, enjoying the scenery, maintaining his truck. Even shooting wasn't his particular strength.

When my uncle drove me from Kentucky to Illinois, his car

broke down in Bloomington. We had to stay for three days. That's why, Fanton, ever since I was little, I'd wanted to return to Bloomington one day. It's the reason I came to live in Bloomington. I'd often visit the places I went with my uncle, for while we were there, he would take me out walking every day—from the hotel to the restaurant, and from there to the mechanic's, and from there to lots of other places. My uncle seemed as taken with Bloomington's beauty as I was. He told me its name came from "Blooming Town"—a blossoming town, and also, a town full of flowers in bloom. Actually, we could have left for Illinois sooner, but he purposely stayed on, to see more of that lovely, blossom-filled town.

My uncle had his own children, a boy and a girl. But I wasn't Cinderella. My life was like that of any other kid. I wasn't mistreated, though I was never spoiled either, and my two cousins never regarded me as a nuisance in any way. While my aunt showed signs of wanting to coddle me, my uncle was firm. I would be treated like one of their children, no less and no more. I was conscious that I wasn't actually part of their family, and they also seemed conscious of my outsider status, but this had no bearing on my behavior or theirs. I think it was for the sake of maintaining harmony that Uncle sent each of us to different schools, from elementary all the way to high school. He'd tell the neighbors, "If I had a dozen kids and there were only eleven schools in this town, I'd have to move somewhere else with at least a dozen schools—one for each child."

After graduating from high school, my eldest cousin, Fitzwilliam, went on to study at the technical college in Aurora, Illinois. A year after I started college, my younger cousin, Virginia, began attending a small college elsewhere in Illinois, in Des Plaines. And so, we lived our own lives. After my aunt died, about a year after Virginia left for college, my cousins and I grew even further apart. Even more so when my uncle followed my aunt the next year. My cousins and I rarely met up.

Again, I had the feeling I was all alone in life. There was no one to look out for me except myself, and also no one to hold responsible for what I did in life, except me. With my uncle gone, I felt I had been born alone, had grown up alone, and someday I'd die alone too.

Moving on: I graduated from Vincent College in Dunbar, Illinois, with a two-year degree. But there was nothing particularly exciting about my life. The same went for the three years I worked as a middle school teacher in Kennikat, Illinois. Only when I moved to Hampshire, still in Illinois, to work as an editor for a children's book publisher, did something happen—a fling with a football player. I've told you about this, haven't I, Fanton? Oh, Drummond.

How I suffered. Shame, regret, heartbreak, jostling inside me, rolling into one. And the traces of it lingered for the longest time and refused to go away. Yet it was a wonder that—once the pain and shame and regret had finally passed—our love affair didn't leave a more lasting impression. Or in metaphorical terms—I'd contracted a disease, but at least it wasn't cancer. I hadn't died. I was alive, still standing, had regained my health. I would recall our love affair only once in a while, and only then would it leave a fresh gash on my heart. But even then, the pain would only last for a little while.

Our dalliance was probably something like what happened between Ursula and Skrebensky. You recall it, don't you, oh, Fanton, oh, Drummond? After realizing she may be pregnant, Ursula goes half mad. She feels so tormented she falls ill. But from the way D. H. Lawrence wrote it, you'd think it was nothing much at all.

When I read Lawrence's The Rainbow for the first time, that is, before I read out that passage to you, it amazed me that Ursula's pain and suffering could be treated so, as no more serious than a boil, Drummond. But in the end, like me I suppose, Ursula manages to overcome her anxiousness. Her fling with Skrebensky becomes nothing but a bad dream, and when she sees a rainbow, the dream vanishes and is no more. To her, Skrebensky no longer exists, only nature—which the rainbow symbolizes. Lawrence writes, "She saw in the rainbow the earth's new architecture, the old, brittle corruption of houses and factories swept away, the world built up in a living fabric of Truth, fitting to the over-arching heaven."[34] How astonished I was.

And it still astonishes me, though much of it has faded. Some time ago, I read a Playgirl interview with Margaret Trudeau, the ex-wife of Canadian Prime Minister Pierre Elliott Trudeau. "When I was seventeen, I had an abortion," she proudly declared. Then, with the same note of pride, "The fetus fell out in the toilet at a department store."[35]

Like me, Margaret also had a fling with a football player. But she went into it with her eyes open, whereas I'd been deceived. Then there was Ursula, who half knew and half didn't. For all three of us, the results were the same: no lasting impression was made.

I lived in Hampshire for only two years before leaving for the University of Illinois Urbana-Champaign. I've told you about this, haven't I, Drummond? Fanton. But now I'll tell you the more important parts.

I had an associate's degree in English, but I wasn't satisfied. I wanted to study art. So off I went—only to have a dazzling woman become my object of study instead. She would follow me, at first, hiding behind a tree and watching whenever I sketched in the woods. Over time, she began to show herself, materializing near whatever I happened to be drawing at the time. Then she began standing next to me, and eventually, she would sit at my side. I'll keep her real name to myself, but let's call her Winifred—from *The Rainbow*, like Skrebensky and Ursula.

I didn't pay her any mind at first, but after talking to her, and gazing at her, I found myself in awe—all too aware that, if I desired, I might hold her, squeeze her, pinch her arm, bite her lip. And yet I also felt as if she only existed in the abstract. At times it was as if I could see right through her, all the way to the trees behind. She was solid, transparent, abstract, all in one. There was a magnificence about her. Her body and soul were in perfect balance, and the same went for the solid, transparent, and abstract elements of her being.

She was very reserved, though at times she didn't want to bother with small talk either. She professed not to know much

A photograph and short article clipped from the Indonesian-language magazine *Tempo*, dated September 1, 1979. Below three columns of text is a photograph of a white woman, in profile, with dark hair in a short bob with a wide smile on her face. To her right is a white man, taller than her, with long, lean features, sporting a receding hairline and sideburns, and wearing a suit. The photograph is captioned *Margaret Trudeau*.

The text, printed in Indonesian, reads as follows (translated):

Margaret Trudeau has made yet another shocking revelation. "When I was seventeen, I had an abortion," the ex-wife of former Canadian Prime Minister Pierre Elliott Trudeau said serenely. "The fetus fell out in the toilet at a department store," she went on. "And Pierre asked me never to talk about it."

She even confessed that the man who had gotten her pregnant was a football player. That's what she told *Playgirl* magazine. The mother of Trudeau's three sons (Justin, 7; Sacha, 5; and Michel, 3, who are in their father's custody) then admitted that she'd once been close with the singer Lou Rawls, and that he had asked her to marry him.

"Not only that, I once had a very friendly telephone relationship with Senator Edward Kennedy," she said. It occurred in 1974, when she was getting treated at a hospital to calm her nerves. "He came to see me, and after that, for months, he would call me at different times. We'd talk about love, marriage, and a lot of other things. And he was a man who was capable of loving so very deeply."

She added: "If I remarry, it'll be to someone who's going to be good to me, and who's going to believe in me, and I'm going to believe in him. And most importantly, he has to let me be free, because freedom is everything."

Olenka once read about the exploits of Margaret Trudeau, ex-wife to the Canadian prime minister, in an issue of *Playgirl*. From this, she learned that part of her life resembled that of Margaret's. Margaret's story as it appeared in *Playgirl* was featured in *Tempo*.

about art at first, dismissing her knowledge as not only general but superficial as well. But even so, she could sense my art wasn't any good. This she stated simply, without any hint of false modesty or scorn. As you know, there are those who deploy false modesty as a means to mock others, aka Wayne Danton.

My work really wasn't bad, but it was missing something, she told me. I had talent and skill enough, capturing whatever I rendered with ease. I even had a knack for recalling finer details with great precision. By way of analogy, if I were a reader of a novel, I'd have no trouble recalling specific passages, or events, or the atmosphere of certain scenes. I would have no trouble producing a faithful retelling of the novel. Likewise, in my art, I was able to transfer whatever I sketched onto paper, even in the absence of the object itself. My powers of recollection were impressive, she said.

Even so, I lacked insight. That was my weakness, she stated baldly. It had to do with the neural pathways of my brain.[36] I could study art till I dropped dead, but this deficiency could never be repaired. The only one who could fix it was God. But since God had created me this way, he obviously had no intention of rehauling my neural pathways.

It was these pathways that were the source of what the painter Andrea del Sarto termed "incentives." For example, comparing himself to Raphael and Agnolo (that is, Michelangelo), del Sarto said:

> *incentives come from the soul's self;*
> *The rest avail not.*

Winifred went on, praising my art as "perfection itself." She said my drawings also had a "vitality" about them. But the perfection of my art was its own fatal flaw. I was able to render movement itself—so meticulous was my knowledge of every detail. And the same for del Sarto. He speaks thus of a Madonna he has painted:

> *I can do with my pencil what I know,*
> *What I see . . .*

He could produce a Madonna in a matter of minutes, in the finest detail, down to her very movements. Hence the art critic Giorgio Vasari dubbed del Sarto "the Flawless Painter." But therein lay his downfall.[37]

Winifred's words pierced me to the heart. I was awed by her, respected her, desired her. I longed to kiss the very soles of her feet. I longed for my body and soul to melt into hers, to fuse into one. How delightful it would be to attain oneness with her. In becoming part of her, I would be like her, solid, transparent, lovely, and glorious.

If I wanted to make art as a hobby, go ahead, she told me. I might even illustrate ads for a living. "If you have the talent to make a living from it, then why not?" she said. But if I wanted to be an artist—I'd better stop now, before delusion consumed me. "And if you've come here with the intention of learning something," she said, "you've made a mistake. Your professors are less talented than you."

I'd sensed the truth of what she was saying, long before she uttered these words. I felt vindicated—my instincts were in line with her assessment. But I decided to keep going. I'd drop out only if something better came along.

My friendship with Winifred deepened. We would eat together in the cafeteria, ride our bikes together, play Frisbee, run, do high jump, and all sorts of things. Her every movement filled me with wonder. Sometimes I'd step away from her for a little, just to admire her secretly from afar. When we rode bikes, for example—I'd make up some excuse and tell her to ride on ahead so I could admire her from behind. Sometimes, I'd turn onto a different path, pedal as fast as I could, then return to the same path but heading toward her, just to admire her from the front.

My mouth would water at the sight of her body arcing through the air as she caught or threw the Frisbee. The same when she did the high jump. I yearned to shelter in the shadow she cast passing over the bar. I longed to wipe the sweat from her body, to put on her grubby clothes and feel them on my skin.

If my parents were still alive and knew what I was doing, they would be tormented to no end. They had once wished

I were a boy. A friend of my father's, Uncle Davis, had even told me they had dressed me in boys' clothes as a baby.[38] Imagine their devastation if they could see me now, if the full extent of my feelings for Winifred were laid completely bare.

Winifred became a part of me, and I a part of her. Yet we avoided visiting each other. She never came to my dorm room and I never went to her apartment. For some reason, it felt taboo to enter her personal space. Apparently, she felt the same way about me.

In addition to never visiting each other and meeting only in public places, determined beforehand over the phone, I maintained my privacy. I had a regular activity I would only ever do on my own—swimming. I happened to have a good relationship with the campus swimming pool manager. When I'd put my TV up for sale, he had bought it, and we'd hit it off. Later, he offered me a job cleaning the pool. This gave me the freedom to swim whenever I wanted, since I now had the pool key.

For some reason, I ended up falling in love with one particular corner of the pool. I looked upon it as my very own. When cleaning, I would always start there, and I'd finish there too. Though I would do a thorough job with the entire pool, I would devote more attention to this spot. I'd spend ages relaxing there. And when diving in, it was always from there too. The same when I got out.

To make full use of the privacy I was afforded, I usually swam at night, once the pool was closed to the public. I'd swim around the perimeter, then stay underwater for a long while before returning to my favorite corner to come up for air. One night, just as I was coming to the surface, something grabbed my legs and pulled me back. Down I went. It didn't occur to me in the least to resist the pull. Then something thrust me back up to the surface. My head emerged from the water.

All the lights were turned off, so I couldn't see a thing. Then I felt a tug on my legs again. I went under once more. It went on like this, as if someone were directing my movements, allowing me to emerge long enough to draw breath before submerging me until I nearly ran out of air. Eventually, I was thrust to the surface again with great force, as if I were being shot out of the water. Only then did the person show herself. Winifred! It was none other than her!

She gave chase. And caught me. She released her hold and commanded me to chase her in turn. I gave chase. Once I'd caught her, she struggled and pleaded with me to let her go. I let her go and she gave chase. She caught me. She gazed at me and stroked my face. Before I knew it, I was stroking hers. She kissed my cheek and I returned it. Finally, she kissed my lips. With equal hunger, I kissed her back. We writhed in each other's arms, like a man and a woman. But we yearned for still more.

She pulled me out of the pool. She'd brought a cover-up with her and forbade me from changing out of my swimsuit. She didn't change either. Sharing one cover-up between us, without doing the buttons, we raced to her car. We were still kissing fiercely, even as she started the engine. When we got to her apartment, we took off our clothes. She pulled me into the bathroom, turned on the hot water, and we bathed together in the same tub.[39] Steam darkened the entire apartment. Winifred and Ursula do the same thing in *The Rainbow*, once Ursula and Skrebensky aren't together anymore.

I had never experienced such enjoyment, such satisfaction. I felt wholly a part of her. The pores on my skin were the pores on her skin, my lips were her lips, my arms, my legs, my torso, all hers. She and I breathed with one set of lungs, on the strength of one liver, one brain. Even the blood coursing through our veins was being pumped by a single heart.

Like I said before, I once wondered at how Lawrence could so trivialize Ursula's affair with Skrebensky. Especially since, through their union, they become one with the natural world. For in Ursula's eyes—or so Lawrence would have it—bodily union with nature could only be achieved through submitting her body to Skrebensky. And I would wonder too at how the affair between Ursula and Winifred could ever be branded a "shame."

Only after I got involved with my own Winifred did I come to understand. For a sense of shame was the miserable climax of my affair—like how Ursula feels after getting entangled with the original Winifred. I was ashamed at using my lungs to breathe, and my hands to eat, and my legs to stand. I couldn't bear to look in the mirror and see my face reflected there.

I had indeed attained the fullness I'd desired—solidity, transparence, and abstraction rolled into one. But that was all I had achieved. Winifred's magnificence and glory remained hers. In fact, any magnificence and glory I myself may have possessed had been sucked out of me, into Winifred's body. And I became a slave to her body's beauty, every enigmatic inch.

Seems she felt the same way. We were ashamed to meet, yet we couldn't help ourselves. Her apartment may as well have been mine. In the dorms, I swapped my double room for a single. With no roommate, Winifred could visit anytime. *No duplication allowed* was etched on each of our keys, but we found ways to get duplicates in the end. She could enter my room freely, and I could always go over to hers. And we made an arrangement: whoever was receiving the other should be waiting in her swimsuit, and if it were cold, a cover-up.

My initial belief was that D. H. Lawrence had made Ursula ashamed of what she and Winifred had done merely as a result of the social stigma surrounding such behavior. Around a quarter century before Lawrence wrote *The Rainbow*, Oscar Wilde was pelted with stones and thrown into jail for leaving his wife to have liaisons with other men. After his release from prison, Wilde remained reviled by society. Eventually, he ran off to France—and died in agony in a cheap hotel.[40]

Lawrence himself attracted hatred from all quarters when people got wind that he might be like Oscar Wilde. Though they weren't about to throw him in jail, they were prepared to ostracize him. Yet when he ran away with his professor's wife, everyone simply laughed, as if there were no difference between committing adultery and a good joke.

Now I knew why. What Ursula did with Winifred and what I did with the person I refer to as Winifred was a trespass against human nature. Whereas what Ursula did with Skrebensky, what Margaret did with that football player, and what I had done with my own football player—and with you—and even what Lawrence had done with his professor's wife, was merely run-of-the-mill sinning, Fanton. Not transgressions against nature, Drummond.

Winifred came to the same conclusion. She told me I was free to determine my own future. However, she also suggested I hurry up and get married so I wouldn't continue to commit the same kind of transgression.

As for herself, she would marry anyone whom she thought a reasonably good match. One of the challenges people faced these days, said she, was that there was too much freedom of choice. So she wasn't going to be choosy. Wouldn't it be great if getting married were like being born? she said. Out of the blue, here's the baby!—no picking whom to be born to, in what town or country, or even what year. She wished marriage could be the same way—out of the blue, she'd get proposed to and accept, without having to think about who would do the proposing.

So Winifred got married and left me on my own. She sent an invitation, but I sensed strongly that she hoped I wouldn't come. Indeed, upon learning about it, I resolved to watch the wedding ceremony at a distance. I wanted to see whether her body looked just as beautiful in a wedding gown. I wanted to study her, to see if she was still solid and transparent and abstract. I wanted to know if she was still as lovely, still as glorious as before.

Closer to the wedding day, I bought a telescope. I sat on a hill not far from the church. From there, I watched her. She looked like any other bride, solid, tangible, unmysterious, impressive only because of her gown. Her husband was old and balding and reminded me of a horse groomer. The one respectable thing about him was his job. He was an ENT specialist. I bet the sight of him repulsed everyone, including his patients. And I bet Winifred had agreed to marry him because of her desire to get married like being born. There weren't many ENTs in Urbana-Champaign. When she had come down with a bad sore throat, I bet all the other ENTs had been on vacation, so she'd wound up going to him.

After she got married, she avoided me. I did the same. When I ran into her in a clothing store, she asked if I needed any money. If I did, she could help, providing I was willing to leave town for good.

Unwilling to leave on the strength of a bribe, I left of my own free will. From there I went to Chicago. And, like I told you, from there I moved to Skokie. I followed Winifred's advice and got married fast.

If I hadn't met Winifred, I would never have tumbled into my marriage with Wayne. I regard my marriage to him the same way I do my relationship with Winifred—as an abomination. I tried to shape our marriage into something holy and good, and failed because of Wayne.

Anything we did that might result in children—so I kept reminding Wayne—had to be done with care. I urged him to go back to living according to a normal schedule. I was fastidious with my everyday diet, following the advice in my Planned Parenthood booklet. I suggested he bathe before "plowing" me. In my eyes, a child would be the *point*, not the *by-product* of a lustful act. He saw it differently. He didn't want to plan. With the result that, when it happened, I didn't even feel "plowed"—I felt raped.

It happened one night, in the middle of a bad dream—the rape. I was sick at the time. And I needed a lot of rest because, very early the next morning, I had to get up and go to work. I still had money from what my parents left me, but I didn't want to just fritter it away. If I didn't have a job, I'd have felt irresponsible.

I struggled hard to get away. He hit me. He said his mind was all stopped up and wouldn't write. He needed me to oil the cogs, he said. No, I kept saying. It was my fertile period. He could plow me tomorrow, once I'd carried out the sacred act of praying for our future child—that the child turn out healthy, that the child turn out good, in body and spirit. But Wayne didn't care. I was raped.

And that's how Steven came to be born. I hated him from the very moment he began occupying my womb. I was in agony—

physically, emotionally, bodily, spiritually. My health ebbed away. I slept all the time.

Eventually, once there began to be signs that I might miscarry if I weren't careful, I had to stop work and stay home. I spent every day lying down. Not only that, there were times when I was in and out of the hospital.

I'd been wanting to buy health insurance for a while. But Wayne had stopped me, saying he would take care of it himself. But "when inspiration strikes, I can't do anything but write," and he didn't end up doing anything at all. He tried to buy coverage later, but of course, we weren't eligible because I'd already been pregnant for some time. I would have to pay for everything myself until Steven was born.

Steven hated me from birth. When he was brought to me, he would start to fuss. I hated him back. Also, I was sick when he was born and had no energy for anything at all. I vaguely remember hearing the doctor saying he needed to be circumcised, but Wayne refused. And though he didn't say it, I knew why: the desire to write was currently aflame and he didn't want to bother with anything that might put it out.

About five days later, when I was still sick, they gave Steven a blood test. Based on the results, they said he was likely to have a mental condition when he got older. Wayne's response was to grumble: stupid doctor, all he wanted was money. "He's got some nerve. Twenty-five dollars just for glancing at the baby and shaking my hand." He went on, muttering like a lunatic, saying writers were more useful than doctors. Anyone could be a doctor, but not everyone could be a writer, even if they wanted to, he said.

I got sicker still. I had no energy to do anything at all. And Wayne merely stood by and watched. Even when the doctor advised that he arrange a formal examination for Steven, he did nothing. Naturally, he continued to complain about the doctor behind his back.

Meanwhile, Steven's hatred for me grew. He became unsettled whenever I came near. This pleased Wayne. According to him, Steven was a clever boy. He knew how to pick his friends. That's why Steven preferred him over me, he said.

One day, when Steven was one year old or so, Wayne took us out to a restaurant. As usual, I was the one footing the bill, but no matter. What really annoyed me was Wayne. He sat Steven between us. Steven turned his head toward Wayne, and Wayne beamed. I'm sure it was exactly what Wayne intended.

Then Wayne told me to switch places with him. He sat in my chair and I sat in his. Steven stayed in the middle. Then Steven turned toward Wayne again, and like he always did, Wayne praised Steven for being clever and knowing how to pick his friends.

Then Wayne told me to leave the table for a while. Steven laughed with glee. Then when Wayne left the table and Steven began to cry, Wayne looked even more pleased.

Bit by bit, without any formal arrangement, Wayne ended up taking care of Steven all the time. As if they shared some invisible bond. Maybe there's an unspoken desire among the mentally unsound to conspire together against sound-minded people—just look at them.

If you ask me, it would be better if Steven were genuinely mentally ill or handicapped, so he could receive appropriate care. Not like now, technically healthy but always in a daze, not handicapped but behaving like he has no ears or mouth. It's harder to treat.

Just before he turned four, Steven began to have trouble peeing. At times he would squirm in pain. His urine even began to have an odor—like rotten eggs. I once caught a glimpse of a worrying color too.

Wayne did nothing. Whenever I asked about it, he'd just say my wickedness was to blame. I must have poisoned Steven's food, he said. He spoke jokingly, of course, but he'd never been the joking sort, and such people always mean ill when they pretend they're kidding around.

I suggested he take Steven to the doctor. I would remind him what the doctor said when he was born. As usual, nothing I said could move him to act.

In the end, I had to call the doctor. He told me to bring

Steven in the next day. And the next day, Steven refused to let me take him. Wayne pretended to have no idea what was going on. Only when I forced him to take Steven to the doctor did he grudgingly set off. Sure enough, Steven was going to have to get circumcised.[41]

Two days before the procedure, Steven had to get his blood and urine tested at the hospital. I was ready to take him there, but he drove me away. Wayne had to take him. I followed ten minutes after the two of them left. When I got to the hospital, they were still waiting to be called in. Steven seemed disappointed I was there. And when they took him to get anesthetized, he still insisted I stay away.

After they took him to the operating room, the nurse told Wayne to wait in the lobby. We waited almost three hours. Naturally, Wayne fumed the whole time. "Just think," he kept saying. "If I didn't have to be in this damn hospital, boy, what a story I'd have written by now."

Just when Wayne had stepped out to take a walk, the nurse called for one of Steven's parents to come in. I went inside without waiting for Wayne. Steven was crying. The blanket had fallen to the side, leaving his privates exposed. They were wrapped in bandages spotted with blood. He wailed even more at the sight of me. He ordered me to go away and fetch Wayne.

The whole way home, he refused to let me carry him. During his recovery, he always asked for Wayne, despite Wayne not knowing how to do a thing. One time, when Steven was sleeping, his privates got tangled in the blanket. He woke up screaming. Wayne just stood there with his jaw hanging open. Steven didn't want me to come near him, but I had to intervene.

From that moment on, my relationship with Steven, which was never good to begin with, became entirely nonexistent. As for Wayne, he enjoys Steven's dependence on him. He wields it like a weapon—damning proof of what an unfit mother I am, unworthy of being loved even by her own child.

CHAPTER 2

A LETTER FROM A READER

Before I could finish reading Olenka's letter, I was interrupted by my old friend Barbara Atkinson on the intercom. She had buzzed in from downstairs. "It's important," she said.

Soon, Barbara was in my apartment, as slim, pretty, and youthful-looking as always. And as always, she carried a camera. She went over to the window and admired the view. It really was a very good one. You could see everything: Highway 46, the university-affiliated police academy and high school, the highway leading down to Monroe Lake, a small ranch of about three hundred cattle and twenty horses, several residential blocks, the top of South Third Street, and College Mall.

Before saying any more about the "important" business she was on, she told me her husband sent his regards. Then she said her son would be starting at the university high school soon. It was a good school, she said.

"From next week onward, you'll be able to see him from here," she told me.

She said her son sometimes asked about me.

"You should bring him over," I replied. "I can take him flying if he'd like. I was thinking it would be fun to take a ride in a small plane."

She said she'd run the idea by her husband and son.

Only then did she go into the reason for her visit. *The Herald-Telephone*, where she worked as a journalist, had recently become part of the Chicago Chronicle syndicate, which spanned seven states. She'd been assigned the task of answering a reader's question from one of the syndicate's magazines.

It was a simple one, about me: was it true that I'd been involved in making the film *Breaking Away*, and if so, what other things had I done? If I were willing to answer the question and let Barbara photograph me, I'd receive an honorarium of $300.00.

"I could have answered the question myself without contacting you, of course," laughed Barbara. I loved that laugh of hers.

She was the one, in fact, who had covered the making of the film at the time. And her husband had worked with me at the ad agency. I'd even cast her son in a shoe commercial once.

I was more than willing. In no time at all, she'd snapped my photo. I asked her about the reader—which magazine they'd written to, and why they wanted to know. Barbara herself had no idea. It was just that the syndicate had a motto about keeping their readers happy. As a result, they were obligated to provide satisfactory and accurate answers to all questions, even if it was at great expense.

When Barbara went home, I hitched a ride with her. I asked her to drop me off by the woods on campus. As it happened, there was the street preacher again, screeching away. As usual, he acted like everyone listening to him was a sinner.

CHAPTER 3

OLENKA'S LETTER, CONTINUED

I kept walking, straight into the woods. The wind was blowing strong. The leaves were already turning red and yellow and a lot of them had begun to shed. In a matter of weeks, all the trees would be bare. If the leaves weren't raked away, they would be covered by snow and eventually dissolve and become part of the earth. Then the trees would bud again, the leaves would fall again, the snow would come again, and on it would go.

In the middle of the woods I saw a student in a heavy coat singing at the top of his lungs. From the words and the tune, I knew he was practicing a song from the opera *Dr. Faustus.*[i] I'd seen a university leaflet a while ago saying the opera was going to be performed in five months. Legend had it, so read the summary in the leaflet, long ago in Germany, there lived an illustrious scientist named Dr. Faustus—his brilliance the envy of scientists throughout the civilized world. But he was consumed by greed. He sought even greater brilliance, more thunderous acclaim, and unattainable worldly pleasure, even desiring to lie with a different woman—a virgin—every night. And so Mephistopheles arrives on the scene, a powerful demon, known for his cleverness and duplicity, delighting in bringing about the downfall of mortal men.

Mephistopheles promises to grant Dr. Faustus's every request. In return, twenty-four years after signing a contract in his own blood, Dr. Faustus will physically die and his soul will become Mephistopheles's eternal slave. Dr. Faustus boldly accepts the offer. And this was the student who had been cast as

Dr. Faustus. He was making ready to slash his hand with a knife and dip the nib of his pen in the blood.[42]

I kept walking until, finally, I reached the bridge that Olenka had once sketched. The wound it had sustained from the tree was still clearly visible. I sat on the steps leading up to the bridge. Only then did I think back to Olenka's letter.

In the remainder of the letter, Olenka recounted how she'd recently ran into an old friend from Urbana-Champaign. This friend had told her that Winifred's husband was in bad health. Everyone suspected he had cancer. Olenka said she was feeling confused about what to do, and sometimes felt the urge to return to Winifred. She was sure that Winifred now needed her too.

Regarding Wayne, she apologized. "It never occurred to me that he would use what I told him about you as fodder for his fiction," she wrote. What an awful thing to do.

Olenka continued her confession: "My intention was to praise you and condemn Wayne. But Wayne didn't flinch. Instead, he happily listened to what I told him and used his writing to beat you down."

After saying that she always kept up with goings-on in Bloomington from afar, and that she knew the university was staging a production of *Dr. Faustus* in two months, she wrote:

"Actually, Dr. Faustus could have achieved his ambitions without Mephistopheles's help. He had the mind and wherewithal to become a giant among men, if only he'd been patient and willing to work day and night. His biggest flaw was not knowing his own strength. He believed himself stupid without making any real effort to prove otherwise. He wanted to take the easy way out and was tricked into eternal servitude to Mephistopheles.

"It's different with me. I've tried hard work and patience. But I know I'll never have the power to capture moonbeams or snowstorms or the changing leaves in my art. Let's say Mephistopheles really did exist. I'd have more of a right to sign a contract with him. If he were real, I mean.

"But please believe me, I won't attempt the impossible. I'll keep it simple. I'm married to Wayne and there's nothing to be done. Come what may, he's my husband. I'm sure he won't be able to support himself, much less him and Steven. He's capable of earning money here and there, but with the way he lives, it'll be gone in a flash.

"And no matter what, Steven is my son. I know he'll be depending on me for the rest of his life. With Wayne the way he is, who else is there for Steven to rely on? He may hate me, but I'll try to help him through Wayne. I have to think about his future. On that note, Fanton, if anything scandalous should befall me, please forgive me, Drummond."

Something about this last sentence felt incomplete. I had no idea what she meant. Even so, Olenka had returned to reign supreme in my heart. Through no effort of mine, MC had been kicked to the curb. Once again I found myself wondering: why on earth had I rolled from Indiana to Kentucky, back to Indiana, and from here to Illinois?

CHAPTER 4

FLYING

Actually, the traces of an answer were already there in Olenka's letter. But I only put two and two together when I was flying low over Bloomington with Barbara's son. Her son, Arnold, wanted to see the buildings and sports stadiums. Wilson, the pilot of the small plane I'd hired, suggested tracing the paths of highways and roads. I liked the idea. Once Arnold was satisfied, Wilson and I decided to follow Highway 46.

Wilson complained that the citizens of Bloomington thought he was a moron. Though the Republicans had picked him twice to be their candidate for mayor, he'd lost both times to the Democrat candidate, Frank X. McCloskey.[i] Now Wilson was almost sixty. He'd given all that up. "I don't have any more ambitions," he said.

He'd always enjoyed following a road wherever it may lead, even when he was little. He would go down any road, as long as it didn't take him too far and the scenery was good. He never had any particular destination in mind. Then one day his teacher assigned him Lincoln's biography to read. From this point on, his hobby took a specific direction. He was going to trace Lincoln's steps.

Wilson would travel to Kentucky, and from there to Indiana, and from there to Illinois. Those were the places, in succession, where Lincoln had lived. Sometimes Wilson would also head to Washington, since Lincoln had served as state representative for Illinois and would travel to Washington for Congress sessions before eventually becoming president of the United States.

"I never wanted to become Abraham Lincoln. Being mayor

of Bloomington would have been enough for me. I just wanted a small spark from the flame, I suppose—Lincoln's passion, his greatness. But I just wasn't up to it. I guess being a pilot for hire is fine."

Unlike Wilson, I'd never had any ambitions. A quiet life, having enough money, enjoying myself when I wanted—I was content with that. I'd never had any desire to become anyone or anything. And, in fact, this was one of the accusations MC had so vehemently leveled at me that day. She'd said I had no sense of purpose. Though I was asking her to marry me, it didn't come from the heart. I was only proposing to her because she happened to be nearby.

MC had been right. But it didn't matter anymore. I was back in love with Olenka. And what Olenka had written about Wayne being her husband "no matter what," and Steven being her son "no matter what" made me jealous. By right, it was I who should be her husband, not Wayne. What she should have said was that she was filing for divorce in order to pave the way for marrying me.

Like Wilson, Wayne had grand ambitions. And though he wasn't stupid by any means, measured against those lofty ambitions, in my opinion, he had failed. He had the talent to be a good writer but lacked the necessary qualities. And it was this disconnect that would be the ruin of him.

I was the superior one by far. Never had I attempted to become anyone or anything, but I could have if I'd wanted to. Unlike Wayne, I would never neglect Olenka, and if I had any children, I could provide for their future. I may have been lazy, but I wasn't a parasite.

I had rolled from one state to another, compelled by my love for her and the spiritual connection we shared. Though she was nothing like Wayne, she had once been ambitious herself. And though she was still young, she had recognized her limitations, like Wilson had. So, like Wilson, she had given up.

Her determination to make Wayne into a true writer must have sprung from her own failed ambitions. She had tried to live vicariously through her husband. She felt herself to be a nobody, therefore it was her husband who must become someone. At least, this was one possibility. The other, of course, was that she had once genuinely loved Wayne.

It was my sense that Olenka had already seen her failure coming, but thanks to Winifred, it became an inevitability. There was no more point in trying. But then why run off to live with bohemians in Chicago? Was it to forget Winifred—in other words, so she could stop living in violation of nature's laws? Or had she wanted one last shot at having a career as an artist? I didn't know. Whatever the answer, she must still have had occasional longings to become an artist. If not, she wouldn't have gotten mixed up with them.

Perhaps she'd been hunting for a man who could be made into an artist with her support, like what she had later tried to pull off with Wayne. I really had no clue. Whatever was in her mind at the time, I knew this much: she was the self-sacrificial sort. And though it was her own failures that gave rise to this tendency in the first place, nonetheless, I appreciated how clear-eyed she was about it.

As it happened, Olenka's life bore a certain resemblance to Abraham Lincoln's. Her grandfather had rolled from Pennsylvania to Kentucky, from Kentucky to Indiana, and onward from there to Illinois. So had Lincoln, before finally rolling off to Washington to become a congressman, then president of the United States. And I distinctly recalled Olenka once telling me that if she did become an artist one day, she would like to show her work in Illinois, then Washington.

She'd once exhibited her work in San Francisco, but that was because her trip there had been sponsored by friends. And though the exhibition spaces were far better in New York than D.C., she'd never felt very drawn to New York.

I had the strong sense that, like Wilson, Olenka had felt compelled to follow the road where it led—despite her knowledge that she would fail. And due to the spiritual bond I shared with her, I had ended up rolling along the same route. She had also been the reason I'd felt the urge to learn more about who I was. This must have been why I'd wound up rolling to Kentucky to revisit my childhood, whether or not I was conscious of why. And the time I had ended up near Lincoln's birthplace one night—that had also been due to the bond between Olenka's soul and mine.

Before landing the plane, Wilson said he intended to support Robert Young, the Republican candidate running for mayor against Frank X. McCloskey in the upcoming election. He said if McCloskey was reelected, he would run Bloomington even further into the ground. He proceeded to lay out all of McCloskey's faults.

Wilson's arguments were sound. In fact, I had already been planning to vote for Young—but for my own reasons. Young's manner was careless, he could be quick and decisive when needed. I'd observed them during a public debate. Indeed, McCloskey came across as reliable, thorough, and smart. He was well-dressed, his behavior was impeccable, never thoughtless, and his answers to every question were precise. Still, he spent a lot of time thinking before he spoke, and not infrequently, he had to consult the notes he'd prepared. Many of his responses went into great detail. To give one example, when an audience member had asked how many Human Rights Commission meetings he'd attended this year, he'd provided the exact number, along with where the meetings had convened and when.

Young couldn't be more different. He had dressed casually. Unlike McCloskey, when answering questions, he hadn't stood up. Instead he stayed seated, and even put his feet up from time to time. If he didn't have an answer, he'd say outright and without apology, "I don't know." Nor did he care whether people in the audience supported him or not. For example, when a union leader stood up and told him he had their vote, he replied indifferently, "Listen, pal. I'm not going to thank you for your support. If you're only supporting me because you think I'm going to grant you concessions once I'm mayor, you're better off with McCloskey. He's the one who needs votes, not me." The audience had clapped.

Young had my support because I felt we were kindred spirits. He did as he liked and acted only when necessary. This was someone worthy of respect. Not Wayne, Wilson, Jerry, Mike, or Abrolin.

As the plane swooped low over Tulip Tree on its return to

the airfield, I spotted a mail truck parked outside. *Maybe it's another letter from Olenka*, I hoped to myself.

But Olenka hadn't written. I did receive two checks, one for $300.00 from the Chicago Chronicle syndicate, and one for $5,000.00 from *Adventurer's Digest*—a magazine that published true stories of journeys and adventures. Now I remembered: after returning from Kentucky, I'd written an article about the people who drove eighteen-wheeler semitrucks. Unconsciously, I had managed to monetize my spiritual connection with Olenka. Providing I was careful, I wouldn't have to work for another ten months.

Then I thought, *Tomorrow morning, I'll write a check for a thousand dollars and make a donation to Robert Young's election campaign.*

I felt a profound sense of relief upon arriving home, as if I'd just completed some all-important task.

CHAPTER 5

AN EXPRESS LETTER

I carried on as usual. Every night I watched TV until two or three in the morning, sometimes even four or five. I stuck to light entertainment. If the news came on, I'd change the channel. I avoided reading the paper as well.

I'd wake up at around one or two in the afternoon and go for a walk, retracing Olenka's steps. Sometimes, when no one was looking, like a dog, I would sniff and lick whatever Olenka had touched. Hundreds of people after Olenka must have sat on the park bench I licked, but I didn't care. I did the same to the grass in the field, the bridge in the woods, the big rock near the Ballantine building, and other spots.

My only desire was to fill my head with Olenka. When Wilson called and left a message, thanking me for donating to Robert Young's election campaign, I had no interest in calling him back. Young himself invited me to eat a meal with him and I turned that down. The Atkinsons asked me to go picnicking with them at Monroe Lake and I ignored that as well.

Even when MC phoned me from Pennsylvania, I issued short, machinelike replies: "Oh, I'm well. Thank you. And yourself?" "How's your sister?" "And your mother?" "Oh, really?" "Gotten any letters from MB?"

MC gave me her phone number. "Feel free to call anytime. I'm always home," she said.

"Oh, really?"

But I didn't write her number down.

I felt guilty only after I hung up. I'd forgotten to ask her about the crash. The decent thing, at the very least, would have been to ask about it and tell her how happy I was that she wasn't pushing up daisies. I genuinely felt bad about this, but I let it be.

Even if I were to do something, what should I do? My remorse grew with each passing day. I kept hearing her voice as I'd heard it on the phone, gentle, full of compassion, and seeming to reflect a certain regard for me.

Finally, I decided to call her. Though for no clear reason, apart from sheer laziness, I kept putting it off. Until one day I received an express letter from her. It consisted of short sentences, like in a telegram: *Have you ever heard of Jill Kinmont? Talk about reaching for the sky. She should have gone to the Olympics. Instead, she wound up on an Indian reservation in California. And that was the story of Jill Kinmont. Can you imagine? Regards, MC.*

I didn't know what the letter meant, but I sensed an infinite sorrow in its tone. Behind those words were tears. I knew it then—she was handicapped for life.

I didn't know her parents' names, so I ran into difficulty when calling directory assistance at the Aliquippa Central Office in Pennsylvania. "I have about twenty-five numbers here listed under Carson," the operator told me. I also didn't know where I'd put the address I'd asked her to jot down at the airport in Chicago. And the letter she'd sent had no return address.

MB had once told me that MC's father wasn't around anymore. Maybe her mother was listed under her maiden name. I asked the operator to put me through to all the women with the last name Carson. A number of them had children or sisters named Mary, but they weren't who I was looking for. Then I asked to be put through to all the men named Carson. Like before, there were often Mary Carsons in their households too.

Finally, I was connected with a John Rodney Carson. I waited for someone to pick up as the operator stayed on the line. I concluded that John Rodney Carson was MC's late father and that her mother kept the phonebook listing under his name.

I kept trying to call, but the phone kept beeping. Perhaps the phone's owner had deliberately disconnected the line so no one could contact them.

I gave up on phoning Aliquippa and switched to calling reference services at the Indiana University Central Library. I asked if they could look up Jill Kinmont. "Hold on," they said briskly. "We'll check on the computer."

A few moments later, I received the following response: Jill Kinmont, born in Greeley, Colorado, in 1937. Won two famous ski tournaments in 1954: the American Golden Cup and the Ernest Pascal Cup. People thought she would go on to represent the United States in the 1956 Olympics. In 1955 she competed in the Snow Cup Race and suffered a terrible accident that left her almost entirely paralyzed. Now she lives in Bieber, California, and works as a teacher on an Indian reservation.[i] Her story was made into the film *The Other Side of the Mountain* by 20th Century Fox in 1975, starring Marilyn Hassett and directed by Larry Peerce, who also did *Goodbye, Columbus* and *Ash Wednesday.* Just three days ago, the movie played on CBS.[43]

I must have been watching another channel at the time.

CHAPTER 6

ALIQUIPPA

The next day I boarded the first flight from Bloomington to Indianapolis. From there, I hopped on a plane to Pittsburgh. Nothing interesting happened on the way. Though I'd never flown to Pittsburgh before, it all felt routine. Nothing exciting. And I didn't feel anxious about getting there anytime soon.

Upon landing in Pittsburgh, I hailed a cab and took off for Aliquippa. Only then did I start enjoying the trip. I wasn't accustomed to roads like these, winding like rivers, as if formed by nature and not human hands. Most of the trees were already bare. Fall was nearly complete. The scent of dry leaves wafted into the cab, better than the smell of snow, more pleasing even than the vegetal aromas of summer and spring.

Olenka had also loved the smell of dry leaves more than anything else. She'd known why, though: the scent of autumn leaves stirred up feelings of lust. I'd agreed. A tree shedding leaves wasn't a sign of impending death but slumber and rest. This was the point at which new life began, not in spring, like most people thought. True, the first signs of life, in the literal sense, appeared at the start of spring—the sprouting of new leaves and all the plants turning green. But this point marked the onset not of life but of suffering. While other poets with their clichés feted April, the start of that most glorious season, spring, Olenka observed that T. S. Eliot had seen it as the reverse. Hence the opening line of *The Waste Land*:

April is the cruellest month[44]

The scenery changed as we crawled alongside the Susquehanna River, the air and water filthy from pollution caused by the ironworks. The thousands of lights from the gargantuan factory only made everything seem dimmer. It was still morning, but it was as if night had already descended on the world.

The sight I witnessed, as we crossed the bridge, was nothing other than a dead city. The earth was parched. Also visible were a few houses, perched atop a barren hill. Their lights were on, but they reminded me of guardhouses in a graveyard.

According to the cabdriver, over the past ten or so years, the residents of this area had gradually moved away. It made sense, I thought. There was no use living here. The ground did look like it had once been fertile, but it had turned hard and dry over time. Pollution from the ironworks, I suppose.

The only ones who stayed were the factory workers. Even so, once they were able to buy a car, they weren't willing to stay. Better to seek cleaner air and more fertile soil, even if it was farther away. Only the truly indigent, or the ones who loved their native soil with no regard for their health, were willing to remain. If the land were a person, it would be diseased. And so, like someone handicapped for life, the land had been abandoned, just like that. No one could love it anymore.

We went up and down several hills before finally reaching healthier climes. At last, we reached the town of Aliquippa. The driver asked where to drop me off. "The bus station," I replied.

After storing my bag in a locker, I searched for a pay phone. I flipped through the phone book and found John Rodney Carson's address.

I was about to call but decided to go straight there instead. I hailed another cab.

John Rodney Carson's house was situated in a nice neighborhood. A public fountain stood not far away. Down the street from Denim Avenue, where the house was, were several stores and a bowling alley. There must have been rumbling noises all night.

Moments after I rang the doorbell, a woman, not overly elderly, opened the door, asking who I was. When I said, "Fanton Drummond," she replied, "Oh, from Bloomington, Indiana?" Her tone was cheerful and bright.

She invited me inside.

CHAPTER 7

REUNITED WITH MC

It was true. MC was handicapped for life. She would never stand or walk again. She was permanently confined to a wheelchair. Unlike Jill Kinmont, MC hadn't suffered nerve damage. She could still feel whatever she held and wherever she sat. And even though her left arm was broken, she would soon be able to use it as before. But her lip had been torn. The scars from the stitches were still visible. A gloomy expression dominated her features, but to my eyes, she still looked appealing, healthy, and strong. With her physique, she would have made a good horse jockey, if she weren't handicapped.

I found her lip grotesque at first, but I got used to it over time. It even intrigued me the longer I looked at it. I'd seen many people whose appeal stemmed from their disability. This was how it was with MC's lip.

Was I in love with her again? I couldn't say for certain. But the lingering scent of autumn leaves, the parched earth, the scenes both interesting and unenjoyable from the journey just taken all mingled together, coloring my tastes. Lust would well up inside me, followed by disgust, nausea, and pity—sometimes mixing together as one, sometimes in succession, sometimes flaring up spontaneously.

Before she could tell me all about the accident, I had made my decision—if the signs were right, I was willing to marry her.

She told me how, both before this and now, she had rather hated watching TV. But as it was no longer possible for her to pursue all the activities she'd once enjoyed, she had ended up turning to television. One evening, she had seen *Breaking*

Away on NBC. She probably wouldn't have watched it if she hadn't met me.

Because she'd heard so much from me about Bloomington, she paid close attention to everything in the film. And if it weren't for me, she would have simply ignored all the names of the cast and crew. But because she did know me, when my name appeared on-screen, she couldn't forget it. She'd already tried her best to wipe my name from her memory but with no success. Especially now, since her disability prevented her from doing this and that. With nothing else to do, my name kept coming to mind.

She still wasn't sure whether the person named was really me. So she picked up a pen and wrote to *The Pittsburgh Review* to ask. This was the question that had been conveyed to me through Barbara Atkinson. Once MC found out that it really was none other than myself, she regretted her prior opinion of me.

For in truth, since the very start, she'd had the strong sense that I possessed exceptional powers. I was impervious to all weather and circumstance. If the situation demanded it, she bet I could even sleep and walk at the same time. And she believed beyond a doubt that I possessed unwavering courage. On the other hand, and this was her initial suspicion, I lacked the ability to properly channel my abilities. As such, she saw me merely as a professional loafer with no conviction. My own powers were being used by me, she said, to keep myself down.

After learning a bit more about me through that magazine, she began to admire me. If she weren't handicapped, she said, she would have showed up in Bloomington asking for forgiveness. But since she was lonely and couldn't do anything, she could only hope I would be kind enough to pay her a visit. After sending the express letter and omitting her address, she purposely disconnected the phone, so it wouldn't be just my voice that reached her ear—I myself would come. And now that I was here, she expressed her unbounded gratitude.

If I hadn't felt sorry for her, I would have burst out laughing. I was also aware that she had saved my life. If she had accepted my offer to accompany her on that flight, things would have turned out very differently for me. When I asked about it, she replied, honestly, "I'm not exactly sure what happened to the person beside me. I was out for a long time. But from what I found out afterward, he was all right."

Even so, I was still of the opinion that if I'd gone with her, I'd have met a very different end. And from this sprang my firm conviction: I had to marry her. But I had to be careful. One word out of place and I was kaput!

Meanwhile, the urge to nibble her scarred lip washed over me in waves. And meanwhile, the scent of autumn leaves wafted in through the window from the yard. *She must also like the smell*, I thought. *It might be having the same effect on her.* From the way she shifted her arms, I sensed that she strongly wanted to squeeze my hand.

I laid out the bait, and sure enough, she began stroking it. I stroked her hand in return. But still, I worried it was the wrong move. I had to restrain my lustful passions and renew my proposal.

With regards to her future, she told me she had no detailed plans yet. Only that she was resolved not to bother anyone, much less make herself a parasite. As a result, she was thinking about finding a job she could do from home. She'd only leave the house when necessary. That's how it would be, she said. And what kind of work that would be, she didn't quite know yet.

Even so, after watching so many shows on TV, she had the faint sense that she would probably make a good screenwriter. It wouldn't be too hard, she mused, if she had the inclination, and the opportunity arose. Come up with a simple story, slip in some tension here and there, and presto. At base, she said, the plots for TV shows were nothing but a string of unlikely and unfortunate nonsensical events. They had no substance, much less any morals, she told me.

I valued her opinion. She wasn't wrong. But if she really did start writing for TV, I'd feel utterly revulsed. Before her accident, she'd declared her intention to marry some idiot of a professor. She would climb into her grave fully aware it was nothing other than a grave. Now that she couldn't stand or walk, she was resolved to hop into a puddle, knowing fully that the puddle she intended to hop into was hardly a respectable place. Someone like this was only worthy of disgust.

In the present situation, she was no punter, just a pendulum. Our hands caressed, our lips drew closer, our eyes exchanged yearning looks, but my heart remained firmly in Olenka's grip. MC knew I had connections in the film industry. She intended, of course, to use me.

I suspected her faith that she could do so would crumble if I challenged her. Turns out I was wrong. When I released her hand, distanced my lips, and straightened myself, she betrayed no disappointment. Then she gave me a certain look, as if I were the one who needed her. As if she didn't care who I was and what would become of me. Even if I were struck down by lightning, it wouldn't disturb her in the least.

It seemed to me that, in her eyes, I was someone to be pitied. As if, in her heart, she thought that by letting me squeeze her hand and draw her lips close to mine, she was doing me a kindness. Let's say I kissed her. Why, then her letting me do so would be an act of self-sacrifice unrivaled in this world or the next. This was my impression. I felt hurt. I'd never been treated so by Olenka, so why was MC treating me this way?

Well, nonetheless, I shouldn't forget that she had saved my life. I had no right to proclaim myself some unsullied Adam who had never tasted forbidden fruit. And she was no Eve. She hadn't tried to tempt me. It was I who, upon meeting her in Indianapolis and spending time with her in Chicago, had decided to be tempted.

And so, without further ado, I should return the service. I had to protect her and recognize the right she had to make use of me. Olenka could stand on her own two feet. Moreover, she might return to Winifred. Or even, as her letter clearly implied, she might enslave herself to Wayne and Steven again. I had no ongoing expenses in my life apart from spending for my own enjoyment. Olenka had first been ensnared by Winifred, then, because of Winifred, she had been ensnared by Wayne. Let's say Olenka decided to be with me. I would merely be her way of escaping from these two traps. She was still young and strong, capable and able. She could stand firm without me. Consequently, I had to think of what was best for MC.

Lest I forget, too, Peter Yates had expressed his admiration at my skill on several occasions. Without me, he said, the climactic bicycle-race scene in the old stadium would have been a disaster. And he'd already offered to pack me off to Hollywood several times. There was no harm in me helping MC sell what she wrote. She needed my help.

Sure, I'd never read anything she'd written. Nor did I know whether she'd ever tried writing before. Even so, I had the strong sense that she might be well suited for the work. I could help if need be. She was right, writing for TV was a piece of cake. As long as you had a bit of talent and were willing to prostitute yourself, anyone could do it. She wasn't stupid either, so that was good. MB may have been a gong, but her assessment of MC hadn't missed the mark. What MC needed were good connections and clout to help sell her work.

But could I help her without marrying her? I couldn't imagine working with her without making her my wife, or the mother of my children. I had loved her once. Now the flame of my love was restored.

My relationship with her was very different from my relationship with Barbara, even aside from the fact that Barbara was married to someone else. From my very first meeting with Barbara, I'd never had any desire to treat her as anything more than a friend. Let's say her husband were an Eskimo of a certain tribe who practiced the custom of offering one's wife to an esteemed guest. I would never dream of taking the opportunity to pay a visit. Barbara was pretty, capable, and interesting. I admired her. I'd even danced with her a few times. But I had no feelings for her apart from those of a friend. If Barbara and I were in the same line of work and forced to live together day in and day out with no one else around, I was certain I would never have the slightest desire to fall in love with her.

CHAPTER 8

THE SECOND PROPOSAL

I decided to renew my offer of marriage. This time, instead of waiting until she was alone, I proposed in front of her mother and sister. If I hadn't, I probably would have withdrawn my proposal once the first sentence had come out of my mouth. I wanted to force myself to see it through. And I succeeded in expressing myself clearly and methodically.

I made no revisions to my reasons: I loved her, I wanted to marry her, and I wanted us to have kids.

But I felt my words flowed more from my lips than my heart. The Romantic notions that had compelled me to propose to her the first time had already been doused. I no longer wanted to lead a primitive life, living in a cave, eating raw fish, ordering my children to cut down trees. I couldn't even picture what my children might look like anymore.

In contrast, when I was about to propose the first time, I envisioned them clearly—what color loincloth my first child would wear, the ornament in my second one's nose, the way my third child would hold a fish in its grasp if it caught one.

Now, taking MC's hand in mine, all I had on my mind were the autumn leaves and their scent. I thought about pretending to cry so my words would pierce her heart all the more, but then again, it might not help. Also, I planted a kiss on her lips without kneeling and kissing her hand first.

I silently congratulated myself on not kneeling or pretending to cry. I knew I would be embarrassed if I had. Especially when I saw that none of them were weeping for joy or declaring how happy they were. Her mother was smiling away, yes, but I couldn't discern what her smile meant. And her sister, well! She giggled as if someone were tickling her belly.

I regretted proposing. How vastly different it had been with Olenka. In my head, I had treated Olenka as one might treat nature—plowing it, reshaping it, ruling it, owning it, and if necessary, destroying it. A good red-blooded male should rule over his woman like a pioneer over forest and field. Let not a man be like an Indian, instead yielding to nature, worshipping lightning and snakes and bats, then perishing, swallowed up by the wilderness.

Though I did believe that theory and practice sometimes diverged, good practice would always be grounded in sound theories. And on the basis that women should be managed as nature should be managed, I was firmly convinced that Olenka could be made subject to me. I was also convinced that she would desire to be treated so. Hence she was grateful to me for the times I had set her on the dresser, spread her over the ironing board, transferred her to the dining table, and the like.

But this idea didn't apply when it came to my renewed offer of marriage. The moment I uttered the first word, I felt my pursuit of a relationship with MC was merely to fulfill an obligation. I had happened to fall in love with her in Olenka's absence, had proposed to her and had my life saved by her, and now I wanted to return the good deed. The glue that bound all this together—the scent of autumn leaves.

Suppose it were summer, suffocating, murderously hot. The sight of her lip would likely make me sick. Especially since she just sat there all the time in that wheelchair. No playful chasing each other about. I wouldn't murder her one day out of sheer boredom, would I? Simply because she couldn't put up a fight? It was different with Olenka. Any desire to destroy her would stem not from my boredom or her defenselessness, but from the urge to demonstrate my strength.

MC's younger sister, Catherine, was a bright, capable young woman. She seemed to sense the obligatory nature of my actions. When you thought about it, she was the one who'd played a large part in bringing about what happened to MC. To be sure, she herself had suffered a concussion in her own accident, but it hadn't been too bad. She'd fully recovered and showed no lasting effects, except for being unruly and ill-mannered. But according to their mother, she'd always been this way. Their mother said when she was little, she'd liked to climb trees, and pick fights with boys, and meddle with road signs. People from out of town would get lost thanks to her. Even so, continued their mother, she used to win a lot of awards at school.

I could believe it. When Catherine drove me to the bus station to get my bag and took me around some of the key places in Aliquippa, I saw how much people seemed to like her wherever she went. From her conversations with them, I learned she'd already contacted several organizations on behalf of the passengers involved in the recent crash, in order to speed up the process of getting compensation from the airline. She had even asked people to urge the local government to better accommodate the needs of disabled individuals when it came to public places like the bus stops, the shopping mall, the post office, and such. She exuded leadership. People would flock to her, asking her opinion. We went bowling, and even then, she demonstrated great skill and was admired by all.

My second proposal had met with rejection. MC was still certain that, though it was her I was looking at, and though I did so in earnest, I unconsciously regarded her as a stand-in. It was actually somebody else I wished to propose to, she said. But for reasons unknown to her, I was resorting to proposing to that other person through her. I objected, but she wouldn't believe what I said.

Then MC had made a confession—she had deliberately lured me into coming. She'd no longer been able to contain her desire to see me—a desire that couldn't be satiated by a mere letter or phone call. So she had channeled all her effort into bringing me here. As it happened, she'd been watching the biopic about Jill Kinmont on TV. So she'd dashed off a letter and sent it via express mail the next day. She wanted to apologize for her previous assessment of me, but also express her admiration. As she'd said not long after my arrival, I possessed an extraordinary strength of which I myself wasn't aware, or at least had never made use of.

The first part of an article from page four of *Family Circle* magazine, dated November 20, 1979. The title, centered and in bold capital letters, reads, ***HOW TO LOOK, FEEL AND STAY YOUNG—NO MATTER WHAT THE CALENDAR SAYS!***, followed by the byline, ***By Ann Landers***. No images have been included with the clipping.

The subhead reads, in small bold font: ***Walking three miles to and from her office is part of Ann's daily routine to keep fit. Above, right, having hair done. After talking to the country's top cancer specialists, Ann pooh-poohs the notion that hair dye causes cancer. Because she exercises and avoids tobacco and alcohol, Ann eats whatever she wants—even desserts—without worrying about her weight.***

The body of the article reads:

> If you're looking for a magic wand to wave away the years, or a foolproof system guaranteed to double-cross Father Time, you won't find it here. Also, what works for me may not work for you. But I do know that I look younger than my years and have more energy and vitality than most women my daughter's age, so I must have done something right.
>
> Actually, it's not what I've done—it's what I haven't done that's made the difference.
>
> I believe the decision that had the greatest impact on my health, education, and welfare was made when I was 15 years old, while a student at Central High School in Sioux City, Iowa. I decided I would never smoke a cigarette or touch a drop of alcohol.
>
> At the time I wasn't concerned with preserving my youth. (Young people seldom think of how they're going to look 30 or 40 years later.) I was thinking, however, of what I might do to keep myself in mint condition.
>
> I was determined to go through life functioning on all cylinders and accomplish my goal—which was only to save the world.

Cigarettes and booze, I reasoned, had never improved anyone I knew, and it had seriously damaged some. So, I decided to do myself a favor and have nothing to do with either.

I am not now, nor have I ever been, opposed to alcohol on moral grounds, and I'm not a Carrie Nation trying to dry up the world. For those who enjoy a social drink, fine—but a closer look at friends and casual acquaintances has convinced me that a substantial number of very nice people consider themselves social drinkers when in reality they are alcoholics.

Skin Tips: It takes no special insight to realize that nothing brings on wrinkles, circles, bags and yes, added pounds in all the wrong places—like alcohol. And wine, my friends, is alcohol. Lately, white wine has become the thing to ask for at cocktail parties. Granted it does sound softer and more ladylike than whiskey or gin, but if you drink enough white wine, you will get just as bombed, and it will do your body just as much damage as vodka or bourbon.

A woman's skin can be a prime factor in determining whether she

There the clipping ends. In the bottom left corner is a brief bio for Ann Landers: *Ann Landers' advice column appears in over 1,000 newspapers, which makes her the most widely syndicated columnist in the world. Her latest book is the "Ann Landers Encyclopedia," published by Doubleday & Co.*

The above article was shown by MC to Fanton Drummond when he paid her a visit in Aliquippa, Pennsylvania.

In order to explain what she meant, she reached for a copy of *The Pittsburgh Star*. Inside was a column—*Ask Ann Landers*—by Ann Landers, of whom, in fact, I had already heard a lot about. According to Barbara Atkinson, Ann Landers wrote an advice column for a press syndicate that received letters from readers. Ann Landers's responses, said Barbara, were published in over a thousand different newspapers, weeklies, and magazines across the country.

MC showed me one of the letters. The writer recounted how, three years before, she'd hit a cyclist with her car. The victim had died on the spot. Everyone who'd witnessed the accident said she wasn't to blame. The writer herself knew it was the cyclist who'd been in the wrong, but to that very day, and perhaps for the rest of her life, the writer felt she had committed a great sin. She now requested that Ann Landers publish her letter in full, to impress upon readers the importance of riding one's bike with care. The cyclist wasn't the only victim, observed the letter writer. The accident had also brought hardship upon the victim's family and friends, as well as the person responsible for the victim's death.

Ann Landers replied, *Dear Mrs. G.R. in Michigan. Thank you for writing. Your letter is moving and contains a very important message. I agree wholeheartedly and have reproduced your letter in full.*

"What a cushy job Landers has," remarked MC. "Anyone with half a brain could do it."

Then MC reached for an issue of *Family Circle*. In it was a brief article about Ann's everyday routine. It was very straightforward. Like a great many other people, she woke up every morning at seven thirty, walked three miles a day, avoided fatty foods, et cetera, et cetera.

"She seems completely ordinary," said MC. "And her replies hardly point to any brilliance of mind. Catherine bought me *The Ann Landers Encyclopedia* a while ago. Talk about mediocre. I can't help but wonder, of the thousands of people who applied for the job, why pick her?"[45]

MC continued. "The majority of the applicants must have been more than qualified to run the column. But Landers was chosen because she had a certain something. You have something similar."

She went on to confess that she'd been tempted to reconsider my proposal a number of times. She had nearly given in at the airport, when she was about to board the plane. But, again, she'd felt convinced that I was only using her as a stand-in.

Now she was even surer of her decision. Even if she succumbed to the temptation to revise her opinion—that I was using her as a stand-in—she still wouldn't say yes now. She confessed that she loved me at times. Then she said, "I couldn't bear to make you my nurse for life."

With this, her eyes turned weepy and red.

CHAPTER 9

THE COTTAGE

Once we'd all said goodnight, MC invited me to follow her outside to the cottage. By "cottage," she meant a little house situated next to and a bit behind the main house, in the same yard. MC often slept there. She said she even kept most of her belongings inside.

Like a regular house, it had a bedroom, bathroom, kitchen, and sitting room, all of them small.

Sure enough, there were a lot of things that belonged to MC. What first attracted my attention were several photos hanging on the wall. There was one of her late father, one of her mother, and one of herself. Many of them were of herself. Through these photos, I could chart the progress of MC's life. From infancy to adulthood, she seemed the very picture of health. Even so, she looked like the vast majority of people. Like the friends who appeared in the photos with her, there was nothing distinctive about her at all. If all the people from the photos had been gathered together and ordered to run, or swim, or give a speech, the quality of their performances would have been more or less interchangeable.

MC's standing in life differed from that of Olenka's. Olenka was always the center of attention, regardless of time or place. I'd seen photos of her as a community college student in Dunbar, as a teacher in Kennikat, and as an undergraduate in Urbana-Champaign. If all the people in her photos had been gathered together and brought before a panel of judges, the members would have unanimously declared Olenka to be the most captivating of the bunch. She had the effect of rendering everyone around her meaningless. In this respect, she differed from MC. Even Catherine had more personal charm.

I turned out the lights and headed to bed. In the distance I heard the rumble of bowling. I wondered at how the Carsons could feel so much at home here. An idea sprang to mind. In the morning, I would suggest that Catherine make use of her connections to shift the bowling alley elsewhere. Whether or not she succeeded, the proposal would be sure to attract much attention. I had learned, from her conversations with her friends earlier, that a charity would soon be donating a motorized wheelchair to MC. Neither MC nor their mother knew about it—it was Catherine's secret, her way of making recompense for MC's condition, which she felt partly responsible for.

Apparently, or so MC had related to me, Catherine thought I wouldn't make a good husband. A friend, maybe, but a husband, wait and see, was what she'd told MC. Catherine knew I was capable of acting more and talking less, but in her opinion, when it came to MC, I was all talk and no action. I may have made the trip all the way from Indiana to Pennsylvania, but that was no guarantee that I'd always put MC's interests first.

Before my visit, when MC had told her sister and mother about meeting me and how I'd proposed in Chicago, MC told me that Catherine had said, "We should meet him first." And once I was here, Catherine's first remark had been, "I like him. He seems mischievous. Like me." Their mother on the other hand, according to MC, had wanted her to accept my proposal from the very start.

I couldn't sleep. At first I blamed it on the roar of the bowling alley. But then I thought it might be the insufficient pillows—like Wayne had written about. Then I really couldn't fall asleep.

After turning on the lights again, I studied any photos I'd missed earlier. One of them was large and had been hung at the very top. It was a photo of the Carsons' house, along with the cottage.

I stood on a chair and took the photo in my hands. I noticed it then—there was a difference between the parts of the wall

MC could and couldn't reach. This photo, for example. It was covered in dust. If she could stand, the photo would probably be as clean as the other, lower, objects. I felt sorry for her. Determination rose in me again. I had to do better with this second proposal of mine.

True, the way she'd looked at me earlier had wounded me, all after I'd squeezed her hand and nearly kissed her. But not anymore. She'd been right. It was I who needed her. Must I really spend the rest of my days taking walks, sitting around, watching TV late into the night or early morning and sleeping till noon? If I were responsible for her care, my way of life would undergo a radical change. Even more once we had a child. Since she couldn't do anything, it would be me who would bathe it, who would take it to the doctor if it got sick, who would carry it around the house morning and night.

The more closely I studied the photo of the house with its cottage, the more clearly I remembered having seen something similar before. When and where, I couldn't recall, but the house I was thinking of had also been at the corner of a three-way intersection, also with two doors, one on the side facing its cottage and the other in front facing the front yard. The house had sat higher than the two roads bordering it, so there had been steps leading out to both sides. Like this one, that house had also had an attic situated toward its front. The shape of the house had reminded me of a Gothic structure. Like this one, it had also been painted a grayish green. The walls had also been partially overgrown with ivy, and the chain-link fence had been thick with it as well. Perhaps I had seen the house in person, or else I'd seen a picture. Even its cottage had resembled this one, with two doors, their placement being such that one served as a front door and the other the back.

But the more I thought about it, differences also came to mind. Unlike the other house, the garage in MC's yard wasn't located in front of the cottage. Also, MC's garage was made of smooth planks, not like the garage in my memory, whose bottom portion had been built out of logs.

More importantly, they felt different. MC's house had a fresh, vibrant quality to it, not because it was located on a busy road, but because the house itself didn't give off the impression of gloom and death. If the house were placed on a hill buffeted by cold, bleak wind, the house's presence would make the wind immediately subside.

Different indeed from the house in my memory, whose atmosphere evoked only lethargy, sorrow, and groans. If that house were moved to a peaceful hilltop, its presence would give rise to gusts of strong wind. And if the house were relocated to tropical climes, giant bats would start breeding in the attic, turning the place into a kingdom for their kind.

I felt tired and was ready to try going to bed again. But when I turned out the light, I felt someone yank my hair from behind. I turned around but no one was there. I climbed into bed and got under the covers.

Meanwhile, the bowling alley thundered on. I kept perfectly still. Then I tried to yawn. But I couldn't sleep. MC had been right—I really was capable of sleeping standing up or walking if I had no choice. But that was only if I managed to get to sleep. If I was having trouble sleeping in the first place, well, I would be like now—more ruled by my longing for sleep than ruling over it.

I got up again and turned on the light.

In the kitchen I saw the same thing: all the places within MC's reach were clean. The higher the place, the dirtier. I had no doubt that MC cleaned diligently, but after her accident, what could she do? I pitied her. Again I was determined to renew my offer of marriage. I would care for her and love her, I would make her the mother of my children. All this I would do so she wouldn't have to suffer anymore.

I boiled some water to make instant coffee. I spooned a good amount into my mug before pouring in the boiling water without adding any sugar or cream. This was how Olenka liked to take her coffee. Olenka liked her tea the same way—bitter, no sugar, no cream, and no lemon either. She'd even use two tea bags, to make it even bitterer to the taste.

She did it on purpose, to remind herself life wasn't always happy. It pleased her, to celebrate life's torment with a bitter drink. Whenever waiting for the bus, sitting in the park, or lying in the grass, she would make chewing motions with her mouth, like a cow at rest. In this way, she told me, she would always be aware that she must be patient, must endure in the face of sorrow and misery.

At times I sensed that, through her efforts to stave off torment, she was actually seeking it out. She herself had said it once—that she had spent her whole life celebrating her suffering, the only way to banish her torment being to constantly remind herself she could never be free.

To be perpetually aware of her suffering—therein lay her only escape.

After drinking my coffee, I went over to the bookshelves. Since the books were so numerous and there wasn't much room, many of the books had been placed high up. It was the same situation, the higher the place the dirtier. Yet again I trotted out my firm intention to renew my proposal. Now, I got out a feather duster, stood on a chair, and began dusting the places high up. Suddenly, I felt a tug on my right ear. Who was it? I looked to my right but there was nobody there.

I could tell from MC's book collection that she had a practical bent. While she did have poetry books and novels and works about philosophy and art and the like, most of her collection were how-to books: fixing houses, repairing cars, gardening, making children's toys.

I also found *The Ann Landers Encyclopedia*. I looked inside. Nothing groundbreaking. MC was right—anyone with a decent education who put their mind to it wouldn't find it difficult to compile a similar book.

Once I'd finished dusting a few spots, I chose a book at random and brought it to the sitting room. I happened to turn to the poem "Rabbi Ben Ezra," by Robert Browning, the Victorian poet. The opening lines reminded me of something. They were as follows:

Grow old along with me!
The best is yet to be.

CHAPTER 10

LET AGE APPROVE OF YOUTH

Now I remembered. The old house in my memory was the Lockridge house on the corner of South Stull and Maxwell Lane in Bloomington. There, Ross Lockridge Jr. had written the bestselling novel *Raintree County*. MGM had made the book into a film starring Elizabeth Taylor and Monty Clift.

I'd never seen the film myself, but according to Peter Yates, it had been a box-office hit in the fifties. He was still living in London at the time and hadn't become an American citizen yet. He said the five biggest cinemas in the city had played the film, each one for a full-year run. I'd also heard elsewhere that the film had done extraordinarily well in Honolulu and New York.

A few years ago, I went to see an exhibition of Lockridge's old things at the Bloomington museum. Photos of the Lockridge house from every angle were also on display. There were also photos of the garage where he killed himself. The exhibit included what critics had written about Lockridge too. Generally speaking, they praised him as a genius. If he hadn't died by suicide, he might have written several more books, vastly superior to *Raintree County*, his sole work. Also on display was a sundial, its shape reminiscent of a piston. It was on a pedestal and could be moved around. According to the exhibition booklet, the sundial was a family heirloom, from when the family had lived in Boston. The sundial had made it into the film as well. On the face of the sundial, below the numbers, were inscribed the opening lines of "Rabbi Ben Ezra."[46]

The poem was interesting, as it turned out. Old age, as the poem would have it, was confined to the flesh. The soul itself would never know death. Death was actually the beginning of life. *Like the autumn trees*, I thought to myself.

The poem went on to aver that, since the flesh was bound to perish, life after death would be far better. It would be the true birth of the human soul. As such, the poem ends on this note:

Let age approve of youth, and death complete the same!

While I was at the exhibition, and a few days later, when I visited the Lockridge house and walked around, I hadn't given much thought to the matter of suicide. Neither the exhibition nor the house had left much of an impression. Which was why studying the photo of MC's house hadn't brought the Lockridge house immediately to mind.

I read the poem over a few times before turning my attention to the story of how it came to be written. It had been published in 1864, not long after the poet's wife had died. His wife, Elizabeth Barrett Browning, had also been a poet. She was more famous than her husband at the time. Poetry was also responsible for bringing them together. Since Elizabeth was incapacitated and confined to her wheelchair, Browning was unable to court her anywhere but the house. Faithfully, Browning would wait on his beloved at the house on Wimpole Street where she was living at the time. Despite this, Elizabeth's father wouldn't give them his consent. They were forced to elope without his knowledge.[47] After they got married, out of consideration for Elizabeth, they stayed in an apartment on the ground floor. And wherever they moved, they would never occupy an upper story.

My mind wandered as I read the account of their courtship. None of it seemed to stick in my brain. Only when I came across the photo of Elizabeth sitting in her wheelchair did my thoughts fly to MC—disabled, unable to clean or dust any place beyond reach of her chair, unable to leave the house, unable to get into bed without help.

Now, I may not have been a poet, and MC may not have been anything more than the practical, handyman type, but what was wrong with loving her as Browning had loved Elizabeth Barrett? There was no doubt that she needed assistance and someone to rely on. But, like Elizabeth, she also needed love. And I was certain a woman's happiness lay in having children. Why not serve as a tool to make her happy? I was capable of assisting her, loving her, giving her kids.

She was entitled to all the same things as she would be if she weren't disabled, and it was my responsibility to provide her with them. She was behaving like a pendulum, but it was my duty to make her a punter. If I didn't, I would only keep returning to Olenka. With her in my life, Olenka would have to make herself scarce. I wouldn't allow myself to be a victim, not Olenka's or MC's. It was I who would determine what I would become, a subject not an object.

The roar of the bowling alley had long ceased. There was nothing good on TV. Listening to the radio was tiresome too. Meanwhile, the wind outside blew something fierce. I could hear its mournful voice from inside. And the scent of autumn leaves stole in.

I made my decision. It was time to act. I had to go to MC's room. I was prepared to act like a burglar or thief. If she put up a fight, I'd have to resort to rape. I would plant my seed in her womb this very night. Like it or not, I would assign her the task of carrying on the Drummond family name. If the child was a boy, I would call him Robert Young Drummond, after the Robert Young I was backing for Bloomington's mayor, with the addition of my own surname. If the child was a girl, I would call her Elizabeth Browning Drummond, after Robert Browning's wife, with my surname added. Both Robert Young and Elizabeth Browning had possessed lofty aspirations in addition to principles. They'd both been very capable too. I wanted my children to be like them.

So I walked to the mirror and took off all my clothes. I scrutinized every part I could see. In a matter of moments, my life would change. And I was ready to be transformed.

Carefully, I washed my whole body, dressed myself neatly, and knelt. I prayed, "Oh God, grant me good seed. Grant me choice land where I may scatter the seed bestowed by You. Keep my seed safe from all manner and deed of evil, and in the same way, keep the land where I plant my seed from wickedness too."

I wasn't just kneeling anymore. I was also pressing my forehead to the floor. Again, as before, I had the sense that something was missing. I didn't know what.

As such, I didn't feel entirely ready. What else I needed to do, I couldn't say for sure. I needed something to strengthen my resolve. And, for some reason, my hand touched that same book of poetry. And my gaze fell on the line *the instant made eternity.* It was from another Browning poem, titled "The Last Ride Together," about the final ride of two people in love. There were times in a person's life when an instant could determine their entire future. And everyone, especially if they loved each other, must meet these moments head-on. This could be the instant in my own life that would change the course of my entire life. And this was exactly what I was hoping.

So off I dashed to the main house.

CHAPTER 11

LEAVING MC

The wind blew hard. I crossed the yard and gently knocked on MC's window.

Her voice was soft. "Fanton?"

"Yes, Mary."

This was the only time since meeting her in Indianapolis that I had called her by her real name.

"Hold on."

From the sound of her voice, I knew she was having trouble opening the window.

Eventually, it opened a crack. I opened it wider. Then, like someone trying to snatch a maiden from a den of thieves,[48] I leaped in. The scent of autumn leaves, carried by the wind, leaped too, filling my body.

Mary pulled my arms toward her and began chewing on my lip. The world was transformed into a paradise. I could live there for eternity.

She rested from gnawing long enough to say, "I knew you would come, Fanton. It's why I told Catherine not to help me into bed. I've been waiting for you."

Then she recommenced her chewing.

Sure enough, she was still in her wheelchair. She smelled wonderful. I felt her clothes with my hands and knew she was dressed nicely. She wasn't lying. She really had been waiting for me. I was sure that her world had been transformed into a paradise too. It felt like she wanted to turn me into chewing gum, so she could chew me to her heart's content. It was as if she wished I were a giant, so she could curl up in my bowels and fall asleep. From time to time she would fondle my ear, then gobble it up like someone ravenous for salad.

I was just about to carry her to bed when she refused. With a look of disdain, she condemned me, accusing me of regarding her as a mere concubine. She commanded me to confess who it was—the woman I saw as my true wife.

"There's no one else," I said, before urging her to say yes and marry me.

"Only when I find out who she is, and speak with her, and learn her opinion of you, will I consider your offer," she replied.

"Then why invite me in? Why suck my soul dry with those lips of yours? I hate self-destructive people, but I hate people who hurt others even more. That's what you're doing now. You're hurting me."

She then admitted that she was walking things back. Before, she'd tried to trick herself into believing she didn't love me. Now she was trying to be honest with herself and acknowledge that she did. But she, too, felt hurt. She felt I was deceiving her.

Suddenly, I was overcome with nausea toward her. She seemed to see everything as a single, straight line. All she knew was how to go forward or backward. To her, everything was crystal clear. The idea that anything could be a circle—a chicken and egg situation—was lost on her. Let's say she'd been confused about whether she loved me, and whether I was deceiving her, and whether it was love or pity that had driven her to kiss me, then I would have respected her more.

It was my belief that a great struggle was going on inside her regarding me. But both the reason for her struggle and her method of struggling were feeble. For both within her and in her view of me, there was no mystery whatsoever. She'd already known that she loved me, but then she'd tried to deceive herself. Then, at last, she had admitted she loved me; yet she also knew there was someone else tucked away in my heart, and was forcing me to confess what she already knew to be true. This was the manner in which she evaluated everything—based on what she already believed to be true. She would often pretend—like how she'd pretended not to love me. She preoccupied herself not with wondering why she held certain principles, but merely whether those principles were correct.

I knew that anyone who wanted to have children was responsible for ensuring their God-given potential. Only under pure, clean circumstances could I spill my seed. Only in this way would my child grow to attain any degree of godliness, any purity of heart. If I already had doubts about the soil into which I wanted to slip my seed, my children would be devoid of such potential. Accordingly, I had to back out.

I told her frankly that I didn't like her attitude. I also told her frankly that I wasn't going to go through with my wicked intention to rape her after all. Furthermore, and this was the important part, I told her frankly that I loved someone else. "It's true," I said. "I'm not sure whether I love you or not."

She was silent at first. Then she squeezed my hand. Then she asked, "In that case, in your heart of hearts, there is only one place for me—as your concubine."

"I don't know."

"If I may ask, where is she now?"

By right, I should have answered, "Near me. Always near me. Earlier, she even yanked my hair and tugged my ear." "Dunno," I replied instead.

"What if I took back my rejection? Would you still take me as your wife?"

"No."

"What if I surrendered my body to you now? Would you still want me?"

"No."

"Because we might as well? Purely for fun?"

"No."

"What if I said I were willing to bear you children without becoming your wife?"

"*I* wouldn't be willing."

"Would you still be willing to kiss me? Just one kiss? And nothing more?"

"I would not."

After bidding her goodbye, she asked if there was any chance that I might someday change my mind. "No," I said.

"What if I were to propose to you? To be my husband?"

"I would say no."

"Do you think we can still meet up? As friends? As pals?"

"No."

"You wouldn't be willing to be friends?"

"I would not."

"Even though I'm disabled? And as such, unable to look for you? In the hope that you'll take pity on me?"

"No, I feel no pity."

"All right, Fanton. Let me ask you something else. Don't you feel responsible for my unfortunate state? Don't you feel like you're one of the reasons I'm now handicapped? Not the only reason, but the main one?"

"No."

"All right, Fanton. Let me be frank. I've been attracted to you since I first laid eyes on you at the bus station in Indianapolis. MB didn't say anything about it, but she knew how I felt. That was why she kept coaxing me into getting to know you better. I knew she was coaxing you into it too. The longer it went on, the more confused I became. That's why I didn't phone my mother earlier. I forgot all about it. Or rather, I didn't forget, just delayed it. I wanted to tell her about you and ask her for advice. Then you proposed. I became even more confused. It was in that state of confusion that I made the phone call.

"That was what happened, but let's say I hadn't been in such a state when I'd received the bad news. I wouldn't have reacted in the same way. If you hadn't proposed to me the night before, I would have remained calm. I can't imagine what I would have done, but I'm sure I would have acted differently.

"I'm not going to say that you're to blame for my misfortune. I'm only saying that if you hadn't proposed I wouldn't have acted like I did. Maybe the end result would have been the same—I might still have flown out, on that same flight, and the plane would still have crashed. But at the very least, I wouldn't have been so confused and panicked during the crash."

"I'm sorry," I replied. "I'm afraid I don't know what to say. Only permit me now to take my leave. You've given me much to think about, I'm sure. But for the moment, please allow me to depart."

We kissed once more. It was only after leaping out the window did I recall how adamant I had been about not wanting to.

CHAPTER 12

NAUSEA

So strong was the scent of autumn leaves. I knew the time had come. I had to find Olenka. I was sure she had yanked my hair and tugged my ear for a reason, beyond merely wanting to bother me. Her astral body wouldn't be roaming around trying to find me if it weren't important. I had to get back to Bloomington. Perhaps a letter from her was waiting there.

As it turned out, I wouldn't need to go all the way to Bloomington to learn her news. In the meantime, without leaving a message for the Carsons, I took off toward the bowling alley in search of the nearest pay phone. From there, I called a cab and asked to be taken to the Pittsburgh airport. I would leave for Indianapolis on the first flight out.

It was nearly dawn when I reached the airport. I had to hang around for a while. Like the time I'd ended up in the Indianapolis bus station overnight, I wandered about again, exploring every corner of the airport.

With nothing better to do, I bought a newspaper from one of the vending machines. Then I skimmed through it, also out of boredom. I came across a short article, which reported thus: an amateur artist turned art forger had been caught operating out of Washington, D.C. The forger, whose initials were OD, came from Indiana. She preyed mostly on the rich and famous.[49] The article mentioned several of them, including Senator Kennedy from Massachusetts; former CIA director George Bush; former secretary of the treasury Connally; Elizabeth Taylor's husband, Senator Warner from Virginia; White House chief of staff Hamilton Jordan; and several others who made regular trips to Washington. But since the injured parties had all said, "Never mind," the case was considered closed. Nor would they return the artworks they'd bought. In fact, they declared themselves in awe of OD's talents.

Who else could OD be but Olenka Danton, Wayne's wife?

The article went on to report that, yesterday morning, the forger had been found unconscious in her hotel room. It was generally supposed that she had accidentally taken too many sleeping pills. The police, however, emphasized there were no signs of a suicide attempt. The article gave both the name of the hotel and the hospital where she was undergoing treatment.

I would have thought that such news would leave me greatly shaken. But I was only mildly surprised. Even my decision to head to Washington instead of Indianapolis as originally planned stemmed not from being shaken up, but merely from wanting to follow events from up close. I was devoid of any desire to sweep Olenka off her feet and spread her out on the floor or ironing board or dresser or anywhere else. I had become indifferent.

My passion for Olenka had truly shriveled up. And if I were a writer like Wayne and given the opportunity to mine Olenka's life circumstances for material, I wouldn't make this episode in Olenka's life the story's climax. On the contrary, I would make it the denouement, that is, part of the falling action, the point in the story where the reader has ceased to care overly much about Olenka anymore. And indeed, Olenka wasn't entirely deserving of such attention. The course of her life had been charted, and what happened next didn't need to be discussed at length. For example, if one has a friend who finds out they have cancer, what one should do is express sympathy right away, not wait until they die. The same went for Olenka.

Even so, I couldn't stop myself from wanting to find out what happened next from close quarters. If I were a reader and this were a story, I'd want to know how it ended, even if my interest in the character had already waned. And so, instead of going to Indianapolis, I set off for Washington, D.C.

After keeping the article about Olenka and throwing the

rest of the paper in the trash, I bought an issue of *Family Weekly* magazine. Then I boarded the plane.

I read the magazine on the flight over. A question in a Q&A column caught my eye. It was from a reader in New York named L. M. Westchester, for Paul Findley, a congressman from Illinois. He asked: *Did you really write a book about Abraham Lincoln? What's it called? Did you find out anything new?* The reply: *Yes. The title is* Abe Lincoln: The Crucible of Congress. *As a congressman, he was given a travel allowance of 40 cents per mile. The distance from Washington, D.C., to Springfield, Illinois, was only 1,800 miles, but he fiddled with the numbers, and turned it into 3,252 miles.*[50]

Now that I no longer cared, nothing seemed interesting to me. All the passengers seemed like inanimate objects, as lifeless as the seats in which they sat. And the flight attendants were like female robots. Even their smiles felt forced.

After landing at Washington National Airport, I went to a coffee shop. Only after playing seven games of pinball in a row did I hail a taxi and head to St. Jerome's Hospital. I saw a lot of semitrucks on the way, all of them were in motion, and yet, at the same time, they seemed utterly inanimate to me.

The closer we got to the city, the more indifferent I felt toward Olenka. And MC too. Then I spotted a big green balloon drifting over the Potomac, heading in the direction of Virginia.

I asked the taxi driver if he'd ever heard of the DaVinci.

"No," he replied.

"It made the first trans-America balloon flight," I told him. "It took off in Oregon and landed in Virginia. All the way from the West Coast to the East Coast. How about that."

But I knew full well that neither the driver nor I gave a fig about what I was saying.

As we neared the hospital, I became increasingly aware that I felt rather sick. A physical affliction, to be precise. For instance, though my brain knew the taxi was turning right, I felt like we were turning left. I also knew that the people crossing the road were upright, but I felt they were walking at a slant. Everything I saw was now chaotic, mixed-up, upside down. My interaction with the external world was now pathological,

A brief, rectangular snippet, dated October 7, 1979, from *Family Weekly*, the magazine of the *Sunday Herald-Times*, Bloomington. On the left is a small black-and-white headshot of a smiling, balding fair-skinned man in a suit. The accompanying text, on the right, reads as follows:

> For Congressman Paul Findley (R.-Ill.), author of *Abe Lincoln: The Crucible of Congress*
>
> What *was the most startling discovery that you made about Abe Lincoln*? —L. M. Westchester, N.Y.
>
> - As a Congressman, he padded his mileage allowance. In those days, Congressmen were given $.40 a mile as a travel allowance to commute between their homes and Washington. Lincoln put in for a round-trip mileage expense of 3,252 miles between Washington and Springfield when that actual round-trip mileage figure was only 1,800 miles.

This was what Fanton Drummond read on the flight from Pittsburgh to Washington, D.C.

abnormal. *Nausée* was Olenka's term for it, borrowed from Sartre. One time, Olenka had given me a riddle. There was someone named Antoine Roquentin who would spend his days walking around Paris. Each day, he would go to Café Mably and see a man who always held his spoon in his right hand. One day, Roquentin went into the café as usual, and saw the man as usual. But the man, as Roquentin saw him, was holding the spoon in his left hand as he ate. At that time, he was overcome with nausea.[51] Who was to blame?

The answer was Roquentin. He knew something inside him wasn't quite right. That was how I felt now. I wasn't like Roquentin, of course. Unlike him, I hadn't had a vision of someone falling flat and dropping dishes.[i] Roquentin had, even though he knew the person he was seeing hadn't fallen at all. Nonetheless, like Roquentin, I also felt a *suprême dégoût de moi*, that is, a profound self-disgust.

Consequently, when I reached the hospital, I didn't ask about Olenka right away. It wasn't because I was stalling for time or had forgotten. I simply had no desire to do anything at all.

I walked through the lobby doors and sat down for a while. Then I stood, went to the vending-machine room, and bought some coffee and a pack of cheese puffs. As I was walking back to my seat, I saw a number of people entering and exiting through another door. I had the sense that they were genuinely moving around, while I myself were inhabiting a limbo. As if I were dead and my soul had washed up somewhere, lacking the right to ascend to heaven or plunge into hell. Wayne was right. I suffered from a leprosy of the soul. If my soul were made material, it would be patently obvious that all my digits had fallen off, that the flesh on my cheeks had rotted away, that my legs were about to give way.

Yes, Wayne was right, I thought again. Even so, upon finding both *The Saratoga Review* and *The Atlantic Review* at the hospital magazine kiosk, I felt no desire to buy them. I merely glanced them over and felt indifference, despite the fact that, once again, Wayne had written about the lesions afflicting my soul. Perhaps he was worried I would bring him to court—

Olenka's name had been changed to Olga, my name was now Drumbold, and Tulip Tree had become the Evermann building near the Elberhart Bell Tower. The final paragraph of the story in *The Atlantic Review* read as follows: *Ultimately, Olga was a two-bit whore. She hadn't enough courage to kill herself, not a seventh-of-a-hair's worth. Neither did Drumbold. Something twitched inside them, like dogs on their last legs, on the verge of death—their very souls. And everyone had known it, right from the start, the grim, ghastly disease their souls harbored. So, like wild dogs, they continued to roam.*

He was right. My soul was sick, and it was starting to affect me physically. But the part about me not being brave enough to kill myself wasn't true. More accurately, I'd never given the matter of suicide any thought. And also, I didn't really see much use in killing myself. Like Roquentin, who had declared outright, *Je n'avais pas le droit d'exister*, I, too, felt no right to exist. There was no reason for the universe to continue having me as part of its contents. Yet I believed at the same time that I had no right to make myself not exist. I had come into being without ever asking for it, and it wasn't up to me to undo that.

I should remember, however, that since meeting Olenka, suicide had crossed my mind on three separate occasions. But whenever it had, I'd never felt anxious. I'd never taken an interest in or felt drawn to, much less had any natural inclination to, kill myself. At the Elberhart Bell Tower, Olenka was the one who'd felt anxious. Nor had I felt anxious when seeing the U-505 German submarine at the Museum of Science and Industry in Chicago with MC and MB. The same went for the time Lockridge had spontaneously come to mind.

Regarding the German submarine, the story went as follows: during World War II, it was captured by the United States Navy and towed to British territory. Out of shame, most likely, its captain died by suicide. After the sub was hauled to Chicago, the room where he killed himself was on display for all to see. A museum guide even told us that the captain's ghost could still be heard there, whistling away.

I had my doubts about whether Olenka had really "accidentally taken too many sleeping pills." I also questioned the truth of the police statement regarding the incident, that there had been "no signs of a suicide attempt." People were always giving Olenka the benefit of the doubt. No one ever saw her as anything less than exemplary or good. For example, when Wayne had first told me about Olenka's faults, I'd quietly laid the blame on him. I was sure that if Wayne ever brought Olenka to court and laid out what Olenka and I had done, the jury would determine she wasn't at fault. Olenka's life was exactly as implied in all her photos. If everyone in the photos were gathered together and brought before a jury, all the members would decide that Olenka was the most enchanting of the lot. She rendered everyone around her meaningless. So if she did anything wrong, people would try to protect her and cover up her crime. The hotel staff and police had probably acted out of sympathy for her.

When I asked at the hospital registration desk, I learned that Olenka had left fifteen minutes ago through the side door. I felt no regret, no disappointment. Pent up inside was merely a void. Both Olenka and MC made me sick to my stomach. If I had to eat and look at them, would I even be able to keep my food down? Probably not. Wayne was right. Olenka's armpits were revolting. He was right about her mouth too. It was like that of a venomous snake. I'd seen it with my own eyes. One night, when the sky near Tulip Tree had convulsed with lightning, Olenka had yawned. So I knew beyond a doubt that her tongue was forked and the interior of her throat bright red. True, the lightning had affected my vision, but the impression of her likeness to a venomous snake had been made, and now, it came to the fore once again. She was truly terrifying and, at the same time, repulsive. MC's lip too. Hideous. Even more so in the dark. I regretted ever letting her chew on my lip and gobble up my ear.

So I left the hospital and took a walk. Eventually I hailed a cab and asked to go to the Museum of Natural Arts and Sciences.[ii] I'd heard the DaVinci TransAmerica balloon was there on display.

The DaVinci turned out not to be as big as I'd expected. Its controls were rudimentary too. Piloting a balloon like this wouldn't be too difficult, from the looks of things. Still, I knew I wouldn't be able to fly it, especially not from the West to East Coast.

I bought some coffee, only because my throat was dry and wanted wetting.[52] Then I walked around some more. Suddenly, I vomited. If only I'd vomited up my entire body and soul, how happy I would have been. And if only I could be like the phoenix, bursting into flame and turning to ash, and out of those ashes being born anew. I, too, longed to shatter into pieces, to lose all form.

PART V

CODA

If I were Wayne, after writing the line *I, too, longed to shatter into pieces, to lose all form*, I would stop. The story would end there. I would be careful, knowing exactly where to begin and where to end. I would avoid the nonsensical and insignificant. But I'm not Wayne.

Wayne was always conscious of who he was. Never in his life did he see himself as separate from his identity as a writer, not even for a second. Not so with me. Often, I have no idea who I am, and consequently, don't know what I should be aiming for. I cannot say whether my actions are bringing me any closer to my end goal in life, for that end goal is difficult to discern. As such, I cannot choose my stopping point. I have no power over where my pen may run. If my pen happens to stop here, I will regard this section as a coda. Why? Because my pen has already distilled the entirety of my life into four parts, each with its own themes and problems, the sum of which, together, make up a living organism. To this end, the preceding parts suffice. So if my pen does stop here, this part of the book will serve merely as a coda—to underscore the nature of my being, my status as a living organism.

I have already stated that I find it difficult to discern my purpose in life. Besides that, I also sense something following me, watching me. I've felt free up to now—perhaps too free. I rarely come up against any walls. By giving my conscience the power to monitor my every attitude, opinion, and action, I am able to both condemn and justify whatever I do. As a result, I end up holding dialogues with my own self. Case in point, the masturbatory letters to MC. I've never allowed anyone else to be judge over me.

But over time, the relationship between myself and my conscience has become pathological. There's something upside down about it, which has caused me to distrust myself. I feel like a thief. It doesn't matter whether I acknowledge my wickedness or not, something tells me that I have misused my freedom for the sake of achieving ignoble aims.

Often have I knelt, and looked up at the sky, and bowed my head, and pressed my forehead to the earth, but I have always felt that something is missing still. I know, from glancing through the Quran, that God is sovereign over all. Whom God forgives, and also whom he punishes, lies with him alone. But I also know that "whether ye show what is in your minds or conceal it, God calleth you to account for it."[53] And I must be accountable. Therefore, in my attempt to become a faithful follower, I mutter, "My God, in my utter despair, I still call on You."[54]

Tulip Tree
BLOOMINGTON, INDIANA, 1979

PART VI

OLENKA'S ORIGINS

I wrote *Olenka* in Bloomington, toward the end of 1979. Whether I was in the middle of writing *People from Bloomington* then, I can't exactly recall. If I'm not mistaken, by that time, I'd already finished *People from Bloomington* in part.

As with my other works, I came to write *Olenka* purely by chance. I'd just gone out and was returning home. As I approached Tulip Tree Apartments, where I lived, it suddenly began to snow. And the wind began acting up. I raced inside. As it so happened, the lift doors were about to close. There was a woman in the lift who must have seen my hurry, and she held the lift doors to let me in. Inside the lift, apart from her, there were also three boys, dressed in dirty clothes. Their features resembled the woman's, so I assumed she was their mother. As it turned out, the boys got off on an earlier floor and the woman stayed behind. She told me in brief about who they were. Their mother had abandoned them, and their father worked from morning to evening. The boys were left to their own devices.

For some reason, upon parting ways with the woman, I broke once again into a run, entered my apartment, and made straight for my room. I got out my typewriter and began to write. After a few pages I thought to myself, this short story will be finished in no time. But I couldn't stop. My mind was assailed by an overpowering urge to keep writing, until I was left with no time to attend to any other tasks. Soon, *Olenka* was complete—if I'm not mistaken, in the span of less than three weeks.

If not for that encounter in the lift, I probably wouldn't have written anything. My mind—and hands—would have been drawn into other matters. That I found myself unable to do anything but write shows the extent to which the writing process turned me into an object, as opposed to a subject with control over when I should start writing, what I should write, and when I should stop. And to think it came about by sheer chance.

In itself, a coincidence means nothing, if connections aren't made to other coincidences. I can think of another one, which happened when I was in my third year of middle school, in Salatiga. I was attending a public school at the time, on Jalan Kartini, if I'm not mistaken. I became a faithful patron of a public library not far from the post office where my father was employed. There, I discovered a book of Russian short stories in English translation. With my very limited English language abilities, I managed to finish the book. One of the stories remained fixed in my mind.

I forgot who wrote the story, but I recalled clearly that the main character was a woman named Olga Semyonovna. I remembered well that Olga was always in love with someone, and would adopt the views of whomever she loved to the point of fanaticism. In her eyes, the opinion of whichever man she loved was the highest truth. Unfortunately, the men she loved kept dying. Since she couldn't live without loving anyone, and indeed, no one ever left her alone and unloved, her life became a long string of admirations—of specific individuals whose particular opinions were always irrefutable truths. She married a man who ran an opera, and became fully convinced that to live without opera would be sheer barbarism. When the opera owner died, she married a timber merchant, and insisted that a world without wooden planks was no world at all.

I would often think back to this story. I'd even get emotional when recalling Olga Semyonovna's fate. I deeply regretted not owning the book. The version I'd copied out—painstakingly translated by myself into Indonesian onto cheap paper—I had lost long ago. Dashed were my hopes of ever meeting Olga again.

But time had other plans. A few weeks before I began writing *Olenka*, in Caveat Emptor, a secondhand bookstore in Bloomington, I stumbled across the book for which I had yearned all that time. The child who was lost had now been found.

The story that had so long haunted me turned out to be "The Darling," by Anton P. Chekhov. The protagonist's name was indeed Olga Semyonovna, but this was merely how people addressed her. I finished reading the entire collection in no time without paying attention to what her real name was.

It was only a few weeks after finishing *Olenka* did I wonder where the name "Olenka" had come from. I honestly had no idea. Afterward, I learned that the woman I'd met in the lift was called Anka. This satisfied me somewhat because the name "Anka" sounded similar to "Olenka," but where I got "Olenka" specifically remained a mystery to me.

It was only after I returned to Indonesia and happened to flip through that collection of Russian short stories that I realized that Olenka was Olga Semyonovna's true name. No wonder I'd never heard the name while in America—it was Russian. Subconsciously, I had been inspired to use the name, not due to anything about the name itself, but because of its owner's unfortunate fate.

I then realized that if I hadn't reread that short story about Olga, I would have never written *Olenka*. Or at least, I would have written it using another name. Then again, if I hadn't used the name, I would have probably ended up writing something else.

Upon pondering the matter further, however, I felt some gaps still needed filling in. After all, while writing this novel, I had never thought of Olga once. Also, the Olenka I had written differed from Chekhov's. They differed in character too. Even once I was done writing, I hadn't thought back to her. Only upon learning that Olga was actually Olenka had I realized it fully—that I would have never ended up writing *Olenka* if Olga's fate hadn't been on my mind.

Now I know. Creativity occurs precisely where there are gaps.

Creativity is the act of bringing into being that which is not. And indeed, the Olenka I had written did not exist prior to my writing her. And any connection between her and Olga, both before the novel's completion and afterward, was nonexistent too. What did exist was only an awareness on my part that, if I hadn't read that story about Olga, I would never have come to write this novel. As such, the nature of the connection between Chekhov's Olenka and my Olenka is unclear, and cannot be accounted for. For herein lies creativity. If the Olenka I wrote were merely a literal continuation or manifestation of Chekhov's Olenka, then it would behoove me to call into question the integrity of my creative act. For indeed, a writer is responsible for creating individuals who are distinct from other individuals, who exist in their own right.

Of course, I found it difficult to explain my connection to Olga at first. All I could say was that it was extremely emotional, not intellectual in the least. I sympathized with her, I felt how bitter her life was. The series of happinesses she experienced throughout her life were merely small ripples caused by an underlying condition, that is, her suffering. I had been caught up in her suffering. And being caught up had caused me to become, emotionally speaking, obsessed with her. She came to mind often, and I would feel moved. This suffering, this state of being moved, was also what would subsequently compel me to write *Olenka*.

In trying to trace the matter, I came to realize that there was yet more to my relationship with Olenka. Though I couldn't explain it at first, I felt that Olenka's journey through life was that of a blind person, groping to find herself—a self she had never known and would never discover. Each mania stemmed from a desire to find out who she was. And they were fleeting because she possessed nothing of her own. When it comes down to it, a great many characters in good works of literature possess nothing of their own.

Let's say Olga bore a stamp proclaiming her true identity. It would merely be temporary, like her happiness. Suffering and meaninglessness were the only other things she had. This determination of Olga's to find herself, which flung her time and again into a hollow world, was also what had driven me to write *Olenka*, though I had not been aware of it at first.

Following this, I also realized that there was more to my relationship with Olga. She was a person in her own right—individual, but universal too. Her suffering, her pointlessness, her struggles belonged personally to her, even though they could afflict anyone, at whatever time, in whatever place. If she hadn't had these qualities, I probably wouldn't have developed my obsession with her. And if I hadn't been obsessed with her, she wouldn't have had any power over me at all.

To return to the matter of coincidence, which I've already touched on above: so, what I had initially perceived as coincidence was actually nothing other than affinity—that is, a correspondence between Chekhov's views as expressed in the "The Darling" and my own. Many critics have observed that my characters are bitter, and that life, as depicted in my stories, is always bleak. It has even been said that the worlds I portray are, without fail, terrifying.[i] I myself have often noted that bitterness is a constant theme of mine. My short stories tend to be about the successive ups and downs of individuals as they each attempt to discover who they are. In the end, consciously or unconsciously, each one must face the fact that his or her life is merely a string of emptinesses. They may find their meaning once, and then they die, for the meaning they have found is merely a sham. Such are the characters in *Olenka*, trapped between a desire for self-determination on one hand and utter helplessness on the other. Like the characters in the literary works I admire, *Olenka*'s characters are forced to admit that they are not the architects of their body and soul.

I have tried here to expound on the matter of coincidence, which, as it turns out, is more or less a matter of affinity. I have also come to realize that selectivity plays a large part in coincidence; only that which leaves an impression will influence the writing process, while that which doesn't won't have any effect. In whatever I do, like it or not, I am always engaged in the process of selection.

Like it or not, the coincidences I unconsciously gather together during the writing process have been pre-selected. These form the essential crystals of what I write, which will give my work shape as a whole. As a result, every aspect of what I write possesses meaning. Even parts that seem to bear resemblance to others, or to bear no direct relation to the main matter, are, too, an integral part of the whole. Whenever Fanton Drummond suddenly brings up the books Olenka used to read—obviously, it's for a reason. These books form part of a greater unity inseparable from the novel itself. The same applies to Fanton recounting his childhood as an orphan in Kentucky. Out of the blue, he begins comparing his experience with that of an orphan in nineteenth-century England—for there are indeed differences and also genuine similarities across these disparate times and places. The configuration of society in nineteenth-century England did indeed allow hypocrisy to reign unabated, in religious matters among others. But conditions in the twentieth century, specifically those experienced by Fanton Drummond, render the individual without excuse for the wrongs he commits, for these wrongs are, in essence, now attributable to the doer himself. The freedoms enjoyed by Fanton Drummond and the other characters in *Olenka* also make demands on their consciences.

The literary term for a narrative that drifts or meanders into irrelevance is "digression." If I'm not mistaken, the term already has a formal Indonesian-language equivalent: *lanturan*—that which leads the writer away from the matter at hand. I do not know whether the many leaps I have executed in *Olenka* can be considered digressions or not, for whatever the case may be, everything that winds up in my work has had a very long running start. Even matters that may appear offhand or spontaneous have actually occupied my mind for a good while. For example, technically speaking, I read about Abraham Lincoln's indiscretions as a congressman regarding his travel allowance in the October 7, 1979, issue of the *Family Weekly* magazine supplement for the *Sunday Herald-Times*. This is the article that Fanton Drummond reads on the flight from Pittsburgh to Washington. But I had already heard about the matter long before reading the article.

Another example: the DaVinci TransAmerica balloon passed over Bloomington on the night of October 1, 1979. This is the moment when Olenka leaves Fanton Drummond for good. But the DaVinci would have never strayed into *Olenka* if it weren't for my interest in news about balloon flights. I had even taken a ride in a hot-air balloon over Bloomington a few years prior to writing *Olenka*. I would also watch ballooning competitions, which would take off from outside Tulip Tree. In real life, the DaVinci failed to reach Washington due to the awful weather conditions affecting the whole of the Midwestern United States. But in *Olenka*, the balloon ends up on display in a museum in Washington, D.C., after successfully traversing America's skies. If I had never been haunted by hot-air balloons to begin with, I would never have included the DaVinci in *Olenka* at all.

What happened to Margaret Trudeau, the ex-wife of the Canadian prime minister Pierre Elliott Trudeau, was also something I'd heard a lot about before. Reports of her sensational exploits had often appeared in the media, from first-rate outlets to third-rate ones. One finds many such matters in many literary works, of the same tenor and spirit, even if there is no close correspondence. As such, when Olenka recounts her experience, which resembles that of Margaret's, it was not done lightly.

But let us speak frankly. One cannot trace everything that goes into the writing process back to purely technical matters. A more fundamental matter is responsible, too, namely, the views of the writer himself. As such, I'm not entirely sure whether the leaps in *Olenka*, which appear so spontaneous, can be considered digressions, but if so, these digressions occurred because, from both an intellectual and emotional standpoint, nothing runs entirely straight. For example, someone trying to examine himself will not be able to do so without a set of tools. And one such tool is the comparison of himself with others. So when Fanton Drummond sinks into despair, it makes sense that his thoughts should suddenly fly to the famous clairvoyante Madame Sosostris. He feels fortunate not to have the powers of a clairvoyant, who sees in the world nothing but calamity and destruction. In his complete ignorance, he is free to enjoy life, just as your average plane passenger has no sense of whether something is wrong with the engine. On he flies, never thinking to break into a cold sweat. So it is when Fanton Drummond stays in MC's cottage. That his thoughts should suddenly fly to another house—the Lockridge house, that is—is not without reason. The Lockridge house was once the site of a suicide. Remembering the Lockridge house then stirs him to mull over Robert Browning's poems. And these poems are what give rise once again to his eagerness to have children.

Moving on, I must tell you, as someone who is fond of E. M. Forster, that I especially like what he says in *A Passage to India*—that "most of life is so dull." But when he writes, "there is nothing to be said about it," I hesitate to agree. For we must know that upon plunging into someone's mind, we will discover the richness of their thoughts. They may not have done much, or done anything astonishing, and as such may be boring, but of their thoughts there will always be much to tell. At base, everyone is an Immanuel Kant—the shackles of life constrain him while his mind leaps freely across worlds. This is why a work's literary merit is not measured by its wealth of head-turning action, but rather, how richly it captures the thoughts that flash through one's head.

And once again, there are no thoughts that run wholly straight. Ask any honest person willing to speak openly. He will tell us that the richness of his inner life lies in digression's curves. True, the cleverer a person, the deeper he can dig into a matter, but nonetheless, he will never be able to shake himself of the need to glance right, left, and behind. When, near the end of his life, Kant said, "*Das Gefühl für Humanität hat mich noch nicht verlassen*," a great many references must have flashed through his mind.[ii] As such, digression is more than just a technical matter; it provides a framework for thought.

We ourselves should not be shy to acknowledge that we see a great many correspondences in the course of everyday life, which appear to be coincidences but are actually the result of a network of fine interconnected threads. With every selection we make, we will realize just how many connections there are, which we cannot free ourselves from. Indeed, any wisdom we exhibit in our deeds, and also in our writing, will reflect how keenly we perceive the interconnectedness of a great many affairs.

To return to E. M. Forster, I become still more hesitant to agree when he declares of life, that "the books and talk that would describe it as interesting are obliged to exaggerate." Actually, life is inherently interesting, without need for embellishment, as long as honest, open people are to be found. Indeed, this is the task of the writer—to create such people. Every literary work of merit is, in essence, a recounting of the thoughts and opinions that rage within those who are not ashamed to face up to who they really are. Fanton Drummond, Olenka, Wayne Danton, MC, and the others in this novel don't make excuses for themselves. Their world is limited, confining. But because they don't pretend otherwise, through their eyes we glimpse the horizons of a great many other worlds. They have received their share of beatings in life, and are not ashamed to admit that they are not heroes in the least.

There will likely come a time when I will be held to account for writing about the lives of such flopabouts. My answer is, I have never encouraged anyone to be a narcissist. A narcissist always sees himself as handsome, with no awareness of the disease lurking within. In my writing, I seek to testify to the human condition, that we are creatures, wretched and covered in sores, though glorious and graceful too. Examine for yourself every line of every page of literature's most monumental works. Every word bears testimony: human beings are not agreeable creatures.

Indeed, if we want to see ourselves for who we really are, narcissism will not serve us. Fancying ourselves heroes of the dime-novel variety will not help us if we aspire to become nobler than we are. As the ancient Greeks would say, what we need is catharsis, brought on by a revulsion at one's very self.[iii]

Roquentin in Sartre's novel *La Nausée* experiences a *suprême dégoût de moi*, as does Fanton Drummond at the end of *Olenka*. Their gaze penetrates their bodies, through to that which rages within.

BUDI DARMA
SURABAYA, JANUARY 1, 1982

PART VII

NOTES BY THE AUTHOR

1. That which haunts Fanton Drummond is not mere hallucination—unlike the hallucinations with which, for example, Aldous Huxley in *Antic Hay* (1923) and E. M. Forster in *A Passage to India* (1924) saddle some of their characters. Their characters are pursued by apparitions that don't actually exist, brought about by physical states of being that prevent them from thinking clearly. What Fanton Drummond experiences, on the other hand, stems from his spiritual connection with Olenka.

   There is a Marathi writer from India who, in one of his stories, takes up this subject—the fleeting apparitions that may arise from a shared spiritual bond. This writer, P. S. Rege, was born in 1910, and often wrote under the pen name Roop Katthak. The story of Katthak's I refer to here is "Manu," which was written in Marathi, then translated by the writer himself into English.

   In *Jane Eyre*, the nineteenth-century English novelist Charlotte Brontë takes up the same subject—the fleeting apparitions that may arise from two people in love sharing a spiritual connection (see note 13).
2. While in Bloomington, I met a writer from Missouri. If I'm not mistaken, his name was either Peter Leech or Peter Leach. He had written a short story whose title I can't now recall, which was published in a literary magazine whose name also escapes me. The story made it into an anthology of best stories for the year nineteen-seventy-something. If I'm not mistaken, the anthology title had something to do with the O. Henry Awards. And if I'm not wrong, the annual anthology was originally established in honor of the short story writer O. Henry. Wayne Danton's story, "Olenka," bears resemblance to the story above.[i]
3. Articles and photographs of this preacher appeared frequently in the *Indiana Daily Student*, Indiana University's student-run

newspaper, which has a circulation of fifteen thousand copies. The body language and behavior of those listening to him were similar to what I describe in this novel. People said his name was Max Lynch and that he was formerly a lecturer in mathematics at a college in Terre Haute, Indiana.

4. Perry Miller is considered a pioneering figure in the field of American studies. *The New England Mind: The Seventeenth Century* was published by Harvard University Press in 1939 and is considered a seminal work in the field to this very day. For this novel, I have adapted some of Miller's concepts, combining them with ones from Nathaniel Hawthorne's stories and novels (see note 7).
5. I don't remember exactly which Russian writer this was. In the fifties, a short story by this writer, along with ones by other Russian writers, and, if I'm not mistaken, a few Chinese short stories, were translated into Indonesian by three writers, two of whom were Mochtar Lubis and Beb Vuyk. Balai Pustaka published the collection, if I'm not wrong.[ii]
6. A quote from "The Flea," by John Donne (1572–1631), one of the leading figures of the Metaphysical Poetry movement in England. Key to such poetry was the contemplation of the nature of the relationship between human beings, the world, and God. The physical union of individuals joined in love played an important role in understanding this relationship.

   The writer D. H. Lawrence (1885–1930), whose work I quote several times in this novel, took a similar stance. In the foreword to his novel *Women in Love* (1920), he wrote, "Let us hesitate no longer to announce that the sensual passions and mysteries are equally sacred with the spiritual mysteries and passions" (see note 11).
7. Most of the works written by Nathaniel Hawthorne, the nineteenth-century American writer, concern themselves with seventeenth-century New England Puritan life. One of Hawthorne's forebears was a Puritan judge, who was tasked with trying people accused of practicing black magic and the dark arts. What "black magic and the dark arts" consisted of, exactly, was never clearly defined. The punishment for such crimes was severe, ranging from standing in the sun or getting whipped to being sentenced to death. Nathaniel was disgusted by his forebear's actions (see note 4).

   I met a Ms. Hawthorne in New York once. When I asked her, she replied that she was indeed one of Nathaniel Hawthorne's descendants. This encounter was one reason why writing this novel went so smoothly.

The story "Young Goodman Brown" served as a springboard for my story "Bambang Subali Budiman" (which has been published in *Horison*).[iii]

8. "Life merely delays defeat . . . before, finally, we give in" ("Hidup hanya menunda kekalahan . . . sebelum pada akhirnya kita menyerah"), from "Derai-Derai Cemara" ("Rustling Pines"), by Chairil Anwar (1922–1949).
9. Spoken on October 2, 1979, the day before Pope John Paul II's visit.[iv]
10. Michel, the protagonist of André Gide's novel *L'Immoraliste* (1902), also stands stark naked before a mirror in an attempt to learn more about himself.
11. A version of the views espoused by D. H. Lawrence in *Women in Love* (see notes 6, 21, and 24) appears earlier, in *The Rainbow* (1915).
12. "This is a world loath to reply" ("Ini dunia enggan disapa") comes from Chairil Anwar's poem "Kesabaran" ("Patience").[v]
13. In *Jane Eyre* (1847), Charlotte Brontë (1816–1855) roundly condemns hypocrites who use religion to engage in corrupt, stupid, and disgraceful behavior. Brontë herself held religion in high regard but was disgusted by those who used religion for evil ends.

    In the nineteenth century, such hypocrisy was probably fairly widespread, since religion played an important role in charitable enterprises at the time. Things have changed in Fanton Drummond's time: people no longer need to use religion as a pretext for their dishonorable intentions. Like Olenka, Fanton Drummond will eventually take responsibility for what they have done wrong together, without using religion as an excuse.
14. In ancient Greek mythology, Sisyphus, king of Corinth, was condemned by the gods to roll a boulder up a hill in Tartarus every day. Once the boulder reached the top, he had to release it and let it roll to the bottom. Once the stone reached the foot of the hill, he would have to roll it back up.
15. "Kerikil Tajam dan Yang Terempas dan Yang Putus" ("The Sharp Stones and the Outcasts and the Offcuts")—the title of a poetry collection by Chairil Anwar.
16. *Jane Eyre*, by Charlotte Brontë (see notes 1 and 13).
17. In Hemingway's novel *The Sun Also Rises* (1926), Robert Cohn, an ex-boxer, knocks Jake out cold.
18. "The drizzle hastens the nightfall" ("Gerimis mempercepat

kelam") is a quote from Chairil Anwar's poem "Senja di Pelabuhan Kecil" ("Twilight in a Small Harbor").

19. *The Leatherstocking Tales* are a series of novels by James Fenimore Cooper (1789–1851). They occupy an important place in early American literary history.
20. The novel *Vanity Fair*, by William Makepeace Thackeray (1811–1863), a nineteenth-century English literary work of significance.
21. I have borrowed from the dialogue between Hermione and Ursula, two women who love the same man, Birkin, in D. H. Lawrence's *Women in Love* (see note 11).[vi]
22. Semiramis, Dido, and other heroines were a popular subject of poetry from the Middle Ages, an era when the world languished under the rule of men, and people secretly longed for strong female figures.
23. Hermione's words (see note 21).[vii]
24. With his family, once anything goes wrong, it can never be put right again—this is what Gerald believes in D. H. Lawrence's *Women in Love*. He says this when his younger sister drowns. Soon afterward, his father passes, and in the end, Gerald himself perishes in the mountains, in the snow.[viii]
25. Due to a snowstorm, I once ended up spending a night at the Indianapolis bus station on my way from Aliquippa, Pennsylvania, to Bloomington, Indiana. I have included several of my observations from that experience here. The arm-wrestling match has not been taken from this experience, but from Hemingway's novella *The Old Man and the Sea* (1952), when Santiago is arm wrestling "the negro" in a kerosene-lamp-lit tavern in Africa.
26. The film *Breaking Away* (which was initially titled *Bambino*) was shot in Bloomington during the spring of 1978. It began showing in 1979. Many film critics (including the reviewer for *The New Yorker*) regarded it as the best American film that year.
27. I have often heard this story about the conversation between these two philosophers. The version I include here is taken from Roop Katthak's short story "Manu" (see note 1), which is about a young Marathi man who goes to England to study philosophy.
28. Madame Sosostris and *Tristan and Isolde* I have taken from T. S. Eliot's long poem *The Waste Land* (1922), about the barrenness, meaninglessness, and emptiness faced by humankind in the twentieth century. Wagner adapted the folktale *Tristan*

und Isolde, sometimes referred to as *Tristram and Iseult*, into an opera. T. S. Eliot quotes from this opera in *The Waste Land*.

29. The Surah Al-Baqara, verse 62, translated by Abdullah Yusuf Ali, published originally in 1934 by the publisher Dar Al-Kitab Al-Masri in Egypt and the publisher Dar Al-Kitab Al-Lubnani in Lebanon. This translation of the Holy Quran has undergone several reprints.
30. Held every October.
31. Caesar's wife has a dream wherein something bad befalls her husband. The next day, she forbids her husband from leaving for the Capitol, but he insists on going. In the end, Caesar is murdered in front of the Capitol by Brutus and his accomplices (*Julius Caesar*, by William Shakespeare).

    Ivan Dmitrich Aksionov's wife also has a dream in which disaster befalls her husband. The next day, she too forbids her husband from leaving the house, but he leaves anyway because he feels he must keep the appointments he has made with his customers. In the end he is accused of murdering a merchant who happens to be staying with him at the same hotel. He is hauled off to jail, suffers terribly, and there he breathes his last (Tolstoy's short story "God Sees the Truth, But Waits").

    The inspiration for Olenka's mother's dream came from Tolstoy's story and also the atmosphere around Halloween—which I've experienced a few times now in America.
32. Halloween falls every year on the last Wednesday of October. The origins of Halloween are unclear.[ix]
33. Andrew Wyeth's father was killed in a similar accident in Pennsylvania. Wyeth (born in 1917) was considered a pioneering figure in the Magic Realist school of painting in America. Two similar accidents, one after another, occurred in downtown Bloomington a few weeks before I wrote "Orez," one of the short stories in *People from Bloomington* (*Orang-Orang Bloomington*). I have based the death of Olenka's father on the death of Wyeth's father, which, if I'm not wrong, occurred in the fifties.
34. *The Rainbow*, by D. H. Lawrence (see note 11).
35. From *Playgirl*, as quoted by *Tempo* magazine, vol. 9, no. 27, September 1, 1979, page 20 (the "Pokok dan Tokoh" ["Points and People"] section). I have been unable to find the original *Playgirl* interview.[x]
36. Geniuses have unique brain tissue—such was the topic of a con-

versation on NPR (National Public Radio) about the composers Bach, Beethoven, and Chopin. If I remember correctly, I listened to this conversation in the fall of 1979.

37. I have taken this from "Andrea del Sarto," a poem by Robert Browning (1812–1889), published around 1855. Browning took up the subject of del Sarto's life (1486–1531) as related in *The Lives of the Most Painters, Sculptors, and Architects* by Giorgio Vasari (once del Sarto's student). Browning had seen del Sarto's art in person in the Palazzo Pitti in Florence. Like him, I admire del Sarto's art for its detail.
38. When I was little, I lived in a small town in Central Java. My late father worked at the local post office. There was a couple there who wished for a son but had a daughter. Until she grew up (according to my definition of "grown up" at the time), she was always dressed in boys' clothes to fulfill her parents' longings. At the time, such a sight was considered very peculiar indeed (see note 40).
39. A similar scene occurs between Ursula and Winifred in *The Rainbow* (see note 34) when they get caught in the rain. In the end, Winifred marries Ursula's uncle. Ursula is disappointed, not because she is jealous but because she sees such a marriage as irresponsible.
40. Oscar Wilde's parents wanted a girl, but he was born a boy (1854). For years, Oscar was dressed in girls' clothes and treated like a daughter. When he was grown, he would dress in an oversized white robe and pace back and forth delivering lectures on art for art's sake. Though his wife was a sweet, pretty thing, he fooled around with an aristocrat named Lord Alfred Douglas. As a result, in 1895, he was thrown into prison. After his release, still bearing his shame, he fled to Paris, took to drink, and finally died there in 1900.

    The experience of seeing something similar in a small town in Central Java (note 38) and reading Oscar Wilde's life story facilitated *Olenka*'s completion.
41. Due to a cystoscopy indicating a problem with the flow of urine, caused, among other things, by the presence of excess flesh near the glans of the penis (phimosis).
42. I have taken my inspiration not from Goethe's *Faust* but from the play by Christopher Marlowe (1564–1593).
43. Many film critics panned this film, but I enjoyed it. Kinmont has a boyfriend who leaves her upon learning that she will be handicapped for life. She ends up meeting a young man who enjoys

flying small planes. He proposes to Kinmont and she accepts. Before they can get married, he dies when the plane he is piloting crashes, on Kinmont's birthday of all days.

44. *The Waste Land*, see note 28.
45. According to an article on page four in the November 20, 1979, issue of *Family Circle*, Ann Landers's advice column appears in more than a thousand newspapers, weeklies, and magazines, making her the most widely syndicated columnist in the world. She also put together *The Ann Landers Encyclopedia*, which was published by Doubleday & Co. To this day, Landers lives in Chicago. The letter I quote was published in *The Indianapolis Star*, and other outlets, on October 28, 1979.
46. I once saw a book about the Lockridge siblings. The publisher was Penguin, if I'm not mistaken. But my efforts to track the book down have failed. Ross Lockridge Jr. once taught at Indiana University Bloomington, before killing himself for reasons unknown. *Raintree County* was his only novel, published in 1948 by Houghton Mifflin Co., Boston.

    When I was writing *Olenka*, an Indiana University lecturer was occupying the main house, while the side house was being rented to a university student.

    The sundial inscribed with the lines from Browning's poem, which also featured in the film, is now installed in the garden of a professor emeritus who specializes in Romantic literature and who possesses expertise in landscaping.

    The exhibitions I mention in *Olenka* are purely fictional.

    Regarding the poet Robert Browning, see note 47.
47. Many books have been written about the romance between Browning and Barrett. There is also a play, if I'm not incorrect, titled *The Barretts of Wimpole Street*. When I was still a student at Gadjah Mada University in Yogyakarta, I watched a film about their relationship, based, I think, on the play mentioned above.
48. From the title of Sutan Takdir Alisjahbana's novel *Anak Perawan di Sarang Penyamun* (*Maiden in a Den of Thieves*).
49. An art forger who became rich overnight was the subject of discussion on an NPR program I listened to three months before I began writing *Olenka*.
50. This question, addressed to Paul Findley, a Republican congressman for Illinois, appeared in *Family Weekly*, the magazine for the *Sunday Herald-Times*, on October 7, 1979, page two.
51. Sartre's *La Nausée* was originally published in 1938.

52. "The throat is dry and wants wetting" ("tenggorokan kering sedikit mau basah") is a quote from Chairil Anwar's poem "Catatan th. 1946" ("Notes from 1946").
53. The Holy Quran, Surah Al-Baqara, verse 284.
54. "I lose all form / shatter into pieces"; "faithful follower"; and "My God, in my utter despair, I still call on You" ("Aku hilang bentuk / remuk"; "pemeluk teguh"; "Tuhanku / Dalam termangu / Aku masih menyebut nama-Mu") are taken from Chairil Anwar's poem "Doa, kepada Pemeluk Teguh" ("A Prayer, for the Faithful Follower").

Notes by the Translator

PART I

CHAPTER 8: THE ELBERHART BELL TOWER

i. The IU Bloomington campus as described in *Olenka* is partly fiction, partly fact. There is no Elberhart Bell Tower, but its real-life counterpart is the Metz Carillon, named after Dr. Arthur R. Metz.

CHAPTER 11: THE FLEA

i. This is a reference to John Donne's "The Canonization."
ii. A reference to *King Lear*, Act IV, Scene I: "As flies to wanton boys are we to the gods; They kill us for their sport."
iii. From "Hymn to God, My God, in Sickness," by John Donne. The poem also features the speaker likening his body to a map, not unlike the narrator who talks about treating Olenka's body as he would a map.
iv. Interestingly, Fanton's summary of the story is not a strict retelling. It combines the original Hawthorne story with elements of a story by Budi Darma that was partially inspired by "Young Goodman Brown." For further details, see my note to Budi Darma's note 7.

CHAPTER 12: OLENKA LEAVES ME

i. *La maja desnuda* is the painting referred to here.

PART II

CHAPTER 4: MC LEAVES FOR HOME BY HERSELF

i. In real life, the Picasso, also known as the Chicago Picasso, was not taken down. Budi Darma would, however, have been familiar with the controversy surrounding the statue after its installment in 1967.

CHAPTER 5: OVERNIGHT IN INDIANAPOLIS

i. These are two eponymous characters from the stories "Orez" and "Yorrick" in *People from Bloomington* (*Orang-Orang Bloomington*), which Budi Darma wrote during the same period.

PART III

CHAPTER 2: DISASTER

i. Budi Darma was likely inspired by the real-life crash of a DC-10 plane that took place earlier in 1979, the year *Olenka* was written. American Airlines Flight 191 crashed shortly after taking off from O'Hare International Airport on May 25, 1979. Everyone on board died, as well as two people on the ground.

PART IV

CHAPTER 3: OLENKA'S LETTER, CONTINUED

i. Busoni's *Doktor Faust* was performed by the Indiana University Opera & Ballet Theater in 1974, the year Budi Darma started his master's degree at IU Bloomington. According to *The New York Times*, the opera was "staged brilliantly" (Harold C. Schonberg, November 25, 1974, page 38). This staging may have inspired Budi Darma to write this scene.

CHAPTER 4: FLYING

i. Frank X. McCloskey was indeed the mayor of Bloomington from 1972 to 1982.

CHAPTER 5: AN EXPRESS LETTER

i. Three details of the biography given here diverge from fact: namely, Kinmont's birthplace and birthdate, and the town in California where she ended up residing. The rest of the details provided (the ski tournaments she won; the dates of these competitions) are accurate. It is possible that Budi Darma deliberately changed these details, as he has done selectively throughout the novel.

CHAPTER 11: LEAVING MC

i. The exchange here is reminiscent of Jane and Rochester's exchange in *Jane Eyre*, when Rochester is trying to convince Jane to stay after she finds out about Bertha.

CHAPTER 12: NAUSEA

i. The passage from Sartre's novel reads (as translated by Lloyd Alexander): "Suddenly I had a vision: someone had fallen face down and was bleeding in the dishes."
ii. A fictitious museum.

PART VI

OLENKA'S ORIGINS

i. Probably a reference to Harry Aveling's essay in the April 1974 issue of *Horison*—a special edition devoted to Budi Darma's short fiction. The essay is titled "Dunia Jungkir Balik Budi Darma," or "Budi Darma's Topsy-Turvy World." The essay's title is itself an allusion to an essay by Budi Darma, published in *Horison* in July 1971, titled "Sastra Merupakan Dunia Djungkir Balik," or "Literature Is a Topsy-Turvy World."
ii. "The sense of humanity has not yet left me."
iii. It may be useful to refer to Budi Darma's extended note on catharsis in the first installment of his two-part essay "Moral dalam Sastra," or "Morality in Literature," published in the February 1982 issue of *Basis*. The essay contains a discussion of catharsis, relying on an interpretation that emphasized catharsis's morally cleansing aspects.

PART VII

NOTES BY THE AUTHOR

i. The story referred to here is "The Fish Trap" by Peter Leach. It was included in *Prize Stories 1974: The O. Henry Awards* (Doubleday & Company, 1974), and first appeared in the Fall 1972 issue of *The Virginia Quarterly.*

ii. I have not been able to find a collection that matches Budi Darma's description. There does exist a collection of stories from China, *Tjerita-Tjerita Tiongkok* (*Stories from China*), translated into Indonesian by Mochtar Lubis, Beb Vuyk, and S. Mundingsari, and published in 1953 by Pembangunan. A collection of stories from Europe titled *Kisah-Kisah dari Eropa* (*Tales from Europe*), translated into Indonesian by Mochtar Lubis, was published the previous year, in 1952. Other collections of stories by Russian authors were published during this period, too, including a collection of eight Russian short stories, *Delapan Kisah dari Rusia* (*Eight Tales from Russia*), translated by Bagus Siregar.

iii. The story referred to here, "Bambang Subali Budiman," was published in the October 1981 issue of *Horison.* It was the only story Budi Darma wrote during his graduate studies in Indiana that was not set in America. A loose translation of the story's title would be "The Wise Bambang Subali"—"Budiman" being an honorific for a wise or intelligent person derived from Sanskrit, an Indonesian equivalent to the Puritan title "Goodman."

iv. John Paul II's visit to New York spanned two days, from October 2 to October 3, 1979. During this visit, he made two separate visits to St. Patrick's Cathedral, where he was received by the Archbishop of New York, Cardinal Terence James Cooke. I have not been able to find the exact quote referred to by Budi Darma in his notes.

v. I have opted for a more poetic-sounding translation of these lines, but more literally, the translation would be "This is a world loath to acknowledge a greeting."

vi. The relevant lines from *Women in Love* occur in the chapter "Woman to Woman" and read thus: " 'Yes,' said Hermione slowly—'I think you need a man—soldierly, strong-willed—' Hermione held out her hand and clenched it with rhapsodic intensity. 'You should have a man like the old heroes—you need to stand behind him as he goes into battle, you need to *see* his strength, and to *hear* his shout—.' "

vii. The relevant lines from *Women in Love*: " 'Then he is so changeable and unsure of himself—it requires the greatest patience and understanding to help him. And I don't think you are patient. You would have to be prepared to suffer—dreadfully. I can't tell you how much suffering it would take to make him happy.' "

viii. From the chapter "Mino": " 'There's one thing about our family, you know,' he continued. 'Once anything goes wrong, it can never be put right again—not with us. I've noticed it all my life—you can't put a thing right, once it has gone wrong.' "

ix. Although this is not strictly accurate, Halloween did indeed fall on a Wednesday in 1979, the year Budi Darma wrote *Olenka*.

x. As Budi Darma explains, he did not actually read this interview firsthand. This quote is from the interview as paraphrased in *Tempo* magazine, which appeared in the novel as a clipping. The original interview appeared in the September 1979 issue of *Playgirl* and was written up by Celeste Fremon. A comparison between the *Tempo* article and the original interview shows that the quotes in *Tempo* aren't strictly quotes that have been translated from the English-language original—rather, they are a combination of paraphrase and quoted text.

ALSO AVAILABLE

People from Bloomington

Translated by Tiffany Tsao

Set in Bloomington, Indiana, where the author lived as a graduate student in the 1970s, this is far from the idyllic portrait of small-town America. Rather, it's a place where the solitary can all too easily remain solitary; where people can be obsessively curious about others yet fail to form any genuine connections. Budi Darma paints a realist world portrayed through an absurdist frame, morbid and funny at the same time.

PENGUIN CLASSICS

Ready to find your next great classic? Let us help. Visit prh.com/penguinclassics